by Marti Leimbach

DYING YOUNG

SUN DIAL STREET

Sun Dial Street

SUN DIAL STREET

MARTI LEIMBACH

NAN A. TALESE

DOUBLEDAY

NEW YORK
LONDON
TORONTO
SYDNEY
AUCKLAND

PUBLISHED BY NAN A. TALESE/DOUBLEDAY
a division of Bantam Doubleday Dell Publishing Group, Inc.
666 Fifth Avenue, New York, New York 10103

DOUBLEDAY and the portrayal of an anchor
with a dolphin are trademarks of Doubleday,
a division of Bantam Doubleday Dell
Publishing Group, Inc.

Book design by Marysarah Quinn

Library of Congress Cataloging-in-Publication Data
Leimbach, Marti
      Sun dial street / Marti Leimbach — 1st ed.
         p.   cm.
      I. Title.
   PS3562.E4614S86   1992
   813'.54—dc20   91-41300
                                                CIP

ISBN 0-385-42255-5

10   9   8   7   6   5   4   3   2   1

FIRST EDITION

*This book is dedicated to Lenny and Mary, who inspired it,
and to Alastair, who made it fun to write.*

SUN DIAL STREET

PROLOGUE

After my father died, my mother hired a U-Haul trailer and parked it outside our house, which was in Kingston. She bought reams of bubble wrap and Styrofoam peanuts, rows of cardboard boxes, great balls of twine. She had the ambition to load the trailer, floor to ceiling, wall to wall, stacking boxes and bureaus, sealed crates, locked trunks, suitcases all filled to creaking.

The plan was a move westward, a journey along Route 80 as far as Salt Lake City and then south to Los Angeles. She meant me, too. She meant I had to move. In point of fact I had not lived with these people—my family—for years. I had no intention of moving anywhere. But Mother asked me to spend a few days helping her pack, so I did. I thought it my duty to try to convince her to move someplace local—to Weymouth or Milton or Braintree. If she must be closer to a city, move to Boston, I suggested. But she would not budge.

"L.A. is crowded, polluted, full of crime," I told her.

"Oh yes, I know. I bought a rape whistle," Mother said. "Mind the step, Sam."

We were making our way up from the cellar, hauling a steamer trunk. The staircase was narrow and the trunk was awkward and large. Mother went ahead of me. I took a step when she took a step. I pushed when she pulled.

"Didn't Charles Manson live in Los Angeles? And Thomas 'the Gore' Gordon? What about the famous ice-pick case?"

Mother took a step. Another.

"Sam, that's a ghost story," she said. "The *ice-pick* case."

We reached the top of the stairs. She looked at me reassuringly.

"Mickey Mouse lives in Los Angeles," she said.

It was November, but already autumn had dead-ended with the coming of not just frost but a snowfall. Mother made a great show of how this was the last time she'd need her winter coat as Los Angeles would be eternal summer, terrific sun, with none of the capriciousness of Massachusetts weather. She set out in a bright red, ankle-length, all-weather parka, bending flaps of cardboard and securing them with packing tape so they formed boxes. She prepared squares of bubble wrap and measured space in the trailer. She ignored the snow and took only brief pauses through the morning to show my sister and me her wet hair, her dappled hands, her coat now drenched at the shoulders.

My sister, Ginny, fifteen, was disappointed by the weather, as she had planned to run away, which required bicycling. She felt better when she discovered that road conditions were so bad that travel by any means was unlikely for the moment. Ginny listened to the report on the radio, rooting for more bad weather. "Go, snow," she said into her Walkman.

The next day there was no snow, but rain came in torrents

and a large maple branch fell onto the flat top of the trailer, landing in such a way that none of us could remove it. I should mention that we were camping out in the downstairs rooms of the Kingston house, which had been half gutted by fire two weeks previously and still smelled like charred wood, melted plastic, and the chemical the firemen used to destroy the flames. Looking back on it, I can't imagine what Mother was packing anyway, as the fire had consumed the two upper floors of the house and what wasn't destroyed was filthy with smoke. But when it began hailing—on the third day—I felt truly sorry for Mother, who sat at the kitchen table with her chin in her hands. We'd forgotten to put plastic underneath the boxes we'd made, and small leaks in the trailer became streams of rain that destroyed all of our work. The forecast was for continued showers.

"It's a sign from God that we were meant to stay here," Ginny said. She was reading a paperback with a missing cover. She read stacks of these books, toss-outs she never knew the titles of, that she found in dumpsters behind Kingston Mall.

"We can't stay here," Mother said. "There's no house here."

"We could use the insurance money to check into a hotel, and then we'd get maid service, fresh towels, and shampoo in miniature bottles," Ginny said. "I've always wanted that."

The nights were very cold, and as the central heating had been destroyed by the fire, we were dependent on a quartz heater that flicked on and off at night. This worked okay, but Mother feared it because it was a fire hazard, and so she could not sleep. We, who could sleep, were kept awake by Mother's insomnia, and Ginny began drinking from a pint bottle of a nighttime cold remedy, which made her more or less a zombie all the time.

"Don't take that stuff," I told her.

"It's Johnson and Johnson. Perfectly safe," Ginny said.

I made a move and she swatted my arm.

"Touch this bottle and I'll gnaw off your hand," she said.

Next we discovered that the trailer was stuck. I hitched my father's Oldsmobile to it, accelerated slowly, but the trailer wouldn't budge. I tried again but the Oldsmobile's wheels sank into mud. I wedged the tops of garbage cans beneath the tires, and when that didn't work, I tried flattened cardboard boxes and wooden planks. I reversed the car and rocked it back and forth, I got mother to drive while I pushed. Finally, I gave up and for all I know the trailer is still sitting in Kingston, because at dawn on the sixth day Mother decided we were going to leave no matter what.

"I can't stay in this house one more hour," she told me.

"Mom," I began—but I stopped. The move was no longer a cheerful adventure into a new life. Mother didn't look like an adventurer anymore. She looked like a widow who didn't want to live in the house she had once lived in with her husband.

"Get your sister," she said.

I found Ginny sleeping next to the heater. I scooped her up, blanket and all, and took her out to the garage, where Mother sat in the car, studying a map of the United States.

"I think she'll be fine in back, don't you?" she asked.

I put Ginny in the back seat, arranged the pillow, and tucked the blanket around her. I closed the door and looked at my little sister. Her face was so clear and white, her eyelashes so long across her cheeks; she could have been five instead of fifteen.

Ginny refers to this moment of departure, which took place mostly during the haze of sleeping potion, as her kidnapping. She planned to escape at the earliest possible time, probably at a service station, but discovered that every town they passed, from East Coast to West, was even bleaker than the one before. And so she endured the week-long journey to Los Angeles, chain-smoking most of the way with Mother, who also chain-smoked. Each of them, hoping to annoy the other, refused to open a window and the car became a sort of mobile ashtray.

Luckily, I was not there.

"Well?" Mother said. She had the car keys in one hand, lipstick in the other. She dabbed at her lips. She peered into the rear view mirror and rubbed away a stray bit of color at the corner of her mouth. "Aren't you even going to bring a change of clothes?"

"Oh no . . ." I said, backing away.

"What kind of family would we be without you?"

"Mother, I am twenty-five years old. I have a job. Obligations. I have a lease and people who depend on me. I have a girlfriend."

None of this was true but the morning was gaining some momentum, the sky pouring more and more rain, and Mother was worried that Ginny might wake up and wage her own protest. So there wasn't very much time to argue. Mother turned on the car, rolled down the window, and squinted up at me. She said, "Sam, your father died in this house, a matter of feet from where you're standing now, and I have not seen one tear from you, one moment of sorrow. You put your baby sister in the back seat like she's some pile of dung—"

"I wouldn't put a blanket over dung."

"—like a pile of dung and then announce you're leaving this family."

"If I'm leaving then why are you in the driver's seat?"

"Oh, you're too smart for me. Judge for yourself. When we're gone and you're standing in this garage, feeling *relieved*— no, don't say anything—when you are *happy* that this old lady and this teenage girl don't live near you or your precious city, then you tell me who's leaving who."

Mother was right and she knew it. Before she rolled up the window she gave me a look, and I did not kiss her. I did not wave her away or smile. I was too busy imagining the opening that would come with her absence. I was thinking how very fortunate I was that just when I thought my mother and sister were to become a burden to me, they voluntarily disappeared.

We had witnessed my father's death and were freshly linked by it. We had seen the great, unthinkable thing as though with one eye. Everything changed when he died. It was as though the days of the calendar were renumbered, starting again from that day—as though a fifth season had been added to the year. Our lives were divided and the seam between before and after was a wound that we now shared, an unwellness that we blamed one another for. I wanted to leave it, to bring it all to an end. Just then I wanted very much for Mother to drive away.

I watched the Oldsmobile make its way down the street that had once been my neighborhood. I watched Mother and Ginny's departure through the rain. I figured that freedom from my family would be only temporary and Mother would return. I expected a call from somewhere real weird and far and hopeless, a phone booth in Sioux City or a weigh station or an all-night coin-op food bar. I figured she'd get so far and then change her mind, become hysterical, petrify Ginny, and telephone me. My mother had never done anything herself—she'd always had my father.

My father had "systems." His toolshed was a monument to order. He had complicated arrangements involving the cleaning rotation of his work shirts, the preservation of leather shoes, the storage of greatcoats and earmuffs in summer, cotton blazers and tennis shorts in winter. We owned a lot of objects that were not things in themselves but a means for storing other things. House keys were labeled in code. The car was serviced every three thousand miles. He was frugal to a fault and would use the same razor until it made ribbons of his face. Pipe smoking was his one messy habit. When Ginny or I went to him with problems or homework or any of our infinite requests, he was always sitting in his leather recliner, pipe smoke in a stagnant cloud above him, a newspaper folded into neat quarters.

But the systems that were most important were those that involved Mother. He could predict Mother's moods, knew exactly how long a depression would last, when to call the doctor and when not to. He had a system for her pill taking and a system for her meals, which became tricky when the drugs were particularly strong. He'd been able to make it seem to Ginny and me that there was nothing difficult about having a mother who was manic-depressive. Her illness was just one of the great many aspects of life that needed management and a system. He guarded that system above all others, and silently, selfishly, we loved him for it. If there was a guilt greater than the one I felt for letting Mother go as far away from Kingston as she could get without wings or paddles, it was that secretly I felt it was unfair that Dad died. If it had to be one of them, it should have been Mother. It seemed to me she had taken up so much room with her life; we always had to fit around her, to surrender to her more powerful needs. It seemed that my father had been living half-days and leap-year months, that he had been robbed of his time, and that no system, no matter how elaborate, could protect him from her thievery.

This is not what I think now. This is what I thought the day Mother rolled out of the driveway and I returned to my life in Boston, to the cat that I thought was male until it had kittens in my laundry basket. To the rainy city in which I hid myself, hoping that things would get better and that Mother wouldn't come back, which it turned out she never did.

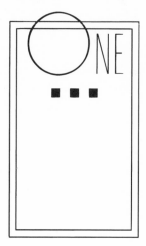

ONE
∎ ∎ ∎

There are certain things about your family that become a part of you and that you cannot change, not through a new choice in geography or an opposing political view, not through education or the violent seizure of interests that are deliberately and radically different from those held by a father, a mother, a sister. Your family is etched onto you like a tattoo, something that can make you ashamed or proud. But it is there anyway, occupying a space just beneath the skin, at once both a decoration and a scar.

This was told to me by the woman sitting next to me on the plane, an older woman wearing lots of rings and what I guess you'd call a brooch. She had a cloud of white hair. Her mouth formed a box when she spoke. She had gotten on the plane in New York and had talked through most of the trip to Los Angeles. She gazed out the window with a startled expression as the glass filled with the city below us, all streetlamps and neon.

She said, "Of course you think your family is insane; I think the same of mine. But you mustn't avoid them because of that."

"It's different for me," I explained. "There's real psychosis, a medical history."

She scowled and shook her head. "No, no," she said, as though I hadn't understood her at all. "Take my own parents, for instance. My father was a poky little man. He didn't speak to any of his children, but he made elaborate dollhouses for us out of cigars. Now you tell me, is that normal? Is that *safe* for a child? My mother collected hats. We had a room of six hundred when she died. Gave them all to charity."

Her name was Celia Lawson and she was on her way to visit her daughter, who had married someone she didn't like and moved to Los Angeles, a city she didn't like.

"Great distance and foul spouses are still no reason for family dissension," Celia told me with a wise look. "Of course, my daughter wouldn't dream of visiting *me*. I have to fly three thousand miles to see *her* every year. Meanwhile she produces child after child with a man I wouldn't have inside the house. She's the same way she was as a teenager, when she used to put her cigarettes out in egg yolk because she knew it would rattle me speechless."

"My sister is like that," I said. "Always putting her cigarettes out in breakfast cereal, Gummy Bears . . ."

"Oh dear," Celia said.

She was afraid of airplanes and ordered gin and tonics the entire trip, hoping they would lend her some courage. I bought the drinks for both of us, doling out fives from a roll of bills I'd extracted from the automatic teller machine, nearly closing my account, just hours before. It had been my father's habit to pay for women no matter the circumstances, and it was mine, too. Celia Lawson had plenty of money, you could tell. The seat she had been assigned was in first class, but she'd found the people in first class boring and decided to try her luck in coach.

"My daughter knows this man," she said. She pointed at the signature line of a letter I'd been reading. "Are you very friendly with Mr. Igleton?"

"I don't know him," I explained. Eli Igleton was the owner of the restaurant in Hollywood where Ginny now worked. He had sent me some demo tapes of bands he knew in L.A., suggesting that I see about finding them work on the East Coast. "He's a business contact."

"What sort of business?" Celia asked.

I explained that I had a job managing musical acts—rock bands, jazz, a trio of country-western singers all named Henry. But things had been sluggish recently, and the demos Eli sent were so strong that I reasoned it was worth a visit to Los Angeles to try to sign the bands on.

"Well, I'm fairly certain that he and Lucy used to be friends," Celia said. "Isn't that a coincidence? Of course, I think we have a tendency to underestimate the frequency of coincidence. Did you know that two out of every hundred strangers who meet in America have an acquaintance in common? And ninety-nine percent of the time they will know someone who knows someone . . . well, I won't bore you with it. Would you like to see a picture of my daughter?"

She took a photograph from her bag. It was a few years old; the corners curled. A brown stain marked the back next to the name Lucy, scripted in ink.

Her daughter was very pretty—I told Celia so, and she smiled, working hard to ignore the swaying movements of the plane. As the plane made its final exit from the sky, she clutched the sleeve of my jacket. Then she looked at me like I'd done something wrong to see her like this, to see her frightened. She tossed her head, as though to shrug off some of that fear, and said, "I am hoping to convince Lucy to abandon that pestilence she calls a husband. With so much divorce these days, you'd think she could manage one of her own."

"Maybe she loves him," I said. It seemed immediately a

stupid, ridiculous thing to say. Celia screwed up her face as though the suggestion were lewd as well as absurd.

She said, "I love dogs. But in China they eat dogs."

There is a second reason I came to Los Angeles. For a long while I'd had some nagging part of me that didn't feel good about the way my family disappeared that one November morning. And how I'd let them go. The few cards we exchanged over the years hardly made me feel connected to them, and this summer I had felt, for the first time, lonely, a little panicked. I was close to thirty now. What if they died suddenly and I had not seen them? What if I died? Standing at my funeral, a bunch of very nice people would say things like "I rented him his parking space," "I delivered his mail," "He was a very fine customer." There would be women there—maybe— saying, "He was cheap, but consistent" or "We had a wonderful five weeks together."

It was time I saw my family; I could feel that it was time. As we entered the terminal it was all I could do to keep myself from running forward to find Ginny. But while I stood in the crowd at Baggage Claim, I wondered if she would even recognize me. In four years I had taken on a different style of dress, worked my voice out of its regional accent, shaved my beard, cropped my hair.

"Of course she'll recognize you. It doesn't matter if it's been four years or forty," Celia said. "You could have grown cucumbers for ears, had your face reshaped, and worn a fez. Family members sniff you out. There's no escape."

People rushed to their bags, dragging them from the belt. A slim leather suitcase rumbled forward. Celia pointed at it and I collected it for her.

"How old is your sister?" she asked. When I told her, she said, "I can't remember when I was nineteen—not a single fact or detail of it. I think the importance of the teenage years is overrated. Sam, give me your address so the next time I'm in Boston I can visit you."

At the time I was living in a loft space in Boston's South End, a floor-through with tall, elaborate windows, blinding by morning light. It was a converted warehouse, not meant for habitation—or visitors. The toilet was rudimentary, the shower something that I rigged up out of a watering trough one of the Henrys donated. Half the space was cluttered with recording equipment, and to help pay the rent I housed the drying pottery of several of Boston's artists. Pots the size of small dinosaurs, pots the size of your thumb, pots with handles looped like human ears, statues of hermaphrodite cupids, plates, trays, all precious to their creators, dried against the splotched backdrop of sheets, canvas, waxed paper. The bed, a futon with a sunken middle, had been there when I arrived.

"It would be dull for you," I said.

"Dull? You want to know dull? Talk to my son-in-law for five minutes and you'll know dull. Look at him! I don't know how she ended up married to *that*," Celia said, pointing to a man who was making his way through the crowd. "I sent her to Princeton for her bachelor's degree. I sent her to Rome for her master's. She had the finest education money can buy, and *look* what she has brought into our genealogy."

Celia's son-in-law was blond, with a mustache that needed trimming. He smiled a lot. He smiled as he moved through groups of people, gingerly maneuvering through one circle of travelers to get to the next. His jacket was denim, a stonewashed job with a lapel full of buttons—little sayings like "Life's a Beach" and "Don't read this button." A collar flapped beneath his chin, and he wore a chain, several chains, around his neck. He finally turned in our direction and caught sight of Celia, who did nothing whatsoever to indicate where she stood.

"Do you want to know what he does for a living?" she said quietly, almost imperceptibly.

"What?" I asked.

She answered in the same hidden way, without seeming to move her lips at all. "He manufactures those vile chocolate constructions shaped like parts of the human anatomy," she said. In a deeper tone of voice she said, "It's an ugly business." Then she stepped toward her son-in-law and received a sizable kiss on the cheek. He guided her away through the people, and I waved when she looked back, rolling her eyes. She sent me a kiss through the air.

Ginny showed up late, looking a little hassled. I hugged her and she leaned into me, pushing against my chest and locking her spaghetti arms around my neck. She was all ribs and blouse, with a back full of ponytail. She stepped out of her sandals and put her bare feet on the tops of my sneakers.

She said, "Sam, you smell like home."

I noticed she wore a shark's tooth on a string of leather around her neck, and it made me remember how she had been the sort of child who collected shells and birds' nests, harbored broken teeth, a fraction of beehive, petrified wood.

I said, "It's been a long time."

"Well," she said, opening her arms wide and stepping sideways like the models in game shows. She was tall, so tall that even her baggy workman's clothes couldn't hide all that length. She had dark, dark eyes, spiky bangs that made a crescent over her forehead, eyeglasses with thick lenses. She said, "Welcome to the West Coast. A place bursting with young women in bikinis driving Jeeps, where manicurists stay open all night and houses smell of sea air and clay. Mother's house excepted, of course."

Her face was a triangular pixie shape. She was pale as a glacier, and had a similar ancientness to her sad expressions. She looked like a person formed with a paintbrush, not with skin and muscle and bone. She looked so light she could just

13

glide away, recede into the crowds of people claiming their luggage or jump years back in time and regain her status as a little girl. I realized that she was dangerously thin. I held up her wrist, which brandished an array of cloth bracelets. I turned her hand, and I thought her fingers were like fishbones and her skin a seamless membrane.

"I met a woman on the plane," I told her.

"You've become handsome," she said.

Ginny drove the same Oldsmobile that had made its way across the continent years before. The car that had once been the elaborate purchase of my father, who'd broken all his own financial rules to buy Oldsmobile's top of the line in 1972. Dad had driven it proudly, like a statesman or a chauffeur. His job, as a salesman for stationery products—greeting cards, mostly— had required long driving hours. He'd roamed southern Massachusetts, Connecticut, Rhode Island, distributing merchandise, taking orders, and checking the stock in the dozens of stores that occupied his territory. He wouldn't allow us to eat in the car—no drive-throughs, no take-outs—because we might smear something sticky onto the cloth interior. We couldn't jump on the seats because of the delicacy of the cushion springs, and we had to be quiet during the drive in order for Dad to admire the silence of the Oldsmobile's immense, sprawling engine.

"You look so much older," I said. I had to shout a little. On the radio was a classical station turned up loud. Wagner came full blast from four speakers.

"I *am* older," Ginny said.

She had a Diet Pepsi in her lap; she'd rigged up a long straw so she could sip from it in traffic. Across the floor of the passenger's side were piles of cassettes, some in plastic casings, and a map that was folded incorrectly and glued that way by means of dried cola. There was an enormous ashtray, secured to the dashboard with a slab of putty. A rattling sound came from empty soda cans in the back, and a banana peel, spotted black, spilled over the edge of the seat, wagging with the movement of the car.

"Why won't Mom talk with me on the phone?" I asked. I was looking out the window, admiring the boulevard, which even at this late hour was full of shining cars with high-gloss paint, fat radials, fancy cloth roofs folded back so people could enjoy the air. Buildings of mirrored glass reflected headlights and neon. Hills ablaze with the lights of thousands of houses could be seen in the distance.

"It's not you. She's going through this thing where she refuses to use a telephone at all," Ginny said. "But she talks *about* you all the time. She says your name every third sentence, I swear. I don't even exist for her. I'm just the person who takes her to the doctor or to the psycho ward or wherever the hell she wants to go."

"Don't talk like that," I said.

Ginny bolted across three lanes and pulled tight against the guardrail. She turned to me, pushing her head up high, letting her voice rise.

She said, "Sam, *you* haven't been here."

She hurled her Diet Pepsi can onto the road, where it was crunched under the fat rubber tires of a souped-up Bronco.

"She's your mother," I said. But I said it in a feeble way, heard myself and felt ridiculous.

Ginny looked out the window, watching the road. Her hair was so dark that it almost looked wet. The reflection of car lights trailed across her blouse front. She stared away, forgetful of me, suddenly preoccupied, her own thoughts blooming inside her. Then she turned, her face intent, her voice stretched flat. She said, "You think it's so easy to be nice? You won't last five minutes with her."

"Let's not get this way," I said. At this moment Ginny was nobody I knew—not my sister, not my mother's daughter.

She'd grown into a young woman with a magnetism she could not hide and an ache so apparent and so deep that it almost hurt to look at her.

"Drive this thing," Ginny said, pulling her hands from the wheel.

I slid to the left and Ginny pushed herself up and over me. As she slipped across my lap I noticed the boniness of her spine. Also that her skin was cold like a melon and that her back was sweating.

"You're too thin," I told her.

"None of your business," she said, looking away.

I waited for a break in traffic. I was strangely bothered by the clicking of the turn signal. The sound of it, *click, click, click,* made me want to rip open the dashboard. Instead, I changed stations on the radio, switching the brawl scene from *Die Meistersinger* for a song about love strung along with pretty guitar chords. It carried us down miles of highway. Ginny folded up beside me, knees to her face, arms around her head. I reached over, put my hand on top of her head, and left it there.

"Don't touch me," she said, without moving. "And take a right here."

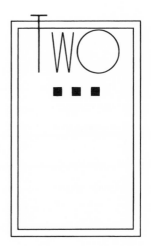

TWO
∎ ∎ ∎

Mother, who these days insisted on being called Jewel, lived in a small, adobe-style ranch house with two bedrooms, an L-shaped kitchen, and a tiny sitting room with a television set positioned exactly where the fireplace would be if there were a fireplace. In a back yard the size of a shuffleboard she grew enormous, gaudy sunflowers in beds she made by filling the centers of old tires with soil. Mother once sent a Polaroid snapshot of Ginny and her outside the front door, waving into the camera like happy people, proud of their small home. But Ginny hated the place and called it the horror on Sun Dial Street, which was not really a street at all but more of an alley, where boys gathered to ride skateboards, shove each other around on the gravel, and beat sticks against trash barrels.

The driveway was a short island of uneven cement. The car barely fit, and when I opened the door I had to be careful not to scratch it against the wrought iron railing next to the house's small front landing. My first thought about the house was that it wasn't fixed on the ground in any normal fashion. It had the appearance of having been dropped carelessly onto the tiny lot and never firmly planted, remaining as if by mistake.

There were lawn ornaments: little gnomes, oversized frogs, painted wooden mushrooms. They gleamed in the moonlight. They looked like toys a child left behind. Ginny pointed at the glow-in-the-dark yellow ducklings that formed a line next to the front door.

"That's Mom's idea of decorating," she said. She was searching her key ring for the correct key. It took a long time to find because the house was completely dark, save for a shine of lavender from the bug lamp outside the living room window. "Meanwhile, half the tile in the bathroom is rotting off the wall."

The bug lamp zapped a mosquito that crashed into its glow. I shifted my duffel bag from one shoulder to the other.

"How is she doing?" I asked. "Is she sleeping? Is she still smearing all those lotions on her skin?" I had brief memories involving trays of softening creams, vitamin E, fragrant oils, whole nights hearing the pacing of Mother's insomnia. Other things.

Ginny was silent, answering me with only a sideways stare. We entered the house, and she fingered the wall for a light switch. I put my bag on the floor and stepped forward into what I guessed was the living room. There were shadows of furniture, and I could make out the V shape of a television antenna. Against the wall were pictures, their glass frames reflecting moonlight. There was a smell like baby powder or like roses, I couldn't tell. The house held both strangeness and familiarity, like a very realistic dream. The darkness of the room made it seem extra tiny, and my vision was restricted in the manner of a dream. Everything was shut in, constricted, absolute. The smell became a heavy, claustrophobic cloud.

Ginny went from wall switch to wall switch; none of the lights worked.

"Mother, is this a fuse situation or did you yank the bulbs?" she asked.

I didn't see Mother. I stood, waiting to hug her if I could find her.

"Try that one," Ginny told me. At my left was the tall stem of a floor lamp. I moved toward it but was stopped by a hand on my leg. I looked down, and there, lying on a couch in the dark, was my mother. Most of her was hidden in a shadow of quilt, but I recognized the shape of her mouth, the long slope of her jaw, the octagonal glasses that I had looked into for as many years as I could remember.

"Sam," she said. "I'm sorry. I fell asleep." She moved to sit up, brushing back one of the strong curls of her brown hair. She had an elegance about her, my mother, a chorus of movements that was both polite and endearing. She held her hands in her lap, for example. She sat with both knees swung to one side and her heels lifted from the carpet.

Tonight she wore a summer dress with a round, embroidered collar. She had on earrings and fancy shoes. She was smiling but worried. She held a finger just above her lip—her habit since a burn she got during the fire in our old house. It made me sad that she was still shy about the scar. Also that it mattered to her even with me. I looked at her and I said what came to mind, the very first thought I had, the very first feeling.

"You're so pretty," I told her.

She touched the collar of her dress, her watchband, her face. She was nervous in a way I was used to seeing but that bothered me fresh every time. I sat next to her and raised my arm over the back of the couch. Behind me, Ginny made an effort with the fifth light switch that would not work.

"Let's not turn on any lights," Mother said. There was only moonlight and a beam from the bug lamp outside.

"I guess we *can't*," said Ginny. She went to the floor lamp, and turned the switch. "Why did you do it, Mother? Why did you take out all the light bulbs?"

"How are you feeling, Mom?" I asked.

"Call me by my other name," she answered in a whisper. "Call me Jewel."

"I hate that," Ginny said.

"It's my name!" Mother said, making her voice whine. She moved closer to me on the couch, casting a glance at Ginny that contained a surprising mixture of enmity and fear.

"Your name is Lois," I said, but gently.

"You too!" she said, standing now. She looked at me, then Ginny, then me again. She wrapped her arms around her stomach. "You can both just leave."

"Mom—" I began, but she interrupted.

"Stop it!" she yelled, putting her hands over her ears. "Just stop that right now."

"Jewel . . ." I tried, but she wasn't listening. Instead she stood and turned away from me, plugging her ears. She spoke in an angry, barking tone. Her words, awakened with rage, were fragmented, disassembled, sounding as though they came from some ruined part of her. She said, "I don't have to put up with—" and then "What you do in your own house—" and then "I've been told by the authorities, by the *authorities!*"

Mother faced the wall, gripped by her own dialogue; I looked around for Ginny, but she was gone. From a hallway leading to the back of the house I saw a spear of light across the tiled floor. I followed the light and entered the kitchen where, on the breakfast table, there were three formal dinner settings with cloth napkins folded into cones on the plates. Above the table was a working lamp. It sent out gold light from six small painted bulbs. The lamp was a pathetic rendition of a Gothic chandelier, enormous and hulking in the small kitchen. Off the kitchen was a small area, almost like a closet but with a door that led outside. I opened the door, pushing it against a stack of trash bags that oozed something brown onto the floor. The outside air took me by surprise and made me realize the staleness of my mother's house, where there was not a single fan or open window. I called out Ginny's name.

The lawn was an overgrown mixture of grass and weeds and randomly planted herbs. I could smell cilantro and basil. I could make out the image of a struggling lemon tree with no fruit, a bush of wild sumac. There was a string of clothesline between metal posts and behind it a hammock stretched between a palm tree and the chain-link fence that surrounded the small yard. Ginny was lying in the hammock. Her hair crept through the netting and brushed along the grass, making a sound like a hiss. She had a penlight in her hand and a paperback face down across her chest. She was looking away from me, behind the line of fence. When I got close to her I could see her eyes were fixed solidly somewhere that was familiar only to her, beyond all stars and atmosphere.

"Has she been like this a lot?" I asked, remembering even as I spoke that Mother had always suffered this way. Mother's headaches could grow instantly into migraines, her moods to "a condition." The only pause in her wavering moods, the only lasting balance, had been in my remembered invention of her. All the miles and days and hours had absorbed what was difficult about my mother, had protected me in my own censored notion of her.

"Only sometimes," Ginny said, and said nothing more.

"How are you?" I asked. I leaned against the palm tree from which the hammock was suspended. I ran a hand up the trunk and, in a casual way, checked the fixture to which the hammock was tied.

"What exactly is it you want to know?" Ginny said in a distant, dreadful way. "How I am feeling this very minute, or how I am in general, or whether I think I've finished growing? Your questions are all too careful, Sam. When did you become such a fucking politician?"

In front of me Ginny was a single long line with her bare

toes sticking up close to my hand. Her glasses, black square frames, were pushed above her forehead and she wouldn't look at me. This was Ginny's most salient characteristic, her ability to both abandon and occupy space, her tendency to draw you in and avoid you at the same time. It was a feature that she'd developed unselfconsciously and that I learned later served her in a thousand different ways, like the camouflage colors of bird feathers. But at the time all I thought was that her silence was terribly loaded, as though it were filled with a prayer.

"What?" she said, though I had asked nothing. She used her penlight to follow the lines of her paperback. I watched her move the tiny bulb against the page; her face seemed tiny beneath the colossal lenses of her glasses. She was all angles and eyes.

Finally I said, "What I guess I wanted to ask was what you were thinking. Maybe I'm wrong, but it seems to me you always have something important on your mind."

"What I was thinking?" Ginny said. She looked away from the book and considered this. "Just then, when you came out here?" she asked.

I nodded. I stepped back, out of the way of whatever thoughts she had.

She patted her mouth and then, speaking through fingers, said, "I was thinking that I am almost twenty and have never had a job I could put on a résumé. I was thinking that you went to college but still all you ended up with was a room in an industrial building that doesn't even have a sink. Meanwhile, all the light bulbs are gone—"

"Ginny . . ." I said. I reached for her, my sister, whom I regarded once, decades ago, as a silly but manageable alien in my home. She'd been brought in one day, wrapped in a pink blanket; I was nine years old and I'd thought, *What's the point of this?* Now I was the stranger; I was new in the house. I had the sudden urge to see Ginny differently, to accept a kinship with her, to be close. I had a flash of remembered feeling, a return to some place in my life that I'd thought had been forgotten.

"Don't be nice," Ginny said. "I just said a terrible thing to you and you're being nice about it. That makes me feel so . . . so trivial. Like anything the baby says is okay because it's re- markable enough that she speaks."

There was suddenly the sound of music from the house, a crashing, ugly cacophony of guitars and drums, feedback, and an extreme use of the synthesizer. Over it came the searing voices of young punk rockers.

"What is that?" I asked.

"Mother has decided that because you manage bands, she needs to keep up with contemporary music. I think she plays it when she cries and doesn't want anyone to hear."

"So she's crying a lot," I said.

"Who can tell? The music sends me screaming for the exits. Come on," Ginny said, swinging her legs over the edge of the hammock. She stepped delicately through the grass, being careful with her naked feet. She was so tall that her length was almost comic. Her hair trailed behind her and she waved her fingers as she spoke. "She made you a dinner—a homecoming dinner, she called it. She's probably upset that we aren't inside crooning over her baked ham."

Mother sat at the kitchen table leafing through a pile of old photographs. When we came in she looked over the rim of her eyeglasses and tucked a lock of hair behind her ear. She looked calmly expectant. There were grade school photos of me with a crew cut, back when my hair was light. Pictures of picnics and birthdays, high school graduations, camping pictures that Dad took of me and Ginny fishing, hiking, complaining. Mother's dinner plate was littered with color slides. She held them up one after another, squinting into the light.

The music was very loud, and I couldn't understand Ginny when she spoke. On the table, in a thick pot blackened from the oven, was a brown, evil-smelling stew.

I sat down. I smiled at Mother, who continued with the slides. Ginny, in the next room, managed to find the record player and end the yelping of a young punker.

I looked at the stew. It had thick blocks of ham, some carrot slices and celery. Against the far side of the pot floated a round white onion.

"Is this for us?" I asked. There were only plates on the table, no bowls. I went to a wall of cabinets and opened door after door until I found the china. From a drawer beneath the sink I dug out three fresh soup spoons. "This was so nice of you, Mom—I mean, Jewel."

When I sat back down Ginny gave me a look as though I were a traitor and a coward.

"I wanted you to have something hot when you got in," Mother said. She was sweet-voiced and solemn. Her hands unsteadily spooned the stew into the bowls, setting one on each plate. "I thought we could look at some family photos."

Ginny stared into her soup bowl. "Mother, please, anything but that," she said. "I think pictures are fake."

"I'd love to," I said. Ginny gave me a look.

Beside Mother was a plastic grocery bag that housed hundreds of pictures, some in envelopes, some clustered with rubber bands. I reached in and scooped up a short stack. Pictures of our old house in winter. Snow, pines, foggy windows. A favorite tree sprang up beside what used to be my bedroom window. In it, the frayed remainders of a kite.

"I saw the garden outside. You do a good job with sunflowers," I said.

Ginny rolled her eyes and I glared at her.

"I like the flowers," Mother said. "They're so tall they remind me of you two. How did I get such tall children," she added playfully, "when I'm such a little woman?"

Ginny poked around in the stew, escorting a lima bean to the edge of the plate and removing all traces of corn. A smile was burgeoning inside Mother, and I waited for her next line, which was an old joke she used to tell me at bedtime.

"I'm a little woman. A little of this . . . a little of that . . ."

I laughed genuinely. At her expression; at her shy, tiny smile. At her mischievous green eyes, that neither Ginny nor I had the good fortune to inherit.

"What's that mean?" Ginny asked. She was too young to remember. By the time Ginny was in grade school Mother had been fashioned into a much different person from the woman I thought of, who had the wonderful, predictable habit of telling stories at night.

The bowl in front of me was filled to the rim, and of course I was not at all hungry. It was after four in the morning eastern time and my stomach felt sour. I knew that I had to eat anyway for Mother's sake. I looked at her and saw that she was very content with her children, one on either side. She leaned back, eyes closed, and I felt special to someone. I felt a way that no friend or lover had ever made me feel, as though there could never be a substitute for my presence. To this woman I was wholly unique, and for a moment I had a brief, exalted understanding of the vastness of a parent's love.

Nonetheless, there was the stew to confront. It had tomatoes and slicks of hot grease. There were potatoes the size of ice cubes and, even worse, a brussel sprout. I looked at Ginny and saw that she had scooped all the tomatoes into a pile on her plate, partitioned the carrots away from the parsnips, unglued the mushrooms from each other, and disposed of the ham. What remained in her bowl was a clear pool of broth.

Meanwhile, Mother seemed to be concentrating on a moment of luxury that took place deep inside her. She had a half-moon smile and appeared almost asleep, she was so still. She kept her eyes closed, her chin tilted toward the ceiling. She looked as though she was listening to some sort of inner music, a private symphony that only she could hear.

"Well, this is really good, Mom," Ginny said, staring into the stew. "You managed to get all four food groups in here."

"Eat your dinner, dear" was Mother's reply.

"Oh, I don't know about that," Ginny said, pushing the bowl back. "It's almost breakfast time anyway, and you know, I've noticed that there's a very fine line between soup and trash."

"You need to eat more, darling," Mother said. "Have you noticed Ginny's new fashion style, Sam? She wears all those boys' clothes that are too big for her. And she hasn't any breasts. Isn't that remarkable? I could have sworn a few years ago she had breasts."

"Mother, you are becoming disgusting again," Ginny warned.

Mother rummaged through pictures, searching. "I'm quite sure that when you were in high school you had breasts," she said. "And stop calling me that name."

Ginny curled her lip, mocking Mother, who finally stopped looking through the pictures. As though coming back through miles of sky and clouds, she looked around the table at us, at the food, at her pile of photographs.

"I'm sorry," she said. "I'm not acting right, am I?"

She placed her hand near Ginny's cheek, but Ginny dodged away.

"I might be ugly but you should see the photos Eli takes of me," Ginny said. She swept her hair to one shoulder in a dramatic way. She smiled with her lower lip pushed out. It was a successful gesture, winning approval from us both, until Ginny noticed that a swatch of her hair had fallen into her soup bowl. She pulled back from the table, doused the end of her hair with a stream of water from the sink, and held a paper towel around the wet end.

"You might try going out with other boys," Mother said.

"I'm not saying there's anything wrong with Eli, but you're so young—don't you think you should be dating boys more your own age?"

"How old is Eli?" I asked Mother. I had the demo tapes in my jacket pocket. If Eli was twenty-two and was already discovering bands as good as these, I was going to retire from the business. I decided this in silence, awaiting Mother's answer.

"I don't know. Ginny, how old is Eli? Thirty-five? Thirty-eight?"

"Oh my God," I said.

"That's it," Ginny said. "I'm going to bed."

"Don't go," Mother begged. "Please, honey, I didn't mean anything."

"Ginny," I said, touching her wrist. I looked at her, hoping she could muster a moment more of patience. But she shook off my hand and disappeared into the dark living room.

Mother frowned. She looked down at the table. My mother had never been a tremendous parent; when we were young she left us for days with neighbors. Sometimes she would drive me to my father's office and leave me at the elevator, instructing me to come home with Dad. To Ginny she had done worse, I'm afraid. But she was a caring, fragile lady, and I could hardly stand the sight of her now, worried that somehow she'd driven away her daughter. I imagined she was recounting a host of memories, remembering good and bad. She might have been thinking of the happy way she thought this evening would turn out, her daydreams while she made dinner, while she zipped the back of her dress, rolled a stocking up each leg.

She finally said, "Ginny's been waiting all week for you to arrive and now I've ruined it for her."

"You haven't done anything," I said, but Mother was busy with her own thoughts.

She smiled. She said, "We've missed you."

THREE

■ ■ ■

For two days the city was covered in a tremendous fog. Mother's house was surrounded with a mist that masked the rest of the neighborhood and it seemed we were living in a world where other people were never seen. The houses on Sun Dial Street were close together and I kept hearing voices nearby but never saw any faces. The neighbor behind us had a dog named Jasper, and she called her dog each morning at seven and each evening at five. Next door a guy worked on his car. I heard tools drop against the driveway, the sound of a hood being closed, the scrape of an oil pan along gravel. An old couple took a stroll after the evening news. Hal and June. I heard the click of their canes, two raspy voices. Sometimes Hal called his wife Juney. There was a gang of teenagers that settled outside at about eleven at night, and the couple across the way made loud, obnoxious sounds during their lovemaking. All of this took place out of sight, behind a veil of gray weather and fog.

I'd rigged up an ironing board as a sort of desk on which I

laid out my scheduling book, Rolodex, notepad. Managers are on call twenty-four hours a day. Three thousand miles make no difference to clients, and I was kept pretty busy. Club owners telephoned collect with scheduling problems, complaints, cancellations. Band members begged directions, guidance, equipment, moral support. I'd bought a travel guide to Los Angeles but so far I'd spent most of my time on the phone.

"Hello, Pelzer, this is Sam. The boys tell me you blew off last night's performance."

Arnold Pelzer was a member of The Fetish, five college guys, all with slick haircuts, leather jackets, shirts with unusual collar and button arrangements and, strangely, the same tendency to lose a contact lens before every performance. They were clean-cut, good-looking boys and, though four-fifths heterosexual, had all the gay clubs wanting them. Unfortunately, Pelzer, who *was* gay, refused to play in gay clubs. Also, he'd recently changed his look, directly violating The Fetish's agreed-upon image. He grew his hair, stopped shaving, went mostly unwashed, and wore the same pair of ripped blue jeans no matter what was spilled, smeared, or rubbed on them.

"Pelzer? Are you listening? I can hear you breathing."

Pelzer answered finally, in a croaky, belligerent voice. "I got lost," he said.

"There wouldn't be a particular reason you got lost, would there?" I asked. But Pelzer wasn't talking.

"Pelzer, are you gargling? I think I hear gargling in the background."

I called back an hour later.

"Pelzer, you cannot refuse to appear in a club after you agree to a booking."

"I agreed before I saw the place. That is not a club; that's a detox center."

"We can't go back on our word with a club manager. It's unprofessional. It's cowardly," I said.

"Fuck that," Pelzer said. "Fuck all that."

■ ■ ■

There was some very bad Scotch in a cabinet next to bottles of even worse plum-flavored wine, apple brandy, Dubonnet, bloody Mary mix and light beer in cans. After about three more calls to Pelzer and quite a storm of alcohol, I looked up and saw Ginny coming through the door. Eli's restaurant required the staff to wear Ray Bans and orange fluorescent jump suits. Ginny's shift ended at two in the morning and she came home smelling like one of the Acapulco drinks with all the sugar and fruit in them. I offered her a nightcap from the selection of horrible alcohol I'd discovered, but she shook her head and said she didn't drink—which I doubted.

"What happened to your mouth?" I asked. Across her lip was a small swelling, dark purple with some blood. She had red wine all down her front, a carton of cigarettes in her hand— Mother's brand—a large brown envelope and a jug of apple cider. In her jump suit she was a floodlight of orange, a walking Popsicle.

"Fell down. This is from Eli," she said, dropping the envelope across my knees.

She put the cigarettes on the coffee table, shook a pack loose from the carton, and tore through the plastic and foil tops. She brought the jug of cider to her lips, swallowed hard, then made a serious attempt to light her cigarette with matches that were damp from the humid air. All the while she watched me, forming some sort of an assessment, though I didn't know what of. I couldn't stop staring at her orange suit. I thought, *Astronaut. Crossing guard.*

"Are you opening it or dissecting it?" she asked, nodding at the envelope.

There was something not quite right with my coordination and I had been ripping little bits from the corners of the envelope without much success. Finally I uncovered its contents:

another demo tape, unmarked except for the label "Demo 4" and the recording date.

Outside there was a swoop of headlights as a car went by. A kid on the corner threw a bottle and someone yelled.

Ginny sat cross-legged on the couch, her hand over her swollen mouth.

There was a long silence.

"What?" I said.

"This is great," Ginny said, smiling. "It hurts to laugh, but you, *you drunk*, I've never seen you like this. It's hysterical. You're absolutely zippered."

She looked at me in that somewhat amused, somewhat disgusted way sober people look at drunk people. It was true I'd had too much. I'd been slouched over the telephone, midway in dialing, and had forgotten whom I was trying to call. Now I focused on Ginny, on the careful way she smoked with her hurt lip, on her long, folded legs. She looked nothing like she had four years ago. She'd grown up while I wasn't around—almost, it seemed, in secret.

"So what's between you and this Eli?" I said.

Ginny looked down, staring at the couch beneath her. She rushed her hands over it as if she was searching for something, a lost earring, a quarter.

"Nothing," she said. "Have you seen my lighter?"

"What's he like?"

"He's like you, a pest." She shook her head, looking down at her jump suit. She ran a hand across the long stain of wine down her middle.

"Okay, don't tell me," I said. I very suddenly felt sick to my stomach. Not like I was going to throw up, but like I wished I could throw up. Behind my eyes was a sharp pain, as though there was something inside my head that ought not to be. Everything bothered me—the smell of the house, the misty air. Ginny had run a clothesline from one wall to the other, and the clothes hanging from it—pantyhose, a blouse, another version of Ginny's dumb waitress outfit—seemed obtrusive, too much to take. What bothered me most, I guessed, was that Mother had gone to sleep around three that afternoon and I'd worked for hours, one eye on her bedroom door, and she'd never even waked up to pee.

"Has Mother always been this crazy, or am I just forgetting?" I asked, turning away. I walked to the kitchen, stood at the sink and dunked my head beneath a flow of cool water. I stayed like that for a while, not caring that my collar became soaked. I swallowed water in gulps. I thought I smelled something in it, a chemical smell. I let the water run in and out of my mouth, as though I were a statue beneath a fountain or a hillside full of rain.

"Hey," Ginny said. She was standing behind me.

I paid no attention, just kept wet. I put my hands over my head and felt water through my fingers. I made it colder so that my scalp ached with it. I felt my stomach turn over and my breath hot with Scotch.

Ginny said, "I find it very interesting that you are a nasty drunk. I wouldn't have thought it. I suppose the answer to your question is yes, Mother has always been this crazy. It's just that when Dad was alive we never noticed as much."

I turned the water off and ran a hand over my hair, pressing out the wetness. I tried to remember years back, exactly how Mother had acted.

"I don't remember her retreating for hours at a stretch," I said.

"You always walked in just before dinner, dropped your books on the stairway, and said, 'Hey, are the folks still alive?' or 'Where's Mom? Is she dead or what?' That's because Mom was asleep."

"I don't remember this," I said.

"And it made me afraid all the time that she *might* die, like I had to be prepared or something. I was so worried about her that it made things worse for me when Dad died. I never even considered him . . ."

I looked at Ginny. The cut on her lip wasn't big, but the rest of her face seemed to shrink away from it. Her hair was flat over her forehead, heavy with restaurant grease and steam. Behind her glasses I could see the tiredness in her eyes. Still, she was very alert, determined to be heard. Across her brow was a deep groove of concern and she stood with one leg pushed out, her arms folded. Her elbows were sharp points and her wrists, so small, made her hands appear oversized.

I told her I remembered now. I told her I could see myself dropping my bicycle on the lawn, closing the front door too hard, leaping up the stairway three steps at a time and calling out for Mother, whose thorough lack of government in the household caused me to tease about the possibility that she was no more.

"So I'm right?" Ginny asked. She pulled the elastic in her hair so her ponytail straightened up. "I'm glad you remember because sometimes I think I just make everything up, you know? I look at those photographs Mom has, of Dad and Mom sitting at the picnic table, or you and me standing together on the front porch, and I don't feel like the pictures are real at all. I think I just dreamed them up, borrowed someone else's memories. Or that I imagined everything."

She pulled out another cigarette and tried to light it with her wet matches, but nothing happened. Then she chucked the matchbook at me and bent over a ring of gas flame at the stove, inhaling clouds of smoke.

"You didn't make it up," I said. "I was there."

"Sometimes," she said. She leaned against the counter, facing me. Outside, the wind picked up, showering the house with loose dirt, a few small pebbles. It was too damp for a sandstorm, but the wind was suddenly strong, extraordinary. It thundered through tree branches, across the broad faces of sunflowers. I heard it rustle through the neighbor's bamboo, and from somewhere far off came a series of notes from a wind chime.

Ginny stood holding her arms across her stomach, her eyes wandering the room. She recounted memories as though she could see our family's short history across the blank ceiling, across the cracked walls of the kitchen, or swimming in the air just in front of her eyes. She went on and on, capturing years inside the span of seconds, summoning up huge events in phrases. I understood then that Ginny's chronicling of her life was a habit, that she conjured up the details of the past decade in pieces she intended to solve, like an algebraic equation, a riddle, or a crime.

"And after Dad died," she said, looked down at her hands, "you were gone."

"I would have visited sooner," I said. "But all the musicians, all the tours."

There had been only one serious musician and one tour: a singer named Courtney Lyons who dropped me professionally and personally the minute she saw the inside of a record company.

Ginny said, "Tours my butt. All you've done for four years is lug around that girl's guitar."

"Mother tells me the only job you've had is this one at the restaurant your boyfriend owns. You go to a career counselor for that?"

"Well, I'm glad we've gone back to hating each other," Ginny said. "It was beginning to be an effort."

It was too late at night to argue. I thought I'd better go back to the living room, unhinge the couch and set up my bed for the night.

"Wait a minute, Sam," Ginny said as I turned to go. "I'm sorry Courtney broke up with you. Frankly, I don't like her music anyway. All those songs about the pill and episiotomy. I think her success is just a fad."

She sat down at the table, pulling her legs up. She kicked a chair out with her naked toe, and I sat down. She leaned toward me and I smelled a faint strawberry from her shampoo, the salt on her skin.

"I don't blame you for not wanting to come here," she said. "I've wished so often that it could have been me who stayed behind. In my head, I've planned a million escapes."

I heard a dog bark, the sound of an engine. I looked at Ginny, but she was concentrating on something else, on whatever was happening outside in the noisy alley or on something deep within her, the kernel of a memory that I could see in her face. She frightened me this way; she seemed so open, so unprotected. I felt I could reach right down inside her and take her heart in my hands. I felt I was looking straight into her, that she had uncovered herself for this one severed moment and anything I might do would be magnified by millions.

Then she leaned back, tilted her head, listened for something.

"That noise you hear," she said in a whisper. "That's Van. He is sitting outside in the car with a double bouquet of flowers for Mother. He's out there waiting to be let in, like a dog, which is what he is."

I watched Ginny as she glided away from me, disappearing into the living room. I heard the front door open, some words, the shutting of a car door, two pairs of footsteps. I listened to everything, to the sound of Mother's bedroom door opening to a stranger named Van, her sleepy voice, the receiving of a kiss. I closed my eyes. For a moment I might have been asleep.

"Sam," Mother said, and I looked up. She was wearing a shimmering bathrobe with lace near the collar and a hair comb with beads sewn in the shape of bows. Against her chest was a fistful of daisies, a flower I particularly despise. Behind her was a man with a white beard and a shirt unbuttoned far enough for me to see a pile of chest hair in the same colorless shade.

Mother introduced him as Van, no last name, no explanation. He had a pudgy, wide palm and made a point of squeez-

35

ing extra tight on the handshake. He had a low forehead and a face full of thick creases. In a very loud voice he said, "Well then, you're here from the East. It was news to me when Jewel told me her boy was coming for a visit. Surprised us all. Tell me then, Sam. Is it Sam or Sammy? Tell me what the hell is new with you then?"

I didn't answer at first. I was annoyed at him for arriving as he did, for interrupting my talk with Ginny. I let his question linger between us while I slouched against the wall, making him nervous with a long stare. He folded his arms and looked away. He moved his hands to his broad hips and swallowed; he looked strangely accused.

Finally I said, "It's three in the morning."

Van looked at me through squinty, sailor blue eyes. His beard, I noticed, was sculpted into a scholarly shape. But he hadn't a bad face and I wondered why I was making him suffer. Poor Van. He was stymied now. He launched into a series of stutters, saying more or less, "Uh-huh. Well, yes, it is. It is, yes, three. About that."

"Mother, why do you have to have *him* here all the time?" Ginny said.

"Be quiet, Virginia," Mother said. "I don't criticize your friends."

"What friends? I have no friends. I'm too busy earning money so Romeo here can drink it up."

"I got two good ears, Ginny," Van said. To me he said, "What's your line of work?"

"Band manager," I said.

"I used to play trumpet, back in the service."

"Van was a Marine," Ginny said. She made like she was holding a machine gun.

"Ginny, that's enough," Mother said.

"How's Doreen?" Ginny asked. The question was for Van but Ginny looked directly at me. "Doreen's his wife."

"Stop," Mother said. She took Van's elbow and led him out

of the kitchen. We heard their voices growing softer and softer, eventually being drowned out by the television—a miniature version of the other one—in Mother's room.

"We could have been more welcoming," I said to Ginny. She'd fired up another cigarette and was smoking ferociously, right down to where the filter would be if there were a filter.

"I hate myself and I hate him," she said.

"How did he meet Mom?"

"In the bin. He fought in Korea and signed up for two tours of duty in Vietnam. Never a problem. Then one day he just freaked out. He thought he was some sort of major political figure. Napoleon? Maybe he thought he was a POW, I don't remember. Anyway, he had this miraculous recovery. He doesn't take meds or anything, lives off a pension. He had the room across the hall from Mom and they watched movies to-gether at night."

"That's sweet," I said.

"Sweet? She met him in an *insane asylum.*"

"Not an insane asylum."

"Dad's dead five weeks and she takes up with that man. By the way, Van has grown kids who despise him, so don't think I'm the only one."

"You need to stop smoking that cigarette or it's going to burn you," I said.

"You can't even get a mortgage in five weeks," said Ginny.

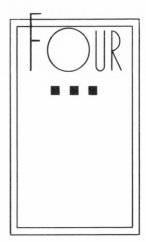

FOUR
■ ■ ■

My country-western trio made a sudden and unexpected campus debut, playing to a full house at Harvard University's Sanders Theater, an elaborate nineteenth-century theater decorated with college insignia, gargoyles, statues, and paintings from all over the globe. It was a place where professors delivered their lectures, where famous political debates had been held. Robert Frost once read there.

Don't ask me. I had nothing to do with the booking. I picked up the phone and one of the Henrys told me in a loud, excited drawl that they'd done two encores and sold 178 tapes after the performance.

"We might be moving up, huh, Sam?" said another of the Henrys, I don't know which one. They all had the same accent. They had moved to Boston from Wyoming when a bottle plant, their employer, transferred 500 of its people.

"You can't tell anything from just one good night," I said. I was tossed on my back, my legs spilling out over the end of the couch. I tried to sound wise, clearheaded, managerial. The truth was that before that day I'd planned to ax the trio. I didn't see a market for country-western. They'd been hanging on by their fingernails.

"You gonna come on back home and do a little hoofing for us?"

Hoofing was the Henrys' word for finding them work. Hoofing was what I did for a living as far as the Henrys were concerned.

"Soon," I said. I promised to make some calls that day, hung up, and began rummaging through my Rolodex.

In fact, I was on the phone to a club in Somerville, a restaurant and bar situation with a big dance floor, convincing the manager what a great act the Henrys were, when Van fired up some sort of electric tool and began hacking away at the hedges on the side of the house. Suddenly the entire house was consumed in the whir and chortle of a saw, which was being powered, I discovered, through an outlet just outside the kitchen window. I leaned out the window and considered unplugging the device. Then I thought better of it. A sudden end to power midway through a branch might cause injury, and worse than having Van around would be having an injured Van convalescing in our living room.

I could see very well what Van was doing now. He stood over a shaggy bush, stabbing at it with the saw. He had a pile of tools by his left foot and an aerosol can of chemical spray hooked to his belt. His entire face was tense and frowning at the offending branches, which dropped one by one to the grass.

I waved, I shouted. He didn't notice. He was too busy defoliating the only real greenery in our yard.

"Oh, let him be," Mother said. She stood next to the stove, warming sirup in a double boiler. She had some sort of mold for tiny candy animals.

"Mother, my business requires that I be able to *hear*," I said.

"Have a toad," she said, holding up a piece of maple cream.

Finally I caught Van's eye. He waved and came to the open window. He leaned against the sill, hands full of hedge clippings, his shirttail wagging over his wide, bulbous stomach. His skin had so many freckles, so many layers of blotchy brown, that he looked like a burn victim. His hair was white and shot through with yellow strands, so I guessed he had at one time been a towhead blond with a fair complexion.

"How is my Jewel?" he asked Mother.

She laughed.

"You wouldn't be making a little lunch for me, would you?" he said in his jolly, nauseating way.

"You'll just have to wait and see," she teased.

Now Van turned to me. "Did you want me for something?" he asked.

I meant to tell him to quit with the saw. But I was mesmerized by how enormous he was. He was such a huge block of person. Everything about him seemed oversized, and it wasn't just because he was fat, though he was fat. Through the thin cloth of his T-shirt you could see all too clearly the outline of his belly button, the crescents of flesh beneath his arms and around his back. I looked at my own stomach, a nondescript plane beneath a polo shirt, without any of the spectacular globular qualities of Van's roller gut. I wondered what it would be like to carry around such weight, to become essentially an orb.

"If you come out a minute, I'll give you a little lesson in weeds," he said, signaling me with his thumb.

"I'd appreciate it a whole lot more if you'd stop using that thing," I said, pointing at the electric saw.

"What? You don't like my Branch Dragon? Let me tell you, Sam-o, this little item is an essential part of my life," Van said, patting the tool with his palm. He stared at me—he had this way of appearing as if he was going to speak but taking a long time to say anything. He patted his shirt pocket, searching for a cigar. He kept looking at me as he wandered his hands through the pockets of his immense shorts, which were strapped to his hips by a tightly clenched plastic belt. After some fishing he came up with a White Owl, which he brought to his lips in a slow way, as though he were considering a matter of importance. Finally he managed his next sentence. He said, "You might consider learning a thing or two about gardening—help your mother out a bit."

"Van, one more scream from that tool of yours . . ." I warned.

He frowned; he looked out over the yard and then back at me. Talking to Van was like conducting an overseas telephone conversation with enormous gaps between phrases. After a long pause he said, "You don't know what is happening here. To you it looks like any old back yard, but there's disease in these greens."

"Undoubtedly. But whatever scourge has found its way into our garden will probably be no worse tomorrow."

"If you're the expert then you tell me, what's this?"

He pushed a swatch of branches in front of my nose, thumbing the leaves, making sure I got a sound inspection of each branch.

"Foliage," I answered.

"Foliage. I got a serious aphid infection happening on this bush and he says foliage. Let me tell you something, Sam-o, let me explain what'll happen if we do what you suggest and ignore this bush."

He went on and on about the hedge, about plants in general. He explained about blight, mold, the importance of earthworms, the chemical properties of pesticides, methods of organic farming, the importance of timed planting. I let him continue because Mother had taken an interest in the conversation. She was listening to him, and so I listened too. I nodded when he defined terms, described leaves and soil types.

Mother seemed so happy that Van and I were talking. She smiled at me and then at Van. I had to let him ramble on—how could I not? The fact was, I couldn't care if the bush were pulped and the garden covered in Astroturf. But when Mother suggested that I help Van with the weeds, you know what? I did it.

Toward afternoon the temperature soared. I tried to get Ginny to go to the beach with me, but she was packing a canvas bag with clothes, jewelry, compacts, mirrors, tubes of color and mascara. Apparently someone was going to take her picture.

"Don't make fun," she said. "This guy has done portfolios for real models."

"I promise after an ocean swim and a short stint on the beach we'll go directly to a photo booth."

Ginny hoisted the bag on her shoulder, teetered some, and let it fall to the floor.

"I think I'll bring a record," she said.

"Come on, a little time in the ocean."

"No, Sam. This is serious stuff," she said. "The photographer taking my picture today did Brenda McCabe's first portfolio."

"Where are you going to be?" I asked.

"Out."

"What if there's an emergency?"

"Don't be ridiculous," Ginny said. She scribbled seven digits on a grocery receipt and held it out for me. "Here. Now please get out of the way."

"Whose number is this?" I said.

"Eli's."

"Eli who owns the restaurant? *That* Eli?"

"He's also a photographer," said Ginny. She began rifling through her record collection. "Don't make comments."

"Well, I'll tell you what," I said, tucking the number into my breast pocket. "As long as this little romance keeps up, you never have to worry about getting fired from the restaurant."

Ginny paused in her search for a record. She balanced a few albums against her palm and looked up at me, narrowing her eyes. "You might as well leave the room because from now on I am not listening to anything you say."

"I have to hand it to you, you are discreet," I said.

She stood up, ignoring me. She looked for her record on her desk, bureau, behind a stack of books by the window, the jumble of clutter by the door. She crouched in front of her closet, pushing against a pile of papers. Her back was a round archway with narrow breadth. She was like a cat on all fours. She scurried across the room and I tagged after her.

"Why all the secrecy? What's he, married?"

Ginny said nothing.

"Profoundly ugly and flatulent?"

She turned away.

"Tell me then. I haven't had any good gossip for weeks," I said. Then in a different way I said, "Really, Ginny, talk to me."

She crawled toward the front of the room, looking under a jacket, a grocery bag.

"Damn," she said.

I said, "Except for the rosy cheeks and your obsession with love duets, I would never have guessed you were in love."

"I am not in love; I have no obsession with love duets," Ginny said. She looked up, scowling. "Stop following me. I mean it, Sam, one more step and I stab your ankle with this ballpoint pen."

"All I'm asking is for you to speak to me. It's been a long time. I would think we'd have something to say to each other."

"Don't pull that," she said. "You didn't come here to see *me*. You came for business reasons."

"That is not entirely true . . ."

"Got it!" Ginny said, lifting a dirty sleeve of white from beneath a stack of newspapers. She shook the record loose, smiling at the label.

"*Madame Butterfly*," I declared, reading over her shoulder. "With a famous love duet, if I'm not mistaken."

"I'm warning you," she said.

Ginny called from her photo session an hour later.

"I'm sorry I yelled at you," she said.

"You didn't yell."

"In my head I was screaming at you."

"Oh."

"Anyway, I think I left my keys at home. Can you take a look for me?"

I told her to hold on and went into her room. I glanced across the dresser and saw a sewing kit, a tub of hair clips, some earrings, a pocket radio. No keys. I dug through her jacket pockets and found them. When I reported this to Ginny, she sighed into the telephone.

"Leave the door open for me tonight," she said. In the background I heard a male voice, some music, something being moved across the floor.

"Say hi to Eli for me," I said. "When do I get to meet him?"

I heard the sound of a match being struck, Ginny's cigarette smoke against the receiver.

"He wants you to come by the restaurant tomorrow to talk about the demo tapes," she said. "You say one word to him about me . . ."

The other thing about Van is that he never went home. It seemed to me that for a married man he had a lot of flexible hours. Even when he did leave, he returned right away, usually before the bug killer or fertilizer or flower feeder or whatever else he sprayed in the yard had ceased to putrefy everything.

"Don't you wonder what this crap does to your lungs?" I asked him. He was standing at the front door, on the other side of the screen, holding a metal container with a spray attachment that looked like a bullhorn. You would think that after so long he'd just walk inside, but no, he stood there and knocked. I thought about what Ginny had said about his being like a dog waiting to be let in. I let him in.

"Nothing wrong with this," he said, holding up his spray can. "It's food for shrubs. Someone outside for you."

In the street just outside our door was a bright pink Cadillac with a woman behind the wheel.

"You know her?" Van asked. "She says she knows you."

I was about to answer no when I realized that the woman in the car was Celia Lawson. I recognized her funny glasses and her particular hairstyle, which made it so her hair never, ever moved. She caught sight of me and blasted her horn.

I charged out of the house and stood by her car. I'd forgotten to put on shoes, and even though it was only nine A.M., the hot pavement stung. I hopped from one foot to the other, speaking to Celia through the car window.

"How did you find this place?" I asked.

"Get in," she said. Beside her was a map of Los Angeles, a crude paper placemat with the name of a doughnut shop across the top; details of the city were illustrated in salmon and green. She put her finger on the control button to raise the window. "I'm losing air conditioning," she said.

I went around to the passenger's side and settled into the white leather of the Cadillac's interior.

"I bought this thing from a rental place called Uncle Sog's. You are never supposed to buy a car that has been used for rental, my daughter tells me. She tells me *after* I've paid four grand," Celia said, accelerating. "And I don't have a license, so alert me if I do something wrong."

We drove down Sun Dial Street, took a series of rights and continued on around again, orbiting my mother's house.

Celia said, "I've been watching a documentary called *The Family in Crisis*. Did you know that the family is in crisis? I used to think that it was just my family that was in crisis, but now I see that historically the family has always been in crisis."

"How long can a crisis last?" I asked. "Isn't a crisis by definition a catastrophe that occurs *suddenly?*"

"That is a point, Sam. But it is a small and insignificant point."

We went round and round, past the UPS building, the all-night taco stand, the car wash.

"If you will give me driving lessons," Celia said, "I'll introduce you to my daughter."

"I'm not sure that's such a good deal for her," I said. Celia had stopped at an intersection even though the light was green. "If you're willing to make a full trade for her, I'm sure you can do better. You might get two hundred or so camels, a dozen slaves—but only if you'd be willing to travel."

"Do you want to know what Lucy's think tank of a husband has spent the past month doing? Trying to sell the school district on the idea that chocolate replicas would best acquaint children with the more discreet regions of the anatomy."

"Celia, I'd love to hang around, but I'm half dressed and there's work to be done."

"I'm surprised he wasn't arrested."

"Celia, I'm getting out."

"You can't. I need an instructor. How about we make an arrangement for a lesson this afternoon?"

"I don't know . . ."

"I have my test in seven days; I'm desperate," she said.

"Celia, green means go."

"I knew you'd be perfect for this job."

"Nice lady," Van said when I returned to the house. He offered me some coffee, which I refused. "How about you give me a hand with the new soil?" he asked.

"What new soil? God, no. Leave me alone."

"Suit yourself, but afterwards there'll be planting."

He went to the kitchen for his coffee and then out the back door to the yard. I decided to wake up Ginny. There was no way I could face Van alone so early in the day.

"Ginny," I said. I tapped her bedroom door with two knuckles. I waited. "Okay, I'm taking a shower but then I'm coming back, ready to assault your morning lie-in. Nobody gets to snooze until noon if I don't. I am the sleep commando."

I laughed gruesomely and sauntered off, heavy-footed. But Ginny did not awaken, not when I showered, when I turned up the volume on the radio, when I stormed through my clothes looking for something to wear.

I walked by her room again and again, making a lot of noise with my loafers. I kept expecting to see her coming through the door, her hair bunched in an elastic band, her nightgown loose around her shoulders. I had a meeting with Eli this afternoon, thanks to her. I hoped he could arrange for me to listen to a couple of the groups I'd heard on tape. Thinking about that improved my spirits. It seemed that for the first time in a long while I was on to some music that had a chance of really making it big, and I was in a big mood.

But then Van decided to take a rest from his gardening. He came into the living room and plopped himself in front of the television. He watched me as I knocked at Ginny's door, shook his head and smiled. I knocked again and called her name, asking if I could come in. I felt very stupid, knowing that Van was sitting ten feet away, listening. He was trying to appear interested in a game show, but he kept the sound down low and I knew anyway he was tuning into my efforts with Ginny's closed door. I could see something of a smirk on his face. After a while he didn't even pretend to be watching the show. He glanced at me in a way that made me feel very creepy. His thick lips were pursed below his mustache and he had this smug, detestable expression. I tried ignoring him but he turned fully toward me. In his palm was the remote control, which he handled as though it were a very important and authoritative prop. He said, "She's not here."

"What do you mean she's not here?" I said. "She's asleep."

"No sir, she's not," Van said. He chuckled in one short breath. He pointed the remote control at the television and flipped a few channels. He brought the volume up and down. Apparently he thought he was hot stuff doing this. With his remote control he seemed to make the statement *I am in control here. I am the possessor of the wand of control, as you can see.*

"Why are you laughing?" I asked.

"I'm not laughing," he said. "I'm telling you she's gone. Her car isn't here, you might have noticed."

"Where is she?"

"If you spent any time around here, you'd know," he said. He turned his head toward Mother, who came into the room, holding a potted plant.

"My little geranium is dying. Can you save it?"

"Of course," Van said. "Give her here, Jewel."

Mother was in a good mood again this morning. We were supposed to be skeptical about her new effulgence. We were supposed to prepare ourselves for another turn. Advice from Wilma, the psychiatric nurse, who came by altogether too seldom but apparently was helpful even so.

But now Mother seemed like the happiest woman in the world, all good news and cheer. She was preparing some sort of meal. Van had promised the day to her and she was celebrating.

"A few more minutes and it'll be ready," Mother said. "We'll all have a nice family brunch."

"Terrific!" Van said and gave me a look.

"That's great," I said.

When she left the room I said to Van, "You're the type of guy who makes lamps out of empty wine bottles and feels strongly about brands of motor oil."

"What does that have to do with anything?"

"I'm just reminding myself," I said. I knocked on Ginny's door again.

Van looked me up and down, let go an enormous sigh and said, "Look, maybe the girl *is* asleep, but she's not here."

"She probably took a taxi home," I said.

Van winced. "Taxi," he repeated.

Finally I turned the knob and looked inside the room. Van was right. No Ginny. The bed was a confusion of sheets and blankets but it was exactly like it had been yesterday and there was no one in the room. I glanced at Van. He was smiling the way you see men smile late at night at girls they don't have a chance with. A voyeur's smile.

I said, "She's asleep, you idiot. Don't disturb her."

I didn't know much about Eli or his restaurant, but it seemed everyone in Hollywood did. I walked down Melrose looking for it without luck but whenever I asked anybody they pointed east, in the direction I was going. I was early for my appointment with Eli, so I didn't mind the walk. There was something very strange about this street. It was lined with shops that sold the type of furniture and knickknacks that were familiar in decades long past. You could buy a peace sign, wide as a beach ball, with heavy blue liquid that moved like lava through the hollowed plastic. Wigs from the sixties. Seventies-style smiley faces in bright yellow. Beads to hang in a doorway. The street was a market for nostalgia, as though the past were for sale inside these Hollywood boutiques. Everywhere there were posters of cartoons and media personalities I had long ago forgotten: The Archie's, Wally Cleaver, Josie and the Pussycats, Mighty Mouse. I saw one guy walk out of a store with a life-size poster of Marlo Thomas from "That Girl."

Melrose was clearly not the sort of place that should be seen during the day. In strong light the elaborate joke of these shops quickly lost its humor, becoming almost tiresome. I got the sense that the street was not in proper form without neon lights, without a darkness that fostered the magic of being able to buy objects of memory. And the people, mostly women, mostly in black leather and long, overdyed black hair, would probably look better at night as well, I decided.

One woman, with a serious crimson-painted mouth, eyed me from the phone booth that had become her leaning post. She stared in a way that some women can, with a sort of stray-dog shyness and willingness to please. I stared back at her as though this happened all the time, as though I'd tossed off chances with other women just a few blocks past. When we locked eyes, I noticed her makeup, which was fluorescent green and brown. She walked toward me, her leather jacket making noise. She had long, heavy legs and she was big, with big shoulders and a wide chest. She stood right in front of me, pressing her lips together. A Marilyn Monroe–style mole was painted on her cheek, and her eyes were heavy with fake lashes. I looked down on her, at her short neck, at her funny painted eyes. I tried to imagine her without the costuming and I decided she was pretty—or that she could be pretty.

"You an actor?" she asked. Her stance was tough city girl. But her voice, I noticed, was young and just a little unsteady.

"No," I said.

"You're someone, right? You're Harry Barton from 'The 'Copters that Kill'?"

"No," I said.

"You a director?"

"I'm nothing," I said. "Nobody. I'm a nullity, a trifle. I'm a thing of naught."

"Asshole," she said. She smiled and I saw her teeth, which were perfect. She looked away, laughing. I saw the skin above each eye crinkle green. I saw a pink log of a tongue. She turned back to me with a different expression, a full-force seriousness. "You a cop?" she asked.

"No. You a prostitute?"

"Yeah, right, fuck you," she said, rolling her eyes. "You got no money, you fuckin' loser."

And then I realized she *was* a prostitute.

"I'm sorry," I said. When I'd gone a few steps, she ran up to me, clumsy on high heels. She spun me around, keeping a hand on my jacket lapel. She looked up at me and I saw her eyes go red, her face get desperate with something crucial and sad. A trauma that belonged exclusively to her. She pulled at me hard and said in a pinched voice, "I'm not a whore."

Eli's restaurant turned out to be a converted warehouse behind several stores. It didn't have much of a sign, really. There was a tiny poster next to a door. The sign said ELI'S. That's all. No opening hours, no reviews clipped from the newspaper. If you didn't know, you'd never guess it was a restaurant.

The place was so dark inside that when I went through the door, I was at once off balance. I couldn't see three feet in front of me and whatever I did see appeared unnaturally dense. I hung back, close to the coatrack. There was music by Ethel Merman, a tune I remembered from dance class when I was six years old. It swam in the air like a voice in a dream. There were lights way off, purple, rose. But they didn't illuminate the air around them. They were bulbs of color against the blank darkness.

A bright orange suit came toward me. At first I thought it was Ginny, but then I saw that this was a smaller suit than Ginny's. At the base of it were tiny shoes. The suit was like a lantern in this dark place. At the end of each arm was a flashlight, dulled electricity through the tiniest of bulbs. Her face, the hostess's face, was hidden. She used her flashlights as though she were landing a plane, instructing me forward, around a curve in the hallway, and up a short flight of stairs.

The light here was better, though still very dim. I saw a

room with a cement floor painted like a children's playground. There were circles for dodge ball. There were hopscotch boards and four-square. The ceiling was a high corrugated roof, as though the place were still a storage facility. Things were hanging in the air, big blow-up replicas of WWI army fighter planes, modern bombers, a helicopter. Arranged next to large square pillars were tables, four to each pillar, with chairs that ranged from piano benches to recliners.

I took a table and told the hostess I was here to see Eli. She nodded, and suddenly the music changed and on came the Monkeys. One wall was a big clock; it said, in block digital letters, FIVE IN THE AFTERNOON.

Eli appeared suddenly, gliding across the room in a swift, bowlegged walk. He wore jeans and a thin cotton shirt rolled to the elbows. He stopped several feet from my table, hesitated, and stepped back. For a moment I thought that it couldn't be Eli and that this man had mistaken me for someone else, which seemed likely in the darkness of the restaurant.

"Are you Sam Haskell?" he asked. "I'm sorry . . . I . . . I'm Edgar Igleton—um . . . Eli. Ginny is around—she'll join us soon, or maybe she will. You never can tell with Ginny. You need a drink, don't you? I'll get you something."

Eli backed a few steps, turned, and then raced across the floor of the restaurant and gave instructions to a waitress. Then he turned again, facing me, and now, stepping slowly, he made his way back. A few feet from the table he froze.

"Do you eat meat?" he asked, the question bursting from him.

"Yes, of course," I said.

The waitress came, bringing a bottle of California wine and three glasses, one presumably for Ginny. We waited as she arranged the glasses and uncorked the wine. I watched Eli, who appeared to be concentrating very hard on the grain of the wooden table before us. He was slim, with a lot of sandy hair and the sort of features that made him seem younger than he was. The waitress poured a small amount of wine into his glass, and he smiled at her and shook his head, gesturing in my direction, and so she did the same for me. I didn't taste it. I nodded and she poured.

"There's such good wine in California," I said. It was from Sonoma County, this bottle. I know nothing about wine but as I drank a bit, I began to understand, for the first time, why some people make it their life's ambition to buy, collect, and drink it.

"Oh, I don't know, you can get a lot of above-average, but . . ." Eli's voice trailed off. Then he said, "Do you like it? Maybe it is very good."

There was a placard on the wall. Evidently Eli's restaurant had won a "best of" award several years running.

"Not bad," I said, pointing up.

"What? Oh, that," Eli said. "Have you been here before?"

"No."

"I guess Ginny doesn't talk much about the restaurant."

"Ginny doesn't talk, period," I said. "She listens to opera at high volume and she scorns food. That's what Ginny does."

Eli chuckled.

"It's true," I said. "Maybe you can give me some advice—she won't talk to me at all."

"About what?"

"About anything. You, for one."

"You want to know how we became friends?" Eli asked. He looked into his wineglass, smiling. "Ginny used to swim in the ocean every night after work, which isn't the safest thing. I told her I had a swimming pool and she could swim there. But she wouldn't. Then one morning—it must have been four A.M.—I woke up. I thought I heard something. When I went outside, I discovered that the plug for the lights next to the hot tub had been pulled out of the socket. There wasn't much of a moon that night, but when I looked hard I could see someone in the pool. Ginny was doing laps, so silently it was like watching a school of fish in a lake. After a few minutes she stopped at the edge of the pool and saw me watching. I didn't want to disturb her, so I went back inside the house. With the spotlights off you can't see anything from the house, so Ginny was able to resume her swim in seclusion. From then on, from time to time she showed up to use the pool. Never said a word. I could always tell because she ditched the lights. One day, months later, she came into my office and thanked me. Then we were friends."

"There's probably no hope for me," I said. "I don't have a pool."

Eli laughed. He was more relaxed now and I began to like him. He was the sort of person I imagine a lot of people liked. We talked about the music business. We compared notes about the club scene in Boston and New York. For someone who had given me several remarkable tapes, Eli knew surprisingly little about the bands involved. I told him how impressed I'd been with the tapes and asked a couple of questions that he dodged, more or less.

"You're satisfied, then. That's great," he said.

"Of course. Is there any chance of hearing them live? Do they play here?"

"Where?"

"Here," I said, gesturing at the space around us.

The waitress arrived with a large tray balanced on her shoulder and set it on a stand. She arranged our silverware and glasses to make room for all the dishes. There were spring rolls, clams on the half shell, a very thin flour tortilla topped with chiles, shrimp, and cheese. Tempura vegetables, a Korean cabbage dish, cold raspberry soup, and a plate of meatballs with three different dipping sauces. Everything was elaborately presented, arranged on colorful plates, scrupulously rolled, folded, balled, sliced and garnished.

"It's a mishmash," Eli said. "Starters from around the world. Is there anything here you could eat?"

I nodded, looking at the food. "This is very nice of you, Eli," I said.

He smiled. Leaning back, forcing his chair to tilt on two legs just like kids do in grade school, he took a long, happy swallow of wine.

"So you're Ginny's brother," he said, as though that were a title, an Oscar, a Pulitzer, a Nobel prize. He looked at the setting that was intended for Ginny. Her glass remained empty, her place at the table unoccupied. "Ginny is completely devoted to your mother, isn't she?" he said.

I wondered if there was an implied criticism in that statement—a parenthetical "and you clearly are not" that was meant to be tagged onto the end.

"My mother isn't always easy," I said. "Ginny does her best."

"Do you mind discussing this? I mean, your Mom is a terrific person, but she has her . . . you know, her bad days."

"I know," I said. I laughed and Eli laughed. "So you've met my mother."

"No," Eli said. "But I wanted to ask you something. Do you think it would help if somebody was there for her all the time?"

"I'm not sure," I said. "She seems to be getting by." I'd about finished off the raspberry soup and was looking at the meatballs with intent. What Eli said next made me nearly choke on my spoon.

"I'd like to hire somebody for that—I mean, if you think it would help."

He was nervous all over again. He brought his hand to his forehead and shuffled through his hair. He held himself stiffly, leaning away from me as though from that vantage point he might better discern my reaction.

"You want to pay for someone to take care of my mother?" I said.

"It's just that Ginny has so much she has to do, as you know, and that's an awful lot of responsibility to have to always take care of another person—"

"Eli," I said, interrupting him. "No. No, thank you."

"I should explain . . ."

"I mean it, Eli, no."

"If you could do me the favor of *considering* it. Just as a gesture of my gratitude for Ginny's work here. A very small . . . gift. Could we call it a gift?"

"I didn't come here to make that kind of deal," I said.

"No deals. It's a gift. I just said it was."

He was upset now, I could tell. He was marking his performance with me and knew that he'd gone wrong. I felt sorry for him but I was also angry. I knew very definitely where Ginny had spent last night and I was amazed that Eli would approach me in this way just hours after waking up with her. I thought his offer was disgusting, no matter how well-intended. I understood one thing very well—he'd undoubtedly made this offer to Ginny, perhaps repeatedly, and he had undoubtedly failed.

"Giving Ginny the use of your swimming pool is one thing, Eli. Money is another. Anyway, this has nothing to do with me. If Ginny asked me about it—and I don't think she will—I would advise her not to accept any of your . . . gifts."

I took the demo tapes from my pocket and laid them out in front of Eli. Suddenly I didn't want any business having to do with Edgar Igleton.

"You are misreading this," he said.

"I don't think so," I said.

FIVE

∎ ∎ ∎

The section of Los Angeles most noted by the world is a small bit of real estate, really only five and a half square miles, on which movie stars, foreign politicians, network moguls, and other countries' cast-out royalty make their homes. It is a very odd thing to see Beverly Hills, because it is so storied, so often alluded to in the media, that inevitably a person feels disappointed when confronted with the famous land itself.

Celia was driving. I held a pamphlet of traffic rules and test questions.

"This isn't so plummy," I said, looking at an enormous, hideous pastel house with oddly shaped archways and light fixtures that were made to resemble torches outside the front door. "Do you think the decoration over the front door has religious significance?"

"High tack," Celia said. "I don't blame you for wanting to get out of here. But you can't leave town until I've passed my driving test. Where on such short notice would I find another instructor?"

"I'm hardly what you would call an instructor."

"Nonsense," she said, nodding at the traffic rulebook. "Read me a question."

"Okay. You are approaching an intersection. The light is red. A policeman is standing at the intersection; he waves you through. Do you, one, wait for the light to turn before continuing through the intersection, two, continue through the intersection as directed by the policeman, or three, come to a full stop at the light and then continue through the intersection as directed by the policeman?"

"Three," Celia said, without hesitation.

"Wrong."

"One."

"Nope."

"I detest rules," she said.

Celia's daughter's house was one of the smaller Beverly Hills homes, which meant it was still colossal. We entered a marble-floored hallway, above which hung a chandelier with crystal trinkets the size of shoes. A small blond child emerged, holding a doll in one hand and a cordless telephone in the other.

"It's Granddaddy," she said and handed the phone to Celia.

"Hello, darling!" Celia said. "I was just having my driving lesson. It's all going very well except my instructor has taken a dislike to his sister's employer and is threatening to return east. No, not to China. To Massachusetts."

Celia snapped her fingers and pointed at me. This was my cue to listen in on the conversation.

She said, "How many tornado warnings in New England? Five in one month? And the mosquitoes are rumored to carry a virus that is undiagnosable *and* untreatable?"

Who knows what he was really telling her? His protests on the other end of the line were muffled. Celia hushed him up. She said, "Have you watered the plants? Don't forget that nasty little fish by the window. No, it's not *our* fish. We don't own fish. Someone abandoned it in the hall and I had to take it in . . ."

She carried the phone through many rooms, talking all the while. I followed her into the kitchen; she pointed at the counter, on which stood bottles of white tequila, rum, vodka, gin, and Triple Sec. There was ice, melting in a tray, and two very tall glasses.

"Of *course* I don't know what kind of fish it is," she said into the telephone. "Does a goldfish have to be gold? Feed it those brown specks in the jar next to its cage. Well, what do you call it if it isn't a cage? Fine, feed it the brown specks in the jar next to its *aquarium* . . ."

I stood at the kitchen counter, pouring shots into glasses. There was a wedge of lime beside the bottles, so I made two very large gin and tonics. I took one to Celia, who finally concluded her conversation.

Another child, a freckled, tiny boy, bounced in. He went over to Celia and said, "Grandma, can I have chocolate?"

"*May* I please have a piece of chocolate," Celia said, pronouncing all her words separately and carefully. "Robert, this is Mr. Haskell."

"You can call me Sam," I told him.

"My real name is Bobby," he said.

"That is because your parents are halfwits, Robert," Celia said. She leaned way over and looked him in the eye. "I had your mother way too late in life. I'm sure there's something chromosomoically incorrect about her and that's why they've named you Bobby. Now, Robert, shake Mr. Haskell's hand."

"He said Sam."

"Shake Sam's hand, then."

Bobby stepped toward me, staring at the ground, and shyly took my hand.

"Say the words," Celia told him.

"It is a pleasure to meet you," Bobby said in a reluctant and unsure way. To Celia he said, "Why can't Granddad come?"

"He's taking care of fish," Celia said. She walked to a cabinet, where she found several boxes of candy. "That was a very good handshake, Robert," she said, handing him an entire box of Almond Roca.

Bobby smiled. He ran out of the kitchen, ripping through the wrapper.

"Don't ask why I try to educate these children," Celia said.

"Nice kid," I said.

"His father doesn't give him a moment of attention," she said. "He's his mother's child a hundred times over."

We took our drinks outside and sat in a small courtyard surrounded by spider plants and ivy, lemon trees in broad wooden buckets and fat flowering cacti. In the far back, next to a stockade fence, was an enormous powerboat. It was white with large blue eyes painted to starboard. Thick cartoon lips were crafted across the front. It was huge, chained to a trailer, and had the words BABY GRACEY on the side.

Celia shook her head, grimacing at the boat. "Don't even mention that monstrosity," she said.

We sat on plastic furniture that was designed in round, space-age shapes. I noticed an animal in the bushes, something like a rabbit but tricolored. It scurried between branches in a movement that was between a hop and a roadrunner sprint, making a noise like a muffled whistle.

"There's something in your hedges," I said to Celia.

"It's a guinea pig—one of the twins' pets. I forget which twin. I convinced the children that it was more properly suited for the out-of-doors. I keep hoping it will run away or drown itself in the automatic watering system but it seems to be thriving out here."

The guinea pig made twitching hops, approaching the patio, but with caution.

Celia leaned over, waving her hand. "Shoo, shoo! Off with you, brute!" Then she said, "It's taken a liking to me—I don't know why. Now what has happened between you and this Eli character?"

She moved her chair closer. Her eyes were light gray, deep set, and beautiful in a masculine way. She had almost no eyebrows at all, which she made up for by having elaborately decorated glasses. Her glasses, which currently hung from a chain on her neck, were bright gold with small, shiny jewels in the corners and ornamentation elaborately etched in miniature across the top.

I explained about Eli as best I could. "Ginny never talks about him, but she's worked at the restaurant for three years and I assume they've been involved right along. But today— now, I can't be sure of why, but today he tried to offer me money."

"Money for what?"

"For my mother's . . . illness. My mother has a mood disorder. The money was for someone to look after her, which is not necessarily what she needs at all."

"Well, I think that's very nice," Celia declared.

"What's very nice?"

"His offering money. I think money is terribly underrated."

"He's never even *met* my mother," I said.

"You know the slogan 'Say it with flowers'? Well, I think it should be 'Say it with money.' "

"That's not the point, Celia," I explained. "I get the feeling there might be conditions attached."

"*Eeeuuw,*" she said, making a face. "Well, you should ask Lucy about him. They were friends before she met Dweedledee and took up housekeeping."

The guinea pig edged toward us again, and Celia pulled it up to her lap. When she stroked its back, it chattered in a contented way. Then all at once there was a tremendous round of snarls and barks from inside the house. The guinea pig sprang from Celia and disappeared into a corner of the yard. The barking went on and on with enormous intensity and then disappeared altogether in a single abrupt moment.

"Damn that thing," Celia said.

"You have a dog?"

"It's the house alarm. If you stand anywhere within five feet of the house you hear a *recording* of dogs."

"Clever," I said.

"I detest it. This must be Lucy. Now, she really is very nice, Sam, and I'm not just saying that because I'm her mother. Lucy has always had a particular charm. Anyway, you two need each other. You just don't know it yet."

I had no time to protest. There were footsteps and then Lucy appeared on the patio, wearing a green-and-yellow warm-up jacket, spandex pants, and a black top. Around her neck were a pair of radio headphones and sunglasses on a green cord. Her auburn hair, wild with curls, was pulled away from her face in a sweatband. Her nose and lips were camouflaged by an orange zinc solution to protect her skin from the sun. She stood with her hands on her hips, one enormous sneaker pushed out. She frowned at Celia.

"Mother, why do you put the alarm on in the middle of the day?" she demanded.

Celia said nothing. She turned her back to her daughter.

Lucy saw that I was present. She came closer, peering at me.

"I don't know who you are, but whatever my mother has told you is a lie," she said. "I did not dance with the Chicago Ballet. I was never Ophelia at the Arena Stage. I am deeply sorry for whatever pretense you were brought here on," she continued, turning to Celia. "Mother, what have you told this man? It was bad enough that you set me up when I was single. Now that I'm married, don't you think you ought to stop?"

Celia remained silent. I explained to Lucy who I was and how I had met Celia on the plane.

"Your mother is taking her driving test at the end of the week," I said. "I'm helping out, that's all."

"Oh, I'm sorry," Lucy said. She put her hand over her mouth, stepping back now, embarrassed. Her voice became a whisper. "I'm very sorry. Sam, is it? I'm really awfully sorry, Sam."

I told her not to worry.

"Mom, I apologize. Mother, I'm sorry I yelled about the alarm. Mom, are you listening? I'm talking to you. Mother? Mother? Can you hear me? My body has been invaded by carnivorous worms. Mom?"

"Sam, let me tell you something," Celia said. "If you ever have children, you'd better hope you die before you get old enough to watch them throw their lives away."

Lucy did something with her mouth that was sort of a smile and sort of a look of disgust. A line of sweat trickled down her cheek and she wiped it away with her wristband. To Celia she said, "See this? This is a house. Inside, you'll find children. There are two parents—"

Celia interrupted. "One of whom still has to sound out his syllables," she said.

"—two parents with nine years of marriage behind them. Now tell me, Mother, what exactly has been thrown away?"

"Darling, I appreciate how hard you've tried. Nobody could blame you."

"Blame me for what? Nothing has *happened*."

"It's stoic, brave. Really beyond the call of duty."

"Mother, I'm married. I have a husband. Someday you might recognize that."

"Oh yes, your husband. While you were out aerobicizing, a young woman phoned your husband."

"Don't tell me!" Lucy said, turning. She pressed her hands over her ears and made fast strides away from us, disappearing into the house.

"She's this close to leaving him," Celia whispered to me, pinching an inch of air between two fingers.

SIX

When I got home, Mother and Ginny were in the living room having coffee with a woman who wore a scarf over her head and introduced herself as Isadora.

"Isadora is a Jehovah's Witness," Ginny said. On her lap was a red book bound in a leatherlike cardboard covering. *You Can Live Forever in Paradise* was written in gold lettering across the front.

"What did you let a Jehovah's Witness in here for?" I said.

"Quiet, Sam," Ginny said. "*Mother* invited her."

Mother said, "Isadora was just explaining how the end of the world is at hand. Go on, Isadora."

Isadora was old; her bifocals edged the tip of her nose, and she was having some difficulty reading from her Bible. She held the Bible well away from her, squinting. Then she asked Ginny if she wouldn't mind reading for her.

Ginny took the Bible, handling it a little awkwardly. She hunched over the pages, reading in a schoolgirlish way, shyly, slowly. Her cheeks went crimson.

"But mark this," Ginny read, "there will be terrible times in the last days. People will be lovers of themselves, lovers of money, boastful, proud—"

"This is ridiculous," I said. "Mother, you don't want to get involved in this crap."

"Isadora has been very nice!" Mother said.

"—abusive, disobedient to their parents—"

"Ginny, stop reading that. You guys are out of your minds."

"—ungrateful, unholy—"

"Ginny, listen to me," I said. "You work till all hours of the night, you starve yourself to nothingness; this afternoon I had a very interesting conversation with your boyfriend, who I think is a pimp, and now *this!*"

I wheeled back, pointing at Isadora. She was a tiny woman with puffy cheeks and dark skin. She had terribly arthritic hands, which she kept folded in her lap.

"Sam, Isadora is our guest!" Mother said. "You mustn't point at her like that."

"Isadora is a missionary. She's used to being chucked out of people's homes," I said.

Isadora spoke to me now. She had a soft voice, a strong Haitian accent. "Young man," she said, "when the war in heaven ended, God hurled demons to the earth. I can see you are feeling strongly the effects."

Meanwhile, Ginny was screaming.

"Eli is not a pimp!" she yelled. She stood in the middle of the living room, her fist in the air. *You Can Live Forever in Paradise* had fallen to the floor. The Bible was face down on the carpet.

"Steady, child," Isadora said. "If you want to be part of God's organization, you must be peaceable with one another."

"He tried to give me money!" I explained.

"I don't believe you!" Ginny yelled.

"For you!"

"You lie. You're a liar!"

"My children tend to argue," Mother told Isadora.

Ginny was on a tirade now. Isadora stood; she touched Mother's shoulder.

"I really must be going," she said.

"Oh, dear," Mother said. "Are you sure you won't stay?"

"See that, Sam!" Ginny yelled. "Mother was enjoying this and then *you* come in and drive Isadora away."

"Good!" I said. "You take a sick woman and feed her to the Jehovah's Witnesses. Great idea, Ginny."

"They'll stop fighting soon," Mother told Isadora. "Are you sure you won't change your mind?"

"Sam, you are the most selfish, brutish . . . !" Ginny stormed into her bedroom, slamming the door behind her.

"They remind me of Paul and Barnabas," Isadora said.

The next day Ginny wouldn't talk to me at all.

I was right behind her as she unloaded the washing machine, emptied the garbage, collected the mail. It seemed all morning I'd been speaking to Ginny's back.

"You have to talk to me again one day," I said. "Why postpone the inevitable?"

"Here," she said, and handed me a pile of towels. "Fold these. Then find a place well away from me and stay there."

I gave up finally and decided to lie in the sun for a while, an activity that I'd wrongly imagined was a big part of life in Los Angeles. I changed into Bermuda shorts and the kind of sandals that they call thongs out here, recent purchases from a beach shop I'd visited with Celia during one of her driving lessons. I found a place in the hammock and stretched out. I was nearly asleep when Ginny found me.

"You could fry an egg on your face," she said, standing over me. "Suntans are so uncool."

"You told me to get lost," I said. I sat up, felt a little dizzy. It was plenty hot out there, but I tried hard to look as though I were enjoying the sun.

"If you want to look good," Ginny said, "lose the shades. Mirrors went out in the seventies."

She was wearing a gray T-shirt, blue jeans bunched at the ankles, with holes punched through the thigh, bare knees. A belt drew in a waistband that had been tailored for someone male and much wider than she. Her skin was cool, creamy. No sun had darkened the perfect crease of her elbows or her long wrists, underscored with veins.

"You don't know this, Ginny, but behind this mirrored glass are minute volumes of Milton and Donne. You may think I am numbing my brain with all this sun and Hawaiian Tropic, but right now I am acquainting myself with centuries of English literature."

"Tanning is for morons," she said.

"If you want an apology, you have it," I said.

"How am I supposed to believe you're sorry when you don't know what you're apologizing for?" Ginny said.

"Ruining your nice time with Isadora?"

"You are hopeless."

"I'm just kidding, Ginny. You're mad because you think I was prying into your very private personal affairs."

"Oh barf," she said. "I'm going inside."

"I'm sorry. Really."

"Sure, like you mean it," she said, but she seemed satisfied. "I'm supposed to tell you that Mom's got her weirdo iced tea mixture and a sandwich inside."

Lunch was tuna, which I downed quickly. Then I headed for the shower.

It was so hot that when I turned on the cold water, it ran warm. The shower head didn't seem to work properly either. It sputtered, hissed air, and sent irregular jets of water to a place just below my sternum. I gave up, went outside, doused myself with water from a rubber hose, and resumed my place in the hammock, water dripping through to a spot of dry earth below.

"You'd better find some shade," Mother said. "You could get

heat exhaustion." She'd brought out an easel, boxes of pastels, crayons, chalk. She had taken up drawing years ago because the rehabilitation center in Kingston had a theory that if depressed people drew, they began to feel better. She was actually quite good. Mother wore a special smock for her artwork; it tied in the front like a cape. She set up the easel, a lawn chair. She wore a hat so large it fanned out past her shoulders. Sunglasses, big squares, took up most of her face. Her lips were white with zinc oxide, and she rigged up an enormous umbrella for shade.

"Or sunstroke," she said.

I tasted the sun on my lips, felt the sweat between my fingers, down the back of my shorts, across my brow.

"I am trying to relax. I've declared a day off."

"What is it you do again?"

"Manage bands," I said.

"Hands? What does it mean exactly to manage hands?"

"*Bands*, Mother. Musicians, people who play musical instruments."

On the table next to Mother were a radio and a glass of iced tea. I listened to the brush of watercolors over paper.

"I've been a manager for four years," I told her.

"Good for you, dear," she said.

"I live in a converted warehouse. Most of the rooms are used as artist's studios. You know Glenn Cray? He used to have a studio there."

"How nice," she said. She took up a charcoal pencil and made light sweeps across a page of manila paper. Above us, skywriters drew clouds in the shapes of the letters K-O-D-A-K.

"There's no heat, of course. Electricity is a variable. I use my microwave for everything except boiling water. And rats do frequent the flat."

"Hmm," Mother said. She poured herself iced tea from a jug resting on the ground.

"There's a lot of drug trafficking on the premises—nothing

dangerous, just crack and heroin. Lately I've been pursued by a Richard Nixon look-alike who claims I was his son in a previous life and who wants to embalm me."

Mother squeezed a lemon into her drink, concentrating very hard.

"I've taken to wearing a hip holster, sitting up all night listening to Gregorian chants. The social worker assigned to me suggests that a lack of quality time with my parents during my early years has caused me to confuse serial monogamy with serial killing. And of course I live on a strict diet of asbestos."

Mother took a long swallow of her iced tea. "My, that's good tea," she said.

"You know, Mom, I think it would help if you listened to a few words I say. Every third or fourth would probably be enough."

Mother looked at me. "Do you microwave the asbestos?" she said, winking.

Eli called that evening. Our conversation was brief.

"You shouldn't think there is any contingency on this money," he said.

"No thank you, Eli."

"You could hire somebody very nice for your mother. I'm not telling you who to hire."

"She's fine. She likes her life the way it is."

"But Ginny has to—"

"Offer the money to Ginny then."

"She won't take it," he said. "Look, you are going to regret this."

"I'm beginning to think there is something very wrong with you, Eli. Where exactly did you get this money? What is it? A drug-running payoff? White slavery fund?"

"I don't run drugs. I don't sell women," Eli said, his voice serious. Then he changed tone, returning now to the begging mode he'd been in. "Think of Ginny. If something happened and she couldn't work for me anymore, what would she do? Where would she get the kind of money she's paid now or someone who'd give her full choice on her hours?"

"Don't make me sick," I said. "And don't expect me to thank you."

"Don't thank me," Eli said, "but take the money."

"I'm just saying it's creepy. It reminds me of something out of 'Fantasy Island,' this random giving of money. I know he likes you, but you really have to wonder about a guy who is trying very hard to peddle cash on your behalf. What's he into, other than food and beverages?"

I was sitting on the toilet, speaking to the shower curtain, behind which Ginny soaked in her bath.

"I resent being trapped like this, Sam. I am cold; I am naked. I hate you for holding me hostage, and if you don't get out of the bathroom right now I'm coming through regardless."

In mock interrogation style I said, "You will be released in time, but first the information."

"Not only is this water cold, it is dirty. I am probably getting an infection. I would get out of this tub right now but I don't know if I can stomach seeing you on the toilet with your pants down."

"Well, that's what you'd see," I warned. "Just tell me the real reason Eli wants to unload a small fortune. For example, tax evasion, counterfeiting. It could be one of these divorce cases where the guy is trying to hide money so that his ex-wife doesn't appeal for more alimony."

"If I get sick, I'm blaming you."

"Rich people don't just give away money. It's strictly a middle-class phenomenon. Rich people hoard. That's why they're rich."

"First, he's not so rich. He's being sued all the time and so he never has any cash."

"Why didn't you say that to begin with? Obviously, he's trying to protect his assets from federal, state, and civil action against him. A normal and honorable American thing to do."

"Do I get to go now?" Ginny asked.

I said, "Just tell me something about Eli and you, anything at all, and I promise I'll hike up my jeans and let you emerge unseen to the warm towel that is waiting for you."

"I hate you, Sam," Ginny said. "I hate you, but I'll do it."

She'd been at the restaurant a week and a half when she first met him. Eli came in carrying crates of strawberries he'd bought from a road stand along Route 101. He carried them proudly, grinning over his purchase. He was handsome, Ginny noticed. She liked it that he didn't seem to care that his hair wasn't combed, that he didn't have the sort of terribly groomed, sculpted body you get from gym workouts. He had casual, offbeat good looks that he completely disregarded. He was proud of the strawberries. Finding them had made his whole day.

It was the middle of the afternoon; the restaurant was slow. Ginny had been folding silverware into cloth napkins and stacking them in a plastic tub. She was nervous about working around Eli; when he came in she dropped a half-dozen forks. But he thumped her on the shoulder as he passed, telling her to help him clean strawberries, and so she followed him into the kitchen.

For Ginny there had been something awesome about the kitchen at Eli's; it was a great big, highly modernized, foggy room full of enormous sinks and hoses. It was red-tiled and had an echo. That day she entered the kitchen with her usual bit of wonder over its many oversized refrigerators, the dozens of carts and tables on wheels. Eli called over his shoulder to the cook, telling him he had a craving for pie.

They stood in front of a pair of sinks, the strawberries red beside them, water flowing soundlessly onto porcelain. Eli rolled his sleeves way above his elbow. There were scars, Ginny noticed, but they were old scars. Around his wrist was an antique watch with fat black numerals. Its leather band, frayed at the seams.

"This way," Eli said. He plucked the green tops from the meat of the fruit with such quickness that Ginny felt clumsy beside him. She tried doing the same. Waitressing at Eli's was a new job, her first job. The skin on her forearm was still marked where they'd done the TB test. Her uniform was so new it made noise when she walked.

"Music!" Eli called, and the dishwasher, Tony, dropped a cassette into his boom box, filling the kitchen with funk. They started dancing right there, in front of a sink full of strawberries. Or rather, Eli began to dance. He whipped off the white apron that had become streaked with strawberry juice, swung his hips to the music, clapped his hands, all smiles for Ginny. She looked at him, astonished, a little afraid. He grabbed her wrist and sent her spinning. She took some steps, hesitated; she felt foolish. She was still holding some strawberries. The cook tapped a wooden spoon to the beat of the music. Eli was dancing in his own odd world. Another waitress came in, her face alight, danced over to Eli and yelled, "Party!"

And just that easily Ginny dropped the berries back into the sink, turning now to where Eli danced with the other waitress. She let her feet flow, gliding across the red tile of the kitchen floor. She felt the beat in her arms, her wrists, her fingers. She moved her hips, shook her hair out of its barrette, a smile emerging. She watched the other waitress dance, a heavy-hipped rhythm with a lot of finger-snapping. She watched Eli, his body both loose and exact. And then she was into the dream of the music, became all forgetfulness and joy. She turned in circles, caught the song in her knees and thighs, held it there. For a moment she felt beautiful.

Eli drew her toward him, his eyes full of discovery.

"He said I was a good dancer," Ginny said to me from behind the shower curtain. "Now do I get the towel?"

SEVEN

■ ■ ■

In the beginning of August, a few months before her seventy-third birthday, Celia was presented with her first driver's license. She invited Ginny, Mother and me to a celebration, but Ginny was at work and Mother had dragged Van away on a trip to Santa Barbara for a flea market. I went on my own, taking flowers.

Lucy and Mikey's house was about seventeen times the size of Mother's, filled with overstuffed furniture, peacock feathers, tables holding candles over which herbs simmered. Narcissus bulbs, sprouting gloriously, were doubled in the reflection of a mirror. The rugs were pastel, as were the walls, and if you stood at one end of the house and peered through the many adjoining rooms, you had the sensation of being surrounded by giant Easter eggs. Bobby and Stacy, Lucy's two youngest children, were already in pajamas when I arrived. The twins were in the basement, screaming at each other over a game of Ping-Pong. Bobby emerged shyly, closing the basement door so that the twins' ravings could not be heard. He asked to be tucked in by his mother.

I sat in a lime green leather recliner across from Lucy's husband, who really did insist on being called Mikey, not Mike or Michael. From the start I thought that there might be something wrong with him. For one, he was overfriendly, too interested, constantly smiling, and yet he said the most offensive and strange things. He had an air of confidence that I found grating. Awfully proud of his appearance, he ran his hands over the muscles in his arms and chest as if they were great prizes. He held his torso in a certain stiff way, as though he were acutely aware of all the layered muscles found there. In fact, he was very small. He had short arms shaped like Popeye's. He wore tennis shorts that were tight and a size too small. The result, in total, was so contrived that he reminded me of a boy's war toy or a parade float in miniature.

As it happened, however, both he and Lucy knew Eli.

"Eli? He went to one of those snotty New York City schools for spoiled kids," Mikey said. He squeezed his right biceps with his left hand, then flicked an invisible speck from his shoulder.

"Chilton Academy," Celia said. "You know the name perfectly well."

"This is the kind of school where there are no grades and students call teachers by their first names. You get the picture, right? A brick babysitter where rich people dump their teenagers."

"Lucy graduated from that school," Celia said.

"Anyway, Eli dropped out of old Chilton," Mikey said. "He came to L.A. thinking that it was *El Lay*, get it? Ha, ha, ha. Also thinking it would be the best place to deal a certain type of luxury psychedelic. He was arrested for dealing and for possession."

Lucy said, "The charges were dropped."

"Only because the police dicked up the investigation—excuse my French. He should have been in prison. The guy's got convict written all over him."

"He was seventeen," Lucy said.

"He was pushing *drugs*," Mikey said.

"Mikey, you haven't exactly devoted your life to good works," said Celia.

"I'm in the candy business. What's wrong with that?"

"I don't know if I'd call it the candy business," Lucy said. "Hershey is in the candy business."

"Hershey isn't the pope. How do you know Hershey doesn't have an entire sideline business devoted to what you call dirty chocolate?" Mikey said.

"Does it?" I asked.

"I'm not saying it does or doesn't. I'm just asking why everyone in this room is a hundred percent sure that all Hershey does is chocolate bars and Kisses? None of us knows what goes on in these big corporations. For all we know, Hershey, Reese, Whitman's, Cadbury, are all doing something we wouldn't approve of."

"Godiva makes chocolate legs," Celia said.

"Bingo! And maybe they don't stop there. Maybe the entire human body is available to the Godiva groupie if he, *or she*," Mikey said, looking at his wife, "can afford it. Meanwhile, they can buy it from me."

"It's disgraceful," Celia said, her head in her hands.

"What you have to watch out for are sharks like Eli. I'll tell you what, Sam," Mikey said. His voice held an air of police authority, as though he were the investigative officer who had uncovered a complex and intriguing crime. "He's gotten himself in trouble with a whole slew of other club owners. The rumor is he let a thousand mice loose in the kitchen at the Go Go Club, and at another place enough *Periplaneta americana*—that's cockroaches to you and me—to sink the business like a stone. Health department closed the clubs right down. Eli might be in some trouble."

"I wonder what the charge would be for putting mice and roaches in some other restaurant's kitchen," I said. I thought it was funny but Mikey was dead serious.

"It's not the police he has to worry about. It's the owners," he said.

"What junk," Lucy said. "I don't believe a word."

"What's not to believe, baby?"

"Don't call her baby," said Celia.

"And you know yourself how badly he treats women," Mikey said to his wife.

Lucy leaned toward me and said, "Mikey has his own little reasons for not liking Eli."

Wedged between Mikey's lips was a bright yellow toothpick. He chewed its end and looked over his left shoulder, plucking a memory from the air. "He once went out with a girl I liked, Flora Martinez. She lived two floors down from me on Beverly Glen. A couple nights after she broke up with him he came over and pissed all over her door."

"Good heavens," Celia said in a bored way. "Doesn't this family have anything more interesting to discuss?"

"Eli did that?" Lucy said. She raised an eyebrow at me. I had found myself wanting to talk to Lucy all evening—a fact I knew I needed to hide from Celia, who undoubtedly was hoping for such a response. Still, I couldn't help watching her. She stood next to her mother now, shifting her weight from hip to hip. She wore cloth shoes and a skirt cut just above the knee. She had muscular dancer's legs that seemed to go on forever. And her voice, octaves deeper than her delicate mother's, her voice was a gift. She drew her hand to her chin, recalling something. "I knew another guy who peed on his ex-girlfriend's door."

Mikey pressed his lips together. "You never," he said. "Who do you know who pissed on his girlfriend's door?"

"I can't listen to this," said Celia.

"Sorry, Mom," Mikey said. He leaned forward, reaching for a pack of Camels on the glass coffee table.

"Please don't call me Mom."

"Oh Celia." He smiled at her and then at me. For a complete idiot he had a lot of guts. He seemed incapable of being embarrassed and so caused others to feel embarrassed for him. He said, "Lucy says Mom and Dad to *my* folks."

"I wish she wouldn't do that," Celia said, and sniffed.

Mikey turned to me. "Can you figure out what this lovely lady has against me?" he asked. He tipped his cigarette, missing the ashtray for about the millionth time that evening. Then he slapped a palm on the table. He stood, making a grand show of offering his hand to Celia. "Let's say you show us all those dance steps you old people do. Let's do it, Celia. Let's dance up a storm."

"It's time for my bath," Celia said.

Celia told me to take her car. I promised I'd bring it back the next day, but she said no, borrow it for a while. Now that she had her license she didn't much care for driving, she said. She held the license in front of her, squinting at the tiny print that stated she was now legally able to drive.

"Lucy says I should be doing facial exercises," she said, assessing the photo.

"What kind of gasoline does it take?" I asked. It was an older car so I wasn't quite sure.

"Perhaps she's right," Celia said, holding the photo at arm's length.

"Leaded or unleaded?"

"What could it possibly matter?" she said, handing me the keys.

When I left I shook Mikey's hand, kissed Celia on the cheek. Lucy was somewhere with one of the kids, so I didn't get a chance to say goodbye to her. I went out to the car. It was just becoming night. The house glowed obscenely with lights so bright they illuminated the entire lawn, right out to the road. The air was cooling now, finally. Over Hollywood Hills the sky was a beautiful blue. I rolled down the windows, checked the fuel gauge.

"Hey," I heard. Lucy bent down so that her face was level with the window. "Thanks for coming over."

"My pleasure," I said. "Where were you? Hiding in the bushes?"

"Yes," she said, as though my question were serious and hiding in the bushes were a perfectly normal thing to do. The house lights illuminated her face, making her eyes seem even larger. I could see that she was a beautiful woman who had forgotten about that beauty. "I know it's none of my business," she said, "but I think you should reconsider Eli's offer. It wouldn't hurt to have the money and maybe take your Mom and Ginny back east. You'd solve two problems. First, you'd have the means to pay a professional to look after your mom. Second, Ginny would no longer be near Eli, so whatever conditions there were on the money couldn't possibly hurt her. Anyway, you don't know for sure if there are conditions."

"Your mother tell you about the money?"

Lucy nodded. "Don't worry, it's not that unusual. Listening to you talk with Mom and Mikey I could figure out that Eli had offered you *something*. He's always doing that."

"Just giving people money?"

"More or less. To Eli, money is kind of a religion. He likes to spread it around."

Lucy swallowed. She fidgeted with an earring. "Look, it's none of my business. Please come over again—if you want to."

"I've got your mother's car. That's kind of a sure bet I'll be back."

"Right," she said. She laughed, and her eyes became long almonds. Lucy's eyes were so pretty it seemed strange that they were anything more than ornamental. That one would be able to see with such eyes seemed impossible. She said, "Well, I guess she can't put one over on you."

"I don't mind," I said.

I waited for her to say something else, but she didn't. I wondered what was next. I couldn't very well drive away with Lucy leaning on the car. I didn't really want to leave anyway but we'd run out of words all of a sudden.

"Mommy!" we heard. It was Bobby, charging through the front door and running full speed to Lucy, his child's arms flailing in the air. "Mommy, you disappeared! Everybody's looking and no one can find you!"

He grabbed Lucy's thigh and put his face right against her. She kneeled down and put her arm around her son.

"I thought you were lost," Bobby said.

"No, no," said Lucy, smiling at me.

EIGHT

■ ■ ■

As had been predicted, Mother's mood changed. I was on the phone, listening to Pelzer's latest complaint about a gig they did and what a dive it was and how bad the acoustics were and how everyone at the club was a drug addict or homeless or trying to rob or rape everyone else, when Mother charged through the front door in a tirade. Van lingered behind.

"You'll probably want to say *adios*," he said, nodding down at the phone. "This might get loud."

Mother stomped through the house, hurling objects, yelling insults. She broke a candy dish, an electric fan, a picture frame, and a small glass pear. She was a magnificent vision of anger, skating from room to room in her billowing sundress, her tiny legs scurrying in and out of doorways. She sat and then stood right up again in an abrupt, alarmed manner. She wheeled around, charging like a bull. Van dodged her, fleeing from one end of the house to the other. I followed as a sort of referee.

Van said, "Let's stop this, Jewel. You know what they say—have a drink and a think before your love life stinks."

"Who?" I asked. "Who says that?"

"Oh sure, have a drink *here*," Mother said. "But you wouldn't dare go out in public with me! It's okay at the beach, where you practically mask yourself so nobody recognizes you but you never take me anywhere *decent*. I'm sure you have other women for that!"

In her hand was a magazine, rolled lengthwise. With each word she spoke she batted the magazine against the back of the television.

"That's not true. I never go anywhere decent with anybody," Van said.

"I'm tired of this, Van, I'm tired—"

"Come on, Jewel, you're gonna ruin the whole evening."

"Mom, I think you better relax," Ginny said. She had Mother's medication in her palm. A glass of water.

"How can you take his side!" Mother yelled.

There was no winning. If we changed tack and agreed with her when she said that Van was lazy or foolish or a Communist or that he'd lost his house or sold his house or that he was an alcoholic, a dabbler, a liar, a bore, or that he was living in debt or living off her, she rallied to his defense. She struck the injured pose of a woman broken by trauma and said, "My God, you don't want me to be happy!" as though she'd just made this unspeakable discovery.

The important details, like that Van was married, were neither acknowledged nor discussed. Mother handled this information very efficiently through concentrating on where Van took her or did not take her.

Still, there are people in this world who quite naturally bring out in others a desire to protect. My mother was one of them. I tried to find ways to make her feel better—to say something, do something that might bring a halt to her unhappiness. Ginny had a different approach.

"God knows where you were last night!" Mother yelled at her.

Ginny sat on top of the kitchen table, her legs crossed Indian-style, a cigarette. "Oh, with the milkman, the pest control man, the dry cleaner, the postman. All the usual rounds," she said. She held up a prescription bottle. "How about some medicine, Mom, before we drown you?"

Van retreated to a lawn chair, taking with him a pitcher of martinis.

"Van, get your ass back in here," Ginny said.

"I've had enough of this," he called through the window. "And I don't need no bimbo minor dictating orders."

Ginny jumped off the table, strutted five monster steps to the window, and said, "Listen, Mr. Universe, we could use a hand here."

"I've done my best already," he said. "I brought her home, didn't I?" He folded his lawn chair and scooped up an armful of gardening paraphernalia—clippers, gloves, trowel. He looped his windcheater over his elbow, fished in his pockets for car keys. "She needs psychiatric help," he said. "She needs to go to the h-o-s-p-"

"She can spell!" Ginny said. She turned to Mother. "Momma, you want to just take one pill at a time. A little water . . ."

"You can't leave me!" Mother wailed at Van. She looked at Ginny, who was dialing the telephone, shrieked, and then went racing through the house like a nervous poodle, saying in various tones, "Oh my God, my own daughter is betraying me. They're just not *human.*"

"I'm calling the *restaurant,* Mother, not the hospital," Ginny called. She leaned out the window and said, "You know, Van, you could do us a favor and slip her those pills."

"I am late already for an appointment," he said.

"Yeah, right, with your wife," Ginny said. Then, to me, "This will go on for a while."

Someone answered on the other end of the line and Ginny explained that she would not be coming in. Evidently whenever Mother had this sort of episode, Ginny had to call work and cancel. Her voice lowered and I assumed she was talking to Eli. She said goodbye and hung up the receiver.

"You know I wasn't made for this," Mother explained to Van, who had made his way back into the house. She stretched herself right up against him, staring with pleading eyes into his heavy, thick face. She was so tiny next to him, and her small frame contrasted with his enormity.

"I'm sorry, Jewel," he said, "but I've got to be on the road."

"Why?" she demanded. "Why do you always have to be on the road? What's so damned interesting on the road?" She slapped his chest, not hard, but hard enough.

Van didn't say anything. He was reaching for the door, struggling to unleash himself from Mother. She hung on, grabbing at his sleeves, at his belt loops. Van gave me a look as though I were supposed to sympathize with his situation. Frankly, he appeared a little helpless. He turned to Mother, putting his hands over her wrists and pulling gently back. He gave her a sloppy kiss on the forehead and wrenched himself away. As bad as he was, he had a heart. When I heard his car pull out of the driveway, I thought that given the way Mother could act up, she was lucky to have anyone at all.

"Well, you've done it," she said, glaring at me as though I were a minstrel performer who had polluted her favorite opera. I edged toward her, hands in front of me, palms up, showing that I carried no weapons, no malice, no harm.

"You've gotten what you wanted," she spat at me, pulling her head back in a mighty theatrical thrust. It was a new stance now. She'd gone from puerile moping to the haughty pose of a grande dame. She swept across the floor, glowering at me from the corner of her eye, and filled the kitchen with her presence.

Ginny was at the kitchen table, charging up a cigarette. Mother stared at her for a long time and Ginny, in turn, sent parades of smoke rings up to Mother's angry, dramatic face. In a flash Mother seized the end of the cigarette and snatched it from Ginny.

"You've burned me!" said Mother, dropping it. She flung herself against the wall, holding her burned hand. Her mouth was twisted down. Ginny had an expression of unholy dread. She stood, reaching for Mother.

"Oh, Mom," she said, patting her back, speaking into her neck. "It's okay. Just a cigarette burn."

Ginny gave me an exhausted, defeated expression. Looking at her, I found it hard to remember that she was so young. Across her brow ran a pattern of fine wrinkles. Beneath her eyes was a veil of blue. She took Mother to the kitchen sink, talking to her all the while in hushed, comforting tones. Holding Mother's hand under the faucet, she gently turned her fingers so the cool stream could soothe the wound. Ginny looked over her shoulder and said, "She's afraid of fire," as though it needed explanation.

After her fight with Van, Mother took to spending vast amounts of time in her bedroom, essentially refusing to leave it. Van made himself scarce—a phone call or two—so Ginny and I created a system to be sure that someone was always home with Mother. I was home in the evening while Ginny went to work and then, presumably, to Eli's house (though she never admitted this). She returned in the morning.

I found the system exhausting. I found myself looking for a way out of the system. It occurred to me that Van had been very instrumental in freeing up time Mother required during these episodes, and as it looked a bit like they were finished, I became sorry I'd been so rude to him.

"I'll go nuts if she wastes one more day in there," Ginny said, pointing at the closed door of Mother's bedroom.

"I agree. We have to get her up and back into the rhythms of the living. What do you suggest? A bomb threat?"

"No," Ginny said, rolling her eyes.

"An actual bomb?"

We pretended we were making breakfast and needed Mother's help with a recipe for crepes. Ginny poured flour into a bowl, sprinkled it with milk, and dropped in an egg. Then she tucked the bowl beneath her arm and took a beater to it. As the batter spun around she called to Mother, asking how much butter to put in the frying pan, how many minutes to cook each side, what consistency the mixture should be. The batter was very thick, looking more like something you'd use to mend sidewalks than cook with. Ginny stood at the door to Mother's room, delivering in her most interested and inquisitive voice a half-dozen questions about how best to transform it into perfect, smooth crepes. But there was no response.

I stood in the kitchen, watching butter sizzle inside the frying pan, become brown, then blacken. I turned off the burner, reheated some coffee. It was only ten o'clock in the morning and already I was exhausted. When Ginny returned from Mother's room, she hurled the mixing bowl into the sink, blasted it with water, and stared into it as the batter washed over the edges.

"This might last days," she said. "Or weeks. If you want to cut out, Sam, go ahead."

"I'm not going to leave it all to you just like that," I said.

"Oh, *of course* not," Ginny said.

"Look, I'm helping," I said.

"I know, I know. And I'm supposed to be eternally grateful."

I made an appointment with Wilma Ramirez, Mother's psychiatric nurse. Wilma worked in a medical building in Culver City, a white building with honeycomb architecture and small windows that looked like portals in a ship. I waited in an office with thick gray carpeting and comfortable chairs that you sank into and did not move in. Wilma brought me coffee with two sugar cubes and granulated creamer in a foil packet on the saucer. She couldn't have been more than forty, but something about her manner made me feel as though I were talking to someone much older. She had a lot of glossy black hair pinned behind her head and wore a pale sweater with a long string of white pearls.

"Have you met Jewel's doctors? Dr. Avery and Dr. Carr?" she asked.

"Her name isn't Jewel," I said.

"I know, but she prefers Jewel."

"Her name is Lois," I said.

"Okay, Sam, we'll begin again," Wilma said. She uncrossed her legs, pulled at a snag on her pantyhose, and fixed the cuff of her sweater. "Have you met Lois's doctors?"

"I don't mean to make trouble, but Ginny isn't a hundred percent with these doctors," I said. "She gets the impression that they overprescribe. Evidently the last time Mother saw Dr. Avery, she couldn't sleep or eat for days."

"It was the Haldol," Wilma said. "A side effect. But usually it's Lois who gets the dosage wrong. It has to be said that your mother is not the best pill-taker."

Since my father died, Mother had either underdosed or overdosed on all her medicine. The medication schedule had been Dad's domain, and it was only in his hands that the dosages were correctly administered. I admitted this to Wilma, who nodded and continued. She conducted our meeting in what I supposed was a professional manner, detailing Mother's condition in a dry, attentive way. She used terms I'd heard before—depression, bipolar disorder, isolated psychosis, mania —in order to describe Mother's condition, or, more precisely, what it was they didn't understand about it. She spoke in a way that made me feel as though the conversation had been choreographed. Or that it had happened before and she was only repeating it. Her explanation was efficient. No extra words, no hesitations.

"I know Ginny does not like the doctors. She was very rude to Dr. Avery when he made a generous visit to your house, as a matter of fact."

"She calls them as she sees them."

"Well, it's clear you two are related. What is it you do again, Sam? Commission musical groups, is it?"

"Something like that," I said.

"And you are out here for some sort of work-related reason, I take it?"

"I had some bands I was interested in," I said. "They didn't work out."

"And you are scheduled to leave when?"

"Today, actually. A few hours ago. I decided to stick around for a little longer."

"Oh," Wilma said. She looked surprised. "It would help, you know, if your mother had someone looking after her the way your father apparently used to do."

"My father didn't always look after her," I said. "He was a salesman. He went away for days at a time."

"What happened then?" Wilma asked.

I tried to remember if we'd had any help—a person who came when Dad was away, a nurse, a caretaker, anyone. All I was sure of was that it hadn't been me. At no time had I taken responsibility.

"She must have taken care of herself," I said.

"Perhaps it was Ginny," Wilma said. There was a silence. "I don't suppose you could conduct your business on the West Coast?"

"No," I said quickly. "No, I couldn't."

"Well, that's too bad. I take it your mother is doing well, however."

"She *was*. But I think it wouldn't hurt for you to come by," I said.

Wilma opened a large calendar and laid it across her desk. "Can it wait until next Tuesday?"

"Not really, Wilma. I'm not sure it can wait till tomorrow."

"I see," she said. She gave me a time, and then, because there didn't seem much else to say, I left.

We tried luring Mother out of her bedroom with Parcheesi, a board game. Ginny swore this would work. We got out the Parcheesi board and parked ourselves on the couch, within hearing distance of Mother's room. We separated game pieces, decided on colors. Ginny took blue for her mood, she said. I was red for my bank account, I told her. We rolled the dice and plodded around the board. We didn't remember how to play. We called out to Mother, telling her how much fun we were having, what spectacular amusement we were able to derive from this mindless activity which was her favorite game, according to Ginny.

Nothing happened. Mother remained quiet; Ginny sighed loudly. A shadow developed between her eyebrows and she frowned at the game board.

Eventually we walked into Mother's room, Ginny's face ablaze with concentration and me feeling like a member of a SWAT team. Mother's bedroom seemed so foreign to me, as full of secrets as when I was a child, but then, those many years ago, I'd had the feeling that the secrets were good ones. The expression on her face was equally mystifying. She lay in bed, looking like someone lost in a city that both intrigued and terrified her. She glared at us and then turned away, moving her head in quick motions like a nervous exotic bird.

Ginny held her hands in front of her and talked to Mother in an exaggeratedly calm way, pausing distinctly between words and sentences.

"We were wondering if we could visit with you awhile," she said. Beneath the covers, Mother was so small. Her bedspread was printed with large blue and yellow flowers that curved over her legs.

"Draw the shades," Mother said.

There were three short windows in the bedroom. Ginny went to the far one and pulled the blind way down, pressing out the late morning sun, which was already full and sizzling away. I looked out the near window at Mother's tiny lawn, helpless beneath the glaring sun, and calculated the number of days before it would collapse into a turf of dust, no matter what Van sprayed on it. I took hold of the shade and it rolled out unevenly. I had to trick it into staying down. Ginny wrestled with the third, finally using a coffee mug as a weight, pinning the vinyl to the sill. When we were finished there was only a thin bar of light at the base of each window. But the heat seemed anyway to come clean through the walls.

"See this," Ginny said. She took a silver-framed photograph from the dresser and brought it over to Mother. The photograph was an old one. There was Dad in a golf hat, a yellow one with a striped ribbon wrapped around its center. He had an arm around Mother who was facing him, smiling. Her hair was shorter in the photograph. She had a floppy collar, a strand of aqua beads. Even then there had been a hint of her extraordinariness, an orange decoration—a brooch?—in the shape of a daffodil pinned breast-high. And in her hand was something that looked like a harmonica.

"Here you are when you were happier," Ginny said, pointing to the photograph. "Do you remember when this was taken? You and Dad were going to a summer party. You wore a white dress with pleats down the front. Dad had that stupid plaid shirt we all made fun of. Don't you remember? He wanted to wear his golfing hat because he'd sunburned his head and didn't want everyone to see his peeling scalp. You told him that was ridiculous. You said, 'If you wear that hat people are going to mistake you for the gardener.' And then you laughed and I took the picture."

"Hmm," Mother said. She wasn't listening. She had the vacant response that characterized her bouts with depression. I touched Ginny's elbow.

"Well, we'll go now, Mom," Ginny said. She looked at me and began walking backward out of the room. "We'll be just outside if you need us."

In the living room her expression changed. I saw the tension in her face. She went over to the Parcheesi board and, in a sloppy way, began putting the game back into the box. She threw the plastic pieces into a bag, dropped in the board, and then dumped the cards over the top. But the box wouldn't close. She slammed down the top and tried to force it shut, but of course the effort was a failure and she had to take everything out and try again. She stood, held the box over her head, and tipped it so the entire contents fell over the carpet. The cards sailed through the air; one of the dice rolled under the couch. Then Ginny got on her knees and began, in precisely the same manner as before, to put away the game.

I went over and put my hand on the back of her neck. I knelt behind her and rubbed the space between her shoulders. "Look," I said, picking up a short stack of cards. "Forget about this."

"I hate that woman in there," Ginny said, glancing toward Mother's bedroom.

"No you don't," I said. "You love her. You always have. One of the failures of love is that you never think you are doing it very well. But you, Ginny, are a very good daughter."

Ginny fixed her attention back on the task of cleaning up the game. She ran her fingers over the carpet, feeling for the dice, for board pieces, rubber bands.

"I'm tired of being a good daughter," she said. "I am about to become a real bitch of a daughter."

"Oh yeah?" I said, laughing. "What are you going to do?"

"First thing," she said, fixing the cover on the box, "first thing is I'm going to take this Parcheesi set out to the road and run it the hell over."

Wilma arrived at nine o'clock the following morning. She helped me pack a bag for Mother. Toothbrush, shampoo, hairbrush, going-home clothes. They were gone within minutes, it seemed.

I waited for Ginny. She slunk in an hour later, leather jacket in hand, uncombed hair and underwear hanging out of a bookbag.

"You look wanton," I said.

She halted in the doorway. Her eyes widened. Worry lines creased her forehead.

"She's gone, isn't she?" Ginny said.

"A few days, no more. They've got to examine her medication," I explained. "She's got a private room anyway."

"I could kill you, Sam." She dropped herself on the couch, which was still in bed mode, heaped with sheets and pillows. "I would, too, but I just don't have the energy. You don't know what you've done. She'll be a Vulcan when they're through with her."

"It wasn't my choice. It was Wilma's recommendation."

"Don't even talk to me," Ginny said.

She went into her room. I heard drawers open and shut, the sound of wire hangers clanging together, zipping and buckling. The door to Ginny's bedroom opened and she appeared, bearing an enormous old suitcase with a broken handle.

"Let me guess, you're running away from home?" I said, trying to get a smile from her. "Last time you planned that, it started to snow."

"Leave me alone," Ginny said, even-toned. She stood in the doorway, glaring. She pointed at me and her finger was like a loaded gun.

"Wait a second," I said and went to where she stood. "Come on, Ginny. Don't leave. We did the best we could with Mother, but enough's enough. She needed a doctor."

She stepped away from me. I took her elbow, but she yanked it away. She went through the front door and I followed her out to the landing, where the morning sun was hot already, though tempered by breeze.

"You're always right, aren't you?" I said. "I forgot that there is this cosmic rule that says you are always right about everything."

"How about the rule that you get to make all the decisions?" Ginny said. "Behind my back."

"I have a vote, you know. I am her son."

"A vote isn't the same thing," Ginny said, "as a done deal."

"Fine, go ahead. Move out. Take your stuff over to your boyfriend's house or wherever. But I'll tell you what, if you think *I* make deals behind your back, I would think you'd be very interested in what sorts of deals Eli makes."

And then, all at once, Ginny pitched the suitcase over the railing and charged at me. "I'm tired of you talking about that!" she yelled.

She was furious and strong. I had to concentrate to avoid her fingernails, her knees, her quick hands. I crouched against the side of the house, struggling against her body blows. For a girl built more or less like a sliver building she had some power behind her. Outside, where the entire neighborhood could see, it was embarrassing as well as painful.

Ginny let up finally and I turned around to face her. She was staring at the space in the driveway where she'd thrown the suitcase and where it had burst open, scattering clothes everywhere.

There was a long gown in a rose color, laid out as though the invisible woman inside it were curled in sleep. A few panties ruffled edges catching the breeze; some camisoles; stockings. There was other underwear, extreme in design—black-laced bodices and leather G-strings, nipple tassels, suspenders, stuff I hadn't ever even seen on a woman in real life, and all of it being swept by an easterly breeze across the cement drive. It floated into the bushes, across Mother's collection of glow-in-the-dark ducks, out into the street.

Ginny sprang for a lace corset and I followed a scarlet negligee. She grabbed chainmail panties, bras, leather leggings; I chased a velvet teddy. This was not easy stuff to untangle from branches, to retrieve from under cars. I gathered an arm-load of underwear, all of it smelling like leather and sex. All so foreign to me that I felt foolish and naive.

Ginny grabbed it out of my hands and began repacking the suitcase. She threw armloads of underwear into the Oldsmobile.

"Ginny, I think you better explain what—"

"Don't talk!" she said.

"—half of Frederick's of Hollywood is doing in your back seat."

"Shut up! Just shut up!"

"A few minor details, like if you wear all this, then what exactly is Eli's attire? Battle dress? A Tarzan suit?"

And then she hit me. She came right to where I was standing, raised a fist full of keys, and hit me just above my left eye. I spun, holding my eye. I felt the blood coming warm against my palm. I couldn't see at all; I couldn't tell what was tears and what was blood. I got my balance and then, with my good eye, searched for Ginny. I couldn't focus. It was as though my vision were suspended from a chain and dangling in front of me. It was as though objects were images falling across a plane of space before me.

"How could you just pack away Mom?" Ginny was saying. "Send her off! You don't even have the sense to know what you've done!"

I wanted to say something but I was trying to see what Ginny was doing, where she was standing.

"It's just like what you did to me," she said. "Just like putting me in the back of a car and letting me go!"

Finally I got a glimpse of her, blurry and waterlogged. She was backing toward the Oldsmobile. She looked so frightened. I wanted to follow her, but I couldn't. I thought, *Hospital, stitches.* I thought, *Insurance policy, painkiller.*

I heard the Oldsmobile's engine charge up. I heard tires. I lay down on the driveway, my eyes closed. I let myself stay that way for a few minutes and then tried standing. There was some skill in this. My head gave a solid pound. I held the side of my face, pressed a little. It hurt, but in a way I thought it was good that it hurt. I appreciated having an external focus for my attention. The pain across my eye brought everything back to simplicity. To comfort and discomfort. Pain and healing.

I looked up and there was Wilma standing before me. She had Mother's overnight case in one hand, a clutch bag in the other.

"You'll need Tylenol, not aspirin," she said. "Aspirin will make it bleed."

Wilma studied my face. She turned my head, focusing on the area just above my eye. For some reason I noticed her earrings, which were gold buttons with a pearl center. I noticed her eyebrows, how dark they were and how her lashes shone as though they'd been treated with glycerine.

"Your mother needs a few things. Her radio, for one," she said. "Perhaps you can tell me where that might be."

"Kitchen," I said, using the end of my shirt to dab my eye.

Snagged in the front railing was a curious piece of satin underwear, crimson with some black lace. It was hooked on a curl of iron, floating out across the landing in an exposed and incriminating way.

Both Wilma and I looked directly at it. "Is it all right for me to go in?" she asked.

"Of course. Look, this is Ginny's . . . um . . . thing."

"And Ginny hit you like that, too?" she said, not believing.

"No, it was the milkman, the pest control man, the dry cleaner, the usual."

"Radio?" Wilma said.

"Right." I got it for her. A Panasonic with a tape player. I gave her the radio and a half-carton of Mother's cigarettes.

"Tylenol in capsules, dissolved in warm water," Wilma said. She handed me a dinner napkin into which she'd folded ice. "And cold compresses applied to the region."

"You're a walking medical library," I said to her. "Do you come with a card catalogue?"

"Tut, tut," Wilma said. "Go to hell."

There came a time many weeks later, when summer had faded and the hills surrounding L.A. were green, when there weren't any more fights and not a trace of those that had come before, that Ginny explained how she came to have such a stock of underwear. We were driving a road that traversed the San Gabriel Mountains, on the way back from a funeral, which was Eli's own. We'd spent hours outside, being made crazy by mosquitoes. Where we'd been bitten there were drying flecks of blood. Ginny picked at a swollen spot on her wrist.

She began by saying, "He wasn't very nice at first. I think I kind of hated him. But we did stuff together anyway, all related to the club. Once he picked me up from school on the motorcycle. We went up the freeway and came off the Wilshire Boulevard exit, which pissed me off because I knew we were going to Beverly Hills and I was in the worst possible fuck-high-school clothes. It was like him to do that, you know? Not say anything and then show up and want to go, like, try on evening gowns and stuff."

They'd stopped first at the Gallery, which was just a single store then, not the chain it has now become. Ginny was supposed to pick a theme for Chloe, a new girl, who had short, overpermed hair and too much gum to be beautiful. The woman at the counter was Tabatha Marran, the wife of the famous artist Benjamin Marran, who helped design some of the merchandise in his wife's underwear store.

"You are looking for . . . ?" She waved her hand through the air, an eyebrow raised in question, her skirt flowing around legs that were posed just a little defensively.

"Something unusual," Eli said.

"Unusual," Mrs. Marran repeated. She had long fingernails that Ginny guessed were fakes glued to stubby boring normal nails like Ginny's own. She stood in front of an open double-doored wardrobe flooded with camisoles in every conceivable color and style.

"The girl's a little rabbity. We need something to detract from her face," Eli announced.

"We have very nice bra and panties sets . . ." Mrs. Marran began. She looked at Eli queerly.

Ginny was going through drawers of underwear, some satin, some cheap polyester jobs but playfully designed.

"We could use some of these neon blues," she said, holding up a pair.

"You have anything sporty?" Eli asked Mrs. Marran. "Like a corset in Lakers colors with a push-up?"

"Oh, Eli, don't make Chloe wear *that*," Ginny said.

"I don't think so," Mrs. Marran said. "Can you tell me what size?"

Ginny took a pad from her jeans. She leafed through the pages until, way at the back, she found the table where she kept all the dancers' measurements. She tossed the book to Eli, who announced the information to Mrs. Marran.

"Well, we won't have any sets that will fit her," Mrs. Marran said. "You should have the young woman come in."

"Look," Eli said. He reached forward and took Mrs. Marran by the elbows. Eli was like that; he was very into touch. It didn't matter that many people, in fact most people, were not.

Mrs. Marran stepped back. Eli smiled. "We don't bring in the girls. We really can't."

When Ginny looked up she saw Mrs. Marran's surprised face. And she saw Eli, handsome, sandy-haired, round-eyed. So boyish that it might have been he who had been plucked from high school that afternoon. She knew he was genuinely obnoxious.

"You are in the wrong store," Mrs. Marran told him. Ginny went red. They'd been thrown out of places before, but every new time embarrassed her.

"Oh, I'm sorry. I thought this was a lingerie store."

"It is."

"Mrs. Marran, certainly you understand what business you're in. Look around. You aren't exactly selling white cotton, are you?"

"I don't think that matters," Mrs. Marran said. "I would like you to leave now."

She was gracious, Ginny thought. She was struggling with that one little boutique on a road where the rents were high and it was not easy to make it. She didn't know then that the store would take off all through California, would duplicate itself twice in New York City, would gain new addresses so rapidly that it would become impossible to keep all the outlets fully stocked. And yet she wasn't going to let Eli touch her or humiliate her or play with her or treat her like a child.

"We want all those," Eli said, using his thumb to point to where Ginny was kneeling with stacks of lacy panties beside her.

"Just these," Ginny corrected. She was eying the ones in Day-Glo colors, imagining a glow-in-the-dark act.

"We want them all," Eli said. "Don't be upset, Mrs. Marran. We're in the same business, you and me. Granted you are much more civilized about it, much more delicate. And private, too. Privacy is the key to good taste."

"I'd hate to guess what business you're in," Mrs. Marran said. She circled the cash register, the phone at her ear, dialing security.

They left.

Outside, Eli rolled his motorcycle off its stand, straddled it, and brought it gunning over to Ginny.

"Let's go," he said, pulling her on.

"What'd you do that for?" Ginny said. She gripped a scrap of paper with the Gallery's address. "Now we're gonna have to mail-order."

She swung a leg over the motorcycle and Eli took off as she pulled herself onto the seat, inching forward, closer to his hips. The sudden speed knocked her back, snapping her jaw shut so that she bit her tongue.

Eli was angry; he drove fast.

"This is so typical," she screamed into his ear. "Every stupid man I know drives like this."

They took the curves leaning way over. Ginny's eyes filled with sand from the road. A pebble hit her in the neck. She squeezed Eli's jacket, hiding her face between his shoulders. They cruised violently through the crowded streets, the afternoon heat firm on their backs.

"Shithead!" she yelled as he gunned past the UCLA campus, dodging a few students. He rode up the outside line of cars at a stop light, ran the intersection, and headed fast through Westwood and onto the freeway.

It was rush hour and the lanes were tight with traffic. Eli sped between them, using his horn liberally. He leaned forward, his elbows fanned out, and raced among cars, swerving dangerously as motorists changed lanes or slowed down. He took an exit and followed an industrial road under the highway, kicking up mud and dust as he reached sixty, then seventy, on the thin, paveless surface.

When they got back to Sun Dial Street, Ginny spat out the blood from her cut tongue. It caught Eli just above the cheek.

"Drive like that again, I'll pull us to the ground. You might think it's cool to scare me, but I'll trip it up next time and bring us both over a guardrail, get it? Because I don't care, Eli. You are talking to someone who doesn't give a goddamn if the bike explodes into the stratosphere with us on it."

Eli smiled. He'd worked out his anger and of course was now sorry.

"Thanks for the afternoon, Ginny," he said.

"Fuck you," she said, typically. "Buy a goddamned helmet."

After that, slowly, bit by bit, Eli began to fall in love with Ginny, whom he'd made an integral part of his business since the afternoon she washed strawberries with him and who on that day had turned seventeen.

"It took a long time for us to really be friends," Ginny explained to me in the car. "I thought he was scum when I first met him. I thought he was some crusty old Dracula but without the wings."

But the day Ginny's bag burst in the front yard, sending underwear flying, I had no idea where it had come from. I thought it was part of a personal collection, and I thought how very little I knew my sister anymore.

NINE

■ ■ ■

I followed Wilma's advice on the Tylenol, keeping a small supply in my jacket pocket. My head throbbed but somehow the mild, constant pain kept me focused on matters at hand. I needed to talk to Ginny. I drove Celia's car to the restaurant and waited in the parking lot. I thought of ways to approach Ginny so she would listen. Of course, she would *listen*. That wasn't the problem. The problem was that I didn't know what to say. I wanted to understand what was going on in her life and I hadn't any right to ask.

In the end, I didn't even try to talk to her. When Ginny came through the door—this was about two A.M.—I chickened out. I slouched in my seat so she wouldn't see me. When she dumped her shoulder sack in the Oldsmobile and drove down Melrose (at a clip, I noticed), I followed her. I kept the Cadillac a few car lengths behind as she popped onto the 5 Freeway, skirting the outside lane and then switching inside in order to hop ahead all of twenty feet. She exited on a ramp, going awfully fast, went a block eastward, and then followed a long

boulevard that paralleled the main road. Celia's car was wonderful even on patchy roads. It glided over potholes, stones,
fallen hubcaps, aloft on its suspension. Smooth, like an underwater dive.

We traveled down a boulevard banked by industrial buildings with sooty windows. We passed a crumbling pink hotel
that looked as though it had been painted over several times to
hide structural damage, a bar called Ya-Ya's, a homeless shelter,
a taco stand. After a few miles Ginny climbed back onto the
freeway and bullied her way through another half-dozen cars.
She was demonic in this regard, and I wondered if she always
drove this way or if she had figured out that I was following
her.

When she finally stopped it was at an all-night McDonald's
in Culver City, just next to Mother's hospital. It was an odd
section of town, an area near radio stations, restaurants that
were rundown but nonetheless required valet parking, and hor-
rifying stores that sold potions for curing colds, flu, acne, and
impotence in a manner that suggested religion. I stayed on the
street, double-parked outside the entrance to the McDonald's
lot, as Ginny wound the Oldsmobile to the drive-through window and placed her order. It interested me that she would eat
at a McDonald's when she could probably just as well eat at
Eli's. That she ate at all was amazing, so infrequently had I seen
her with food.

The attendant handed her a bag and she drove out of the
McDonald's lot and across the street to where the hospital
stood, brightly lit and towering. She parked near the staff entrance, beneath a lantern that flooded her car with light. She'd
obviously done this many times and was practiced in late-night
visitation. I worried that Ginny would recognize Celia's car, so
I stayed near the edge of the lot. But she didn't seem to notice.
In fact, she didn't look out the window. She put what I think
was a fishburger on the dashboard, undressing it from its paper
wrapper, which she arranged like a placemat. She removed two

flaps of bun from her sandwich and tossed them out the window. Next she scraped away the mayonnaise, dropped a few scraps of lettuce into her mouth, and then, using a plastic utensil, unsheathed the fish from its breaded crust. She was left with a fraction of food, a meager slab of bald meat, which she ate unenthusiastically considering the enormous chore of getting the fish into this state. She didn't even eat the whole thing. She had a bite or two, chucked the rest inside the bag, and then went into the hospital.

I was tired. A car screeched down the road next to me, sending fumes of burned rubber into the air. I made a mental note: Never let your life get to the point where you crouch in the dark part of a hospital lot spying on your sister as she dismantles a fishburger.

And then, that very same car that had belched out fumes and left half its tires on the pavement, made a beeline for me at high speed.

The Cadillac is a luxury car, designed to accommodate long rides to summer homes and ski resorts. It is not equipped for sudden acceleration, tight turns, lots of stop and go. So when Mikey took off in my direction, I had a moment of unprecedented panic, visions of accordioned front ends and emergency-room stretchers.

But the Cadillac was quick, roaring back onto the street as I raced forward, Mikey thundering behind me. I knew it was him because I looked in the rearview mirror and saw his face peering over the steering wheel, angry, determined. He floored his car—a white seventies Camaro—knocking my back bumper twice. I felt the car lurch forward, felt my guts shake. I wondered how long he had been following me. I turned right and headed up the center of a street full of shops, my horn blaring out a warning as I made for the entrance to the freeway. Mikey charged forward, gaining on my right, and knocked the Cadillac's side panel. I fishtailed, swerved to avoid a motorcyclist, shouted at Mikey, who would never be able to hear me. Dozens of horns from other cars blasted as we scrambled along like two outlaws.

I made the freeway entrance with Mikey directly behind me, so close it appeared we were connected. I swooped behind a Mercury Monarch, cut three lanes over and drifted in front of a pickup truck. I couldn't see the Camaro and thought maybe I'd lost him. I changed lanes into the center, eased up on the accelerator, and relaxed into the seat, checking my mirrors frequently. But just when I thought I'd made it, I saw a blizzard of white behind me. Mikey was hot along the shoulder, cruising so fast he had to brake when he saw me, tucking himself just behind my right and smacking the taillight so I heard it burst. He zoomed along the side, even with my car. I was so mad now I jolted right, grazing his left front tire, and got a glimpse of his surprised face. I did it again, scraping the long, low door of the Camaro. He retaliated full force, dropping back behind me and attacking from the other side in a quick maneuver worthy of competitive racing. The Cadillac took a good jab in the left door and nearly knocked into a T-bird that had entered the freeway unaware of the drama unfolding on the overpass above Culver City. I shook Mikey loose form my left, braked suddenly, and then drew up behind him, letting go a battle cry as I took out both my headlights with a hard hit to the rear.

Luckily it was late, so there wasn't too much traffic. I took a sudden right and tumbled down an exit ramp, turning left at the bottom. Up the road was a car dealership—Toyota, not Cadillac. I switched off the lights and hid behind the showroom.

Forty minutes of back roads returned me to Sun Dial Street, and all the time I was conscious of every moving object on the street.

At home there was a light on, which was worrisome, I thought. I approached the house slowly. The door opened and I stumbled back, expecting Mikey. But it was Van. He stood with one hand on the door; from the other hung a six-pack of Schlitz, now half empty. He looked over my shoulder at Celia's car. Lights and some glass were missing; there was a hanging fender and a crater of dented metal across one door. Radiator steam surrounded it like a halo.

"Some lady called and convinced me I should stick around till you got home. Now I see why," Van said. He handed me what was left of the six-pack. "I see you've fallen into some questionable road habits, boy."

There were two "emergency" messages from Celia. I found the note Van left on the kitchen table, a ring of condensation from his beer can clouding the numbers.

Celia, on the phone, said, "It's terrible what I've done to you. It's beyond credence."

"He tried to kill me, Celia. Don't make me guess why."

"It's just an overreaction. I suggested to Mikey that you and Lucy were, well, *seeing* each other."

"You told him we were seeing each other?" I said. "I'm lucky he didn't shoot me."

"So he *didn't* shoot at you?" Celia said. She called to Lucy, whom I could hear in the background. "He didn't try to shoot him," she said.

"Celia—"

"How could I have known he'd react this way? If your body ends up in a canyon or a ditch, I will make huge donations in your name to a charitable organization. Or would you prefer to sponsor an annual prize? A park bench? Perhaps a donation to the preservation of wildlife in the Serengeti?" Celia said. "Sam, you're not laughing."

"Celia, you should be aware that three hours ago, on a crowded stretch of the 405, I completely destroyed your new car."

Celia said, "That's fine. Think nothing of it. Nothing at all. I deserve it after what I've done to you. Ha. Ha."

She said, "You are kidding, aren't you?"

Ginny returned home around noon, slept for an hour, and then began listening to records—all of her favorites. The torture scene from *Tosca*, when Cavaradossi is being persecuted by Scarpia's henchmen, was a favorite. Tosca diving to her death was a favorite. There was a scene from Verdi's *Rigoletto*, the one where Rigoletto comes home to his daughter after receiving Monterone's curse, that she listened to repeatedly. All at such a pitch that the rest of life had to take place either in silence or about forty decibels louder than a normal human voice.

"I'm sorry, Pelzer, I couldn't hear. Did you say exploitation or Presbyterian?"

"Sam," Pelzer said. His voice was weary. He'd missed a performance, a small-sized but big-paying club in Brighton. The club owner was very upset. The rest of The Fetish members were very upset. "I don't want to play music when it isn't the music that is being listened to. You're selling us because we're pretty, not because of the music we play. We could stand there and sing pollywolly doodle and it wouldn't matter."

"But you'd still have to *show up* to sing pollywolly whatever," I said. I had a finger plugging one ear. I'd pulled the phone as far from Ginny's room as I could, but it was no use. Music invaded at high volume. A soprano occupied my eardrum. I shouted, "It's the showing-up part you keep forgetting about!"

"What do you care? Speaking of showing up, you keep saying you're coming back to Boston, but I don't see you here. Don't get me wrong—it's not as if you're missed."

"I don't care what you think of me, Pelzer. But there are four other guys in the band and they are going to keep playing. You're the one who's going to get ousted if you continue ditching gigs."

"It's all the same to you," he said. "You get the same cut."

He said something more but I couldn't understand.

"What, Pelzer?" I called into the phone. "Wait a minute. Let me see if I can get Ginny to turn down *Don Giovanni* over here."

"It's *The Magic Flute*," Pelzer said and hung up.

I knocked on Ginny's door. Nothing.

"Ginny!"

"What!" she said from inside the room.

"I can't conduct any business with this noise!"

The needle swooped across the record, carving what sounded like an impressive scratch. The room went silent. I heard Ginny's bare feet slapping linoleum. The door opened and she stared at me. Behind her head I could see her sewing machine set up, cloth bunched beside it.

"Whatcha up to?" I asked. Beneath the lenses of her glasses her eyes were magnified. Huge and burdened with anger.

"Nothing," she said. "Give me your hand."

I held out my hand and she dropped two earplugs made of yellow foam in my palm.

"Now go away," she said.

It was the end of the afternoon, four-thirty or so, and I was sitting by the radio listening to the smog report while Ginny got ready for work. I had slept for two hours midmorning and then lounged on the couch, reading, dozing, watching television, attending to my easy habit of lingering. It occurred to me that everyone in this house, especially me, acted as though they were recovering from flu, *all the time*. I tried to think of when this flulike behavior had started, remembering weekends when I was still living at home, but nothing specific came to mind. Maybe after years of my mother's illness we'd all just accepted a lifestyle suitable to chronic disorders. Ginny, though, was exceptional in that she *moved*. True, she was usually asleep—or trying to sleep—when she was home, which suited the mode we'd all come to adopt. But at least she left the house, which was more than I could say for myself.

I heard the kettle whistle, water go on and off. Ginny went through exactly the same rituals of waking and going to work, as though she could remember nothing of the events of yesterday at all. As though we'd had no fight, as though there had always been a broken-down Cadillac outside the door, as though I'd always had a slice over my eye. She made no comment, ignored me entirely. I caught sight of her darting between her bedroom and the bathroom, and when the phone rang she was in the middle of drying her hair so I had to plug one ear with my finger in order to hear.

"You're out of your fucking mind," the voice, a man's voice, said.

"Mikey?" I asked, calling over the noise of the hair dryer.

"Let me tell you, buddy, I am carrying around a lot of adrenaline. Things could get pretty bad for you."

"This is about Lucy, right? Whatever it is, I didn't do it," I said.

"Is this about Lucy, he asks. He doesn't have a clue why I'm going to bust his face, but he thinks, he *thinks*, it might have something to do with Lucy."

"I'm innocent," I tell him. "It's all conjecture. Gossip. Malice from wrongful sources. Look, Mikey, this is just like Celia. She's trying to wreck your marriage, or hadn't you noticed?"

"Don't get smart. Watch yourself," Mikey said. "And watch that little slut sister of yours."

He hung up. I put the phone on the ironing board and went to the bathroom, from where the whir of Ginny's hair dryer still dominated the house. I switched off the light, which caused the dryer to go off as well. Ginny looked up, irritated.

The light from the hallway illuminated one side of her face, and she glared at me with suspicion.

"Yes?" she said.

"Thought I'd say hello."

She revved the dryer back up. I sat on the edge of the tub. For a few minutes she ignored me. She stood in front of the mirror, twisting her bangs around a brush and blow-drying them into place. Then all at once she turned to me, exploding.

"WHAT?" she screamed.

"Tell me about Eli," I said, shouting over the noise of the dryer.

"What about him?" she yelled back.

It occurred to me that I didn't know what I wanted to know about him. I just wanted to *know*.

Ginny bent at the waist and tossed her hair over her head. She pulled at it with her fingers and ran the dryer around the nape of her neck. Then she turned off the dryer and looked at me through a veil of slick hair.

"That wasn't him on the phone, was it?"

"It was a guy named Mikey," I said.

"Mikey?" she said. "Oh, he's some flyspeck sidekick of Eli's. Forget him."

"You *know* Mikey?"

Pretending not to hear me, she looked back into the mirror. She flicked a few strands of hair so they lay away from her face and then switched off the dryer. She turned to me and I thought she might say something.

There was a beat of silence, then the phone began again. Its ringing felt like the great boom of ice cracking across a thawing lake.

"Listen," she said in a rushed whisper. She touched my shoulder. "Don't answer."

"When will you talk to me?" I asked.

"When I like you better," she said softly.

She left for the restaurant as the lingering daylight made streaks of yellow, pink, and brown in the sky. Lights all over the city flicked on. Color became remarkable. She left wearing her uniform, carrying the same suitcase that had burst open yesterday, held closed now by a belt. And this time I let her go.

TEN
■ ■ ■

Mother sat in bed with a newspaper and coffee. She wore blue slippers, hospital-issued and made of paper, a pair of khaki pants, and a long cotton sweater. On her wrist was a series of plastic bracelets in different colors with identifying information, listing her name, her doctors' names, the particularities of her treatment. Her doctors wouldn't discharge her until they got her soundly back on medication. The question now was which medication and in what quantity. For four days she'd been bored, tired, imprisoned in bed. But she took it well. Beside her were several well-thumbed paperbacks. Her television had color. On a table that sat on rollers near her bed were a radio, a telephone, a box of Kleenex.

She said, "There we were, having such a nice time in Santa Barbara, and then boom, an earthquake. I just don't understand it."

"Mother, there was no report of an earthquake in Santa Barbara."

112

"There's certain things you just come to expect. Like that the ground below you doesn't move."

"It didn't move. There wasn't a quake on this planet that day—or any day this week, as far as I know."

She asked for water and I went to get it. The hospital's "stress unit" had a tiny kitchen, a galley really, with a sink in miniature and a refrigerator. I searched the cabinet, found a paper cup, and filled it with sink water. An enormous round nurse came in, saw what I was doing, and said "Ice," like an order.

I delivered the water to Mother and she took me in, head to toe, and said, "What happened to your face?"

"Ran into a door," I said. "Anyway, you're the patient."

"Oh," she said, and brushed the air with her palm. "This is nothing. The one last summer was much worse. It was just the earthquake this time, I think."

"Mother, I told you, there was no earthquake."

"And Van and I had been drinking things with rum in them," she said. I gave her a look, but she continued, saying, "And the rum was quite old. Who knows how old that rum was, and anyway, I don't drink very well."

I'd heard this before, so often that it sounded more like an echo of history than a statement.

"You are never sure about these things," Mother continued. "It could be the medicine. I don't think I need medicine."

The radio played show tunes from many years ago. It crackled with interference, and I adjusted the antenna, the tuning knob. "This radio could use new batteries," I said. I found a moment of clear reception.

"Sam, it's plugged into the wall."

"Oh," I said. I put the radio down. "Mom, what do you think about Ginny going out with Eli?"

"They are a peculiar pair. I don't know what to think. I'm

afraid I've always had a live-and-let-live policy. Which is why I am such a terrible mother."

"You're not a terrible mother."

"I should have set down rules. If I had it to do over again, you would both have had a proper bedtime."

"I'm sure that didn't matter."

"And four square meals a day," Mother continued.

"It's three you're supposed to have."

"Three, then. Sam, do you think you could leave the radio alone?"

"There's a switch back here but I can't move the damned thing."

"I would also have forbidden foul language," Mother said. "You know I always wanted it to be different. It was just that you were much better children than I was a mother."

"That's not true; we were awful. We still are. *There*," I said. I'd gotten the radio to play on FM.

"I really wish you'd stop fiddling with that," Mother said.

"Mother, I'm *fixing* it."

She reached over and pulled the plug from the wall, silencing a Stephen Sondheim song. She looked at me, very satisfied now that she held the radio cord in her hand.

"I'm trying to talk to you," she said fondly.

The freeway was jammed tight with Saturday night traffic. The road was nothing but bumpers and tires, headlights against chrome, shadows of drivers, the bug glow of cigarette ends. I looked over the long line of cars in front of me and rolled down the window. The Cadillac was running surprisingly well considering what it had been through. I'd had to replace the headlights, of course. And a taillight. Repositioned the fender. Radiator work would be in order. Maybe a new door.

The highway seemed peaceful now, despite the traffic. I stared into the sky, felt the night air heavy with much-needed rain, and heard music from hundreds of different car radios. I crept forward until an exit appeared, escaped onto Wilshire Boulevard, and headed for Beverly Hills.

At the door Lucy was a single long line of black leotard, her hair arranged on top of her head in a hurried knot. She looked over my shoulder at Celia's car, ransacked and ruined in the drive, and showed no surprise at all.

"Sam," she said. "Well, at least you're still standing."

She smiled and welcomed me inside as though my arriving at the doorstep without even so much as a phone call was a common occurrence. She swung Stacy from the top of the hallway table onto the floor. "Off the furniture, precious," she whispered to the child. Stacy, her face hidden in a Batman mask, held a ray gun and was ready to laser to death all intruders. Her position atop the table had been strategically decided upon. I smiled, showing her my gratitude for being allowed to live, and she gave me a look like maybe next time she'd get me.

"Here's Celia's keys," I said, following Lucy into the living room. "I just need to call a taxi."

I walked through kids' toys, couch pillows, clothes, croquet mallets, popcorn. A plant had toppled over, spilling water and potting soil over the yellow carpet, and the twins were in their underwear, racing matchbox cars over the dining room table.

"Celia is visiting your mother in the hospital," Lucy said. "I'm so mad at her I sent her away. No lie. I said, 'Get out.'"

"Celia is visiting my mother?" I asked.

"Sorry," Lucy said. She stooped by the television and rolled up a red exercise mat. With the heel of her foot she rolled two very small barbells against the wall. "I give aerobics instruction to Nella, the babysitter. She's upstairs taking a shower. Nella has a world-class perfect body but she comes to *me* for fitness." She stood, an exercise mat under each arm. She said, "Once, fourteen million years ago, I wanted to be an actress."

I followed her into the kitchen. "Do you know the name of a taxi service?"

"I don't blame you for wanting to leave immediately. You must hate us," she said. She unwound the knot of her hair and the curls dropped just above her shoulders, red and brown. Across her pretty nose were new freckles from the sun. Her eyes, gray and serious like her mother's, might have been a little angry. "Mikey's not here, if that's what is bothering you. We've been fighting round the clock. I threw both him and Celia out. He took Bobby with him, which just pisses me off. I hope he didn't do that to your eye."

"No," I said. I touched the cut over my brow.

"Have you ever been married?" Lucy asked. She hid herself away in the bathroom off the kitchen. I heard water, the tugging of clothes coming off and on, quick clips of a hairbrush. I called across the kitchen, telling her no.

"Well, never, ever do it," she said, emerging now in a pair of silk trousers and a man-sized ivory shirt. "At first it seems a great idea. You hole up, make a lot of noise about how much you love each other, maybe have a few kids. You think it's going great until you find that all of a sudden words you've used every day of your life have taken on an entirely different meaning. A simple question, 'Did you put gas in the car?' does not mean 'Did you put gas in the car?' It means 'I work harder than you and have less time and still I do everything.' It means, 'You are a bad mother.' "

She concocted a fruit drink, poured it into three small plastic cups, and laid out a plate of animal crackers, which Stacy carried with two hands to her brothers.

"Sounds like a serious fight over a simple thing like gas," I said.

"It wasn't *about* gas," Lucy said. "It was about you. I could kill Celia for telling him this insane lie about . . . well, you know the story."

"I know."

"Anyway," she said. She sat on one of the kitchen stools, her chin in her hands. I heard the kids in the next room, shrieking about what animal they were about to eat. One of the twins was insisting that he get all the elephants. "You want a drink?"

I told her not to move. I opened the refrigerator, found an open bottle of wine, and poured a glass for Lucy. For myself I took some of the fruit drink the kids were having.

Lucy said, "Last week he brought home chocolate for the kids and I wouldn't let them have it because it was, you know, part of a woman. He said, 'Oh come on, to them it's just candy.' But I know better. Kids are very sophisticated these days. They know when they are eating women's breasts. I told him he was disgusting. But the fight wasn't about the chocolate. It was about sex. He *talked* about chocolate but he was *saying* that I don't do it for him in bed anymore. And I was saying that I know he's having an affair with the babysitter."

"Nella?" I said, pointing up to the ceiling, where the faint sound of shower water could be heard. "The one with the body that you instruct?"

"Different one. Nella is a friend," Lucy said. She wiped a lipstick smear from the edge of her glass. "Don't tell any of this to Celia. She's been waiting for a divorce now for nine years."

One of the twins came in for another tumbler of juice. Lucy patted his shoulder as he skirted her. He was at that age when he didn't like being touched.

"I hate to admit this, but Mother knew that any man whose business was to make dirty chocolate was just not right-minded. I used to disagree, but now I don't know. I saw the kids with that ten-pound chocolate breast and I thought, my God, this man, *this man* is what I'm married to? It's not so bad with the boys, but Stacy saw her father breaking pieces off for the others and she backed away. Wouldn't eat a bite."

I thought about Stacy, poised on the table with her gun in her hand. I was another male force making way into her home; no wonder she wanted to shoot me.

"I know you're thinking that I am telling you all this because I want to sleep with you," Lucy said. She leaned forward in her chair. "I don't want to sleep with you, though I admit I thought you were very attractive the other night. I used to use sex as a cure, but not anymore. That's the other part of the fight. Sure, he makes dirty candy, but I *am* dirty. See how it works?"

"What about him and the babysitter?"

"Oh that," Lucy said, shrugging it off. "That's only a recent development."

ELEVEN
■ ■ ■

In the car Lucy seemed all at once very happy. She pointed out her favorite bookstore, clothes store, spot for Sunday brunch. We'd opened the sunroof, bringing stars and moonlight into the car. Lucy turned toward me, her face glowing.

"Silly to take a taxi," she said. "I know exactly where you live. When I first came to L.A. I stayed with a friend on Santa Maria at Ninth. I could have thrown a rock and hit your house."

Lucy's car was a Camaro, exactly like her husband's but light blue, not white. We sat in bucket seats, our shoulders nearly touching.

"In college I was support lead in a show where the lead went on to get three movie contracts, one right after another. The ART in Boston almost took me. This is 1978. And I had three call-backs for *A Chorus Line*. Then I come out here, and boom, my luck plunges." She made a rocket using two fingers and did some very real sound effects as the rocket nosedived into the dashboard. She said, "I know I shouldn't complain. I love my kids. And who knows? Maybe when they're all in school I'll try again."

I told her what I'd seen in the music business—a surplus of talent and meager interest from the powers that dictate success.

We left the highway, rode a few blocks, stopped at an intersection. In front of us, high on a billboard, was an enormous face of Marilyn Monroe.

Lucy told me that Celia had devoted years to carting her from ballet class to drama class to dance class to piano. "I was only seven, but I wanted it very badly, the way some kids do. Poor Celia spent more time in cabs."

When I asked her about her father, she said, "My father? My father is a retired neonatal surgeon—you don't know what that is. He worked harder than anyone; there are children alive today who wouldn't be if not for him. No hobbies, never home. I can barely remember what he looks like. There was a newspaper article about some award he got and it showed a picture, so I guess that's what he looks like."

We passed a doughnut shop, a liquor store, the UPS parking lot with its dozens of brown vans. Finally we rounded the bend onto Sun Dial Street. There were four streetlights along the side of the road, two with the glass knocked out. Graffiti. Trash blowing like sails along the pavement. We parked next to the broken fire hydrant, which had given up all its water and now lay decapitated and dry. A light in Ginny's room shone through the window, but the car was gone.

"I'm worried about my sister," I said. I could see the back wall of Ginny's bedroom, her corkboard of postcards, her 1988 Olympics poster.

"You should be, if she works for Eli," Lucy said. "Not that he's a bad guy or anything, but really, there are people who would love to kill him. Mikey's not kidding that those guys think Eli infested their clubs. Half of them are mob-owned, I'm sure. And places like Eli's attract crazies, druggies, all sorts of ordinary low-life and scum."

"What are you talking about? It's a restaurant."

"You've been there?" Lucy asked, her voice harboring some information. "Which part of Eli's?"

"Of course I've been there. Excellent raspberry soup. What do you mean which *part?*"

"Oh, Sam," she said, shaking her head. She put the car into gear and eased forward. "I think we'd better go to Eli's."

This was the first time I'd heard of the Red Room, the unofficial name given it because of the carpet and wallpaper, which had been a deep crimson before Eli changed it into the glass, brass, and mirrors it is now. Lucy said it was one of the oldest strip joints still in existence in Los Angeles. Eli had managed to avoid all the usual methods police had for closing them down. Through the years he'd watched the competition fall—poor health standards in the kitchen, overcrowding, dirty mixing. So Eli made sure his club was immaculate. There was careful screening of minors, no prostitution, and absolutely no drugs. He exceeded the health department standards in the kitchen, the fire codes in the doorways. No one removed so much as a shoelace offstage. It was a well-run, no-nonsense club with a reputation for high-quality strippers.

"There's just this one thing," Lucy said. We swung into the parking lot. "There is no such thing as a clean club. I'm not saying anything about Ginny."

"Why didn't you tell me this before?" I said.

"I thought you *knew.*"

"Do I look like the sort of person who'd let his sister work in a strip club?"

She drove around the back, where a narrow bit of open space wound left.

Lucy said, "I think you'd be very surprised, the people who've worked in places like this."

She made her way around the cars, lined up in extraordinary numbers, rows and rows wedged together. A single spot-light hung from a telephone pole. A tube of fluorescent blue crowned a short flight of cement steps. There was a red door with a shade drawn on its small window. Lucy told me that this was the way in. Apparently Eli didn't believe in signs at all, not for the restaurant, not for the club.

We parked beside a broken line of wire fence. Lucy balanced the car on an incline so steep that we had to lean way back in our seats to keep from falling sideways. "I can't go in with you," she said. "Not because of why you're thinking. I mean, women go and it's not a big *deal* or anything. And it's a respectable club—as much as these things *can* be respectable."

"You don't have to go in," I said. I did my best to smile at her, though mostly I was concentrating on harnessing the urge to run through that red door. I was convinced, bizarre and wrong as it was, that Ginny was being held hostage inside.

"No, no," Lucy insisted. "You don't understand. I'm not be-ing prudish, Sam, I'm not that way. You see, this is how Eli and I got to know each other. I was dancing in a show, a small show, a show in a theater that folded a month later, in fact. Eli came up afterward and said he knew me from prep school, which he did, and would I dance at his club. I was out of money for the zillionth time and I hated to ask Mother for any. I still won't take a dime from her. Part of the reason I let Mikey continue in that dreadful business is that we don't need any help from Mom anymore. So I danced. I made some money. And that was that."

"You stopped dancing?"

"Right," Lucy said. "And I know this sounds ridiculous, but I just can't walk back in there. Not after so many years. I mean, look at me, Sam, I've got the kids; I teach aerobics. I have—if you can stand this—a position with the PTA. Going back into Eli's will just make me feel awful. It's not that I danced with my clothes off. That's nothing. Dancing is dancing and nobody cares how much you have on. It's that I would have done practically anything for the money back then. That's how poor I was. It isn't that I feel cheap or slutty or whatever those laughable words are. It's that it reminds me how sad and young and poor I was. I look back on that kid I was ten years ago and really, it breaks my heart."

I looked at her. Her hair fell in disarray around her face. She pushed her jaw out in a sort of tough gesture, but her eyes, all memory and circumstance, made me wish I had something right to say to her, something warm and personal. It was just that moment when I should have been able to remind her of some wonderful aspect of herself she'd forgotten. It was just that moment to help her imagine her life from some whole other angle. But I missed the beat on this one. Somewhere else a man in a car was saying just the right thing to a woman who mattered to him. But not here and not me. I just didn't know Lucy well enough.

"Did you meet Mikey when you were dancing?" I asked.

She nodded. "That's kind of when I stopped. Eli and I weren't getting along too well then, anyway. You know, it's funny, because Mikey has this way of reworking it so that he saved me from a life of smut and turned me into some sort of madonna mom. But you want to know something nobody else in the world knows?" She leaned back and took a deep breath. The car was angled so that I had to look up to see her. She said, "I modeled for Mikey's first chocolate sculptures. He will never admit this to anyone, but it was my breasts and thighs and butt that made him the success he is today. There, I've said it."

Now she looked away, running her fingers lightly over her lips. A car behind us began to move, its headlights making crescents across the gravel drive.

And then Lucy started to laugh. She laughed and shook her head. She said, "Go on, then. I'll wait for you here."

∎ ∎ ∎

It was mobbed. All men. Suits, polo shirts, Brooks Brothers ties, string ties. I edged through, very slowly, careful not to knock anyone or spill a drink. Years ago, when I went to a bar like this in Boston's Combat Zone, you had to show ID at the door and buy tickets for two drinks just to get in. I'd been with a friend from college, a hockey player; he got in a fight over a sports issue and we'd both been thrown out. I came home with a loose tooth and the collar of my shirt torn, remembering very little about the girls.

Eli's was more of an upscale establishment. A civilized crowd. Regular patrons. They were loose with their money, had beach tans and fancy watches. They stood quietly together, talking, looking up at the bar with casual interest, as though watching a TV show. From ceiling speakers came a tune from Badshack, a new L.A. band with a broody sound, setting the pulse of the dancing. And there, along a wide strip of shining pine in the center of the bar, a woman danced.

She was so tiny I thought at first she was a child, though a closer look revealed she was well into her twenties. She was slender-boned, with an economy of tightly muscled legs and a round face. She was so small, even way high on the bar, you could see that she probably stood no more than five feet. She wore a sequined outfit; her hair was wound in a sparkling metal comb. Her dancing showed some training. She looked up at the ceiling, out over the heads of the crowd, way against the barroom's mirrored walls. There she found her reflection, and she pushed her hips into a teetering motion, watching herself move. The music was slow, with a heavy back-seat beat. She undid the comb, and her hair, straight and gold, dropped like a curtain all the way to her waist.

The song ended; there was clapping. She came out again, circled from one end of the bar to the other, and pitched her bra onto the base of a spotlight stand. Her hair swam around her face, shook over her back, fell across her breasts. So the hair was the thing about this girl, who was called Tina, I found out after her routine ended.

The next one was Roxanne. Her thing was breasts.

There was Madeline, who was athletic-looking. Cropped hair and triceps that told me she worked out.

Meanwhile I'd bought a beer for seven dollars. I'd searched the bar and found no sign of Ginny. It was an embarrassing situation, having to stalk the corners of the room, the dark areas where people who probably did not want to be seen had staked out a safe, anonymous spot from which to view the dancers. I spent twenty minutes dogging the shadows but discovered nothing except a few annoyed customers. Finally a bouncer gave me a look that said, *Watch yourself.* A fat guy in a Panama hat got up from one of the bar stools and I took a seat there.

I ordered another beer and took great swallows of it, scanning the bar for Ginny. I searched for the area where the dancers hung out, waiting their turn, but saw nothing. Ginny could still be in the restaurant, for all I knew. And it was hard to imagine her dancing. She was a beauty in her own way but starving thin, it was true. I thought about Lucy in the car, imagined for a moment a much younger Lucy dancing in front of all these so far polite but leering men. I imagined her waiting quietly on her naked back as some artist figured the molding that would illustrate her breasts in chocolate. I could just see her, bored, cold, her mind racing through the logistics of the coming week, thinking, *Get that blouse cleaned, send a birthday card to Mother, pay the rent.*

Another dancer came on, and she was so beautiful I found myself gazing at her. And then, in my ear came a single soft hello. I turned, half expecting Ginny. But it wasn't Ginny. It was the girl who'd looked like an athlete, Madeline, now saddling up on the stool next to me. She wore a silk half-shirt and matching black shorts, and her legs, capable, long legs, were dressed in lace.

"It's hot in here," she said. "Makes you thirsty."

I nodded, taking out my wallet. Even as I did it I thought that I must be completely crazy and that I didn't know what I was doing. A woman says, more or less, she'd like a drink. You get the drink. The drink buys her away from someone else for a while. She doesn't want the drink or you or someone else. She wants a job, but this is the best she can do. Clubs like this work within the very tradition handed to us by our forefathers, perhaps just more blatantly than elsewhere. It is hard to believe that even now, as the twentieth century spills over the edge, it all still exists.

The barman shot over with galactic speed, took my twenty, and returned with a champagne glass for Madeline and six bucks for me.

She asked my name and I told her. She asked if I liked her dancing and I said yes.

I thought of Lucy in the car. I pictured her outside, glaring at the red door. So Lucy had wanted to be an actress and she'd wound up here. "Are you an actress?" I asked Madeline.

"What makes you think that?" she said.

"You look like one. You have an actress's presence onstage."

She sat back and took me in. "Listen to you talk. My professional interests, if you want to know, are in chemistry."

There was a silence during which we sized each other up. Or rather, Madeline sized me up and I endured it.

"Where's Eli?" I asked.

"Oh, he's out somewhere," Madeline said, looking around. "He'll be back."

"Do you work in the restaurant as well?"

"Me? No, I just dance. And talk to guys like you."

"Did you start in the restaurant?"

"No," Madeline said, with a lot of pause in her voice. She was curious about my questions. I was making her nervous, I could tell. She ran her tongue over her lips, nodding. She smiled and said, "Oh, I get it. Hello, Mr. Policeman."

"I'm not a policeman," I told her. She sat very straight on the stool. She looked away, then down. She had a scar just below her temple, a white V, half hidden by her eyebrow.

"Eli keeps the restaurant separate. Few of the waitresses ever even come in here. Bartenders occasionally work both sides," Madeline said in a stern voice. "Everyone is over eighteen. We dance, we mix. And you know perfectly well that all that's going on here is a chat. I didn't ask you to buy me this drink. You bought it."

"I told you, I'm not a cop," I said. "Funny you'd say that, because a few days ago someone else thought—incorrectly, of course—that I was a cop."

Then I noticed that the barman was suddenly in front of us. He was a big guy with a heavy face and a collar that seemed too tight around his thick neck.

"Yeah, nobody's ever a cop," he said. He took a fresh beer from behind the counter, opened it, and set it down on the bar. I handed him some money but he waved it away. He leaned over, folding his arms across the bar. "You want to arrest someone? Arrest me. I just stole from the management," he said. Then he walked over to a group of guys in black tie who were drinking at a pace.

There was clapping; the music changed. Now came the sound of a wedding march, and a woman decked out entirely in white lace and satin strolled down the center of the bar, her face as solemn as any bride's.

I closed my eyes. The room became much quieter. When I opened my eyes again there she was, in white, a bouquet in her hands, the train of her dress flowing easily at her feet. She stood right in front of me, her face tilted downward. Her lips were light pink; she wore a circle of flowers around her head.

There was a pause in the wedding march, and then the light sound of a flute drifted through the air. The dancer turned, casting her bouquet into the crowd. Someone from the drunk black-tie group caught it. Then there was the garter, tossed over a shoulder to a bald guy in a paisley jacket. Shouts and cheers. Here came the top of the dress. A corset in white lace. The men called out. The virgin scene was obviously a favorite. In my mind I kept seeing the dancer as she stood above me, acting the part of a shy bride. For a moment I'd thought she was Ginny.

"Okay, I can tell from your face you're not a cop," Madeline said.

The dancer turned, her leg level with her hip. Arms out, twirling.

"She's a feature," Madeline said, nodding up at the dancer. "Came from New York. She goes under the name Sasha. I don't think Eli can hold on to her, so get a good look before she's whisked up by some Hollywood type. I'll tell you something. Ginny does a fabulous job with the costumes."

The sound of Ginny's name, so casually included in Madeline's comments, was freakish to me. I looked at Madeline, who watched Sasha.

"She's a beautiful dancer," I said. Sasha was down to a small, precise G-string, her dress in pieces around her. She was spinning to a Prince song, her chin tilted to the ceiling, her face hidden beneath the white mesh of her bridal veil.

"Yeah, Sasha's a hot shit," Madeline said. She uncrossed her legs and pulled at the top of her stockings. "I hate her guts."

"What does Ginny do?" I asked, trying to sound casual.

"Oh, Ginny I like."

"Yeah, but what does she *do?*" I said. My voice was impatient, which worried me. I sat back on the stool, took a long breath, and stared at the stage, where Sasha did a backbend and somehow, remarkably, a walkover. Her high heels landed on the edge of the dress skirt. She was long-waisted, and you could see her muscles shivering on her stomach.

"She used to dance, I guess," Madeline said. She climbed off the bar stool. "Now she fixes the dress when this bitch walks on it."

■ ■ ■

Outside it had started to rain. Lucy saw me racing across the parking lot and pushed open the car door. I ducked inside, almost hitting my head as I got in. The windows had fogged over, making a world of cloudy glass around us. The sunroof was closed now. Rain came hard against the glass, making lots of noise. Lucy folded a magazine over her knee and said, "Okay?"

I nodded. I told her about the bar.

"Sounds a lot more posh than I remember," she said.

"It's the most depressing place I've ever been," I told her. "Not the dancers—they were beautiful. I've never seen women like that."

"Los Angeles has the best strippers because its a show-biz town. Those girls think they're going to be picked up for TV or movies."

"Does that happen?" I asked.

Lucy laughed. "Yeah, I have to admit that some big lives have begun in places like the Red Room," she said. "And some have ended. I'm surprised to hear you didn't see Eli. He used to be like a *fixture* in that place."

"Is it possible that all Ginny does is costumes?"

Lucy gave me a long look. "No," she said. She turned the key in the ignition, flicked on the headlights.

"Don't go," I said. "I should talk to Eli. Stick around for another half-hour while I find him. I promise I'll make it worth your while. I'll take you to the family shack and give you a tour of L.A.'s poor folk."

Lucy shook her head.

"A deluxe tour in several languages. Afterward, a short discussion period—"

She laughed, saying no.

"Espresso will be served," I said, but she held her ground.

"I have to go," she said in a somber way. "Children."

"Ladybug, ladybug, fly away home," I teased. And then, more seriously, "Mikey already thinks we're having an affair. We may as well be friends."

"Sam, don't start," Lucy said.

"I don't mean it that way," I insisted.

"Of course," she said. "Of course you do."

She put her hand on my cheek. I thought that truly all I'd wanted was some company. The night still had a lot in store for me, and I wished I could hold on to the comrade I'd found in Lucy.

"How did you do this?" she asked, running her finger over my damaged brow.

I shook my head as though I couldn't remember.

"We can be friends. That's what we can be," she said. Then she reached across me and pulled the door handle.

"Well," she said as I climbed out. "Bye."

The first and only time Ginny had danced was on the Fourth of July. She was the opening act and came on to a crowd of thirty, a fraction of the number that would ramble into Eli's after the fireworks had been set off. It was a discreet, conservative way to begin.

Ginny had chosen her own music, her own costume, as she would eventually do for almost every act in the club. She hunted down some music that she hadn't heard any of the other dancers use. Aretha Franklin's "Never Loved A Man" was the first. When the notes first came, slow, rhythmical, chiming in the air, Ginny picked her way delicately across the stage to the small crowd of surprised faces. Strippers didn't usually do slow tunes. And they didn't necessarily dance very well. Ginny was exceptional. Those were the days before she stopped eating, before she began her campaign to look different from the women in the club. Her legs were more muscular then. Her tall body had much more weight on it, a firm palace of muscle and flesh. She took off down the shining wooden dance floor, bending to the song, rising with Aretha's voice, stepping low with the strong piano sounds. The music seemed to push her hips out, her legs forward, sending her into bends and turns. She threw her neck back, showing a long line of throat. Her hair tumbled down her back in curls she'd set an hour before.

The next song was Dave Alvin's "Fourth of July." Eli recognized it after only a few notes. He'd played the song for her at his house less than a week earlier. He'd watched her stretch, pull herself up lazily from a leather recliner, and knock the coffee table. Offstage she was a big clumsy girl, but you put her on a platform free of all the objects that tripped her, got in her way, sent her stumbling, and she was graceful and supreme. Eli had offered the spot to her. She'd taken it, saying something about the money. Nothing had been said about what she planned for her ten-minute debut.

Suddenly the room went dark and Eli looked around, figuring there was an electrical problem. He'd owned and managed the place for so long that the emergency repair numbers flashed across his mind instantly. He got up to use the phone. But then he saw that there were still some lights, glowing deep purple from high above the stage. Then Ginny appeared, a dancer you could not see. Her face, her skin, were undetectable on the dark stage. But she wore Day-Glo underwear, and so the underwear was visible, though Ginny herself was not. She wore a neon orange bra, lime green panties, and bright yellow high-heeled shoes that seemed to carry themselves across the platform, glowing in the darkness. Tubes of blue dangled from her ears, and she'd drawn a slim red line down the back of each leg in a colorful illusion of stocking seams. Her fingers were lit up with pink nail polish; they flashed like ten lights across her face, down her long body, across her hips. Moon-blue bracelets shined from her arms. She was alive up there, turning brilliantly in the dark.

Eli watched her dance. She folded her body down to the

floor, sent herself up again, raised her legs into the air, bent her body back, and let her hips guide her forward. In the dark, as she undid the fastening of the orange bra, he could see the shadows of her breasts, though nothing definite. She held the bra across a shoulder, slid it down to where her breasts sent the fabric drifting over curved darkness, down past a hipbone, across the top of her thighs, finally letting it rest like a bright gold sun in the middle of the floor. The panties came off in the same strategic manner as the bra. Beneath them a G-string gleamed purple and red. The bracelets swung up and down her arm, shaking with the music.

Eli wondered what he could possibly have done in life to deserve the gift of this girl, who had strayed into his restaurant one day and whom he'd immediately found irresistible. Thirty men stood squinting in the dark to see the invisible dancer while on the stage two Day-Glo stocking seams and a pair of yellow shoes shook with enthusiasm to a song of independence.

That night, when Ginny came off the floor, Eli told her everything he'd thought as she moved across the dark stage like a rainbow. That she was young and talented and fearless. That he admired her. She could do anything, he said to her. She could have every dance spot she wanted. She didn't have to mix—he'd make up an excuse to the other girls. It didn't even matter to him that his customers had been a little disappointed not to see her with the lights *on*. It didn't matter that she was seventeen and would be the first and only exception he made to his stringent efforts to be law-abiding. If the police found her here, he'd be back in jail right away. To him, just then, it didn't make any difference.

But he couldn't convince her to dance again.

"That was the worst," she told him. They were in the dressing room way in the back. Another dancer was on now, a girl named Sparrow, who claimed to be part Iroquois, though she was blond. She wore a fringed panty bottom, and her bra was some sort of rawhide. She was dancing to one of the standard songs, something by Santana. It was the regular strip-tease number, with all the predictable moves, a routine that would soon become obsolete once Ginny began constructing costumes for the dancers. But there was no victory in Ginny's voice, no celebration in her face. She was talking so loud she was almost yelling. A couple of the other girls looked annoyed. Eli led her to his office.

"Don't pull on me!" she said, twisting away.

Eli's office was in a far-off corner, so small it could only hold a desk and a couple of chairs. He sat down, letting Ginny rule above him. He put his hands out, palms up. He smiled some.

"I'm not ever doing it again," Ginny insisted. Her fatigues were buttoned wrong at the crotch. A T-shirt covered most of the curls she'd worked so hard for. "All those gross men. I think they are disgusting. Tell me, really, don't you think so? In your heart of hearts, Eli, don't you think these guys are, you know, demented?"

"Maybe," Eli said. He lit a cigarette for Ginny, handing it to her as he spoke. "But all men love naked girls onstage. It's wired into the human genetic structure."

"I quit," Ginny said.

"Fine. You quit. I'm not going to beg you. I'm just going to say that there's a spot for you."

"This isn't a club. It's a homeless shelter," Ginny said.

"You want work? Here's work."

"Admit it, you run a disgusting establishment."

"Fine. I run a disgusting establishment. I'm not tying your arms and making you hang out backstage. I didn't force you to take charge of the clothing stock around here—"

"I need the money," Ginny said.

"Stick to the restaurant if you want. Or do you quit the restaurant?"

"You are a revolting human being, Eli."

"Fine. I'm revolting. Quit me, too."

The thing was that she did quit. She hauled her gear from her locker, took her pay for that week, and went home, not without some tears as she wheeled the Oldsmobile down Sun Dial Street, wondering where in hell she would find another job that paid like that. Maybe, also, feeling a little cozy toward Eli, who'd made her feel for a minute there that she was something special—though for all the wrong reasons, she knew.

Anyway, it didn't last long. She always ran out of money and went back. And Eli—from the moment he saw her, a little ragged, impetuous, careless with herself, worried all the time, he'd known she would return.

That first time she quit he'd stood calmly by her locker as she emptied it of shoes, comb, watch, socks, stuffing them all hurriedly into a shopping bag from a Safeway store. He wrote out a check and signed it without a word, playing along with the charade, the ritual quitting that he knew would be short-lived. He'd been in the business a long time.

Ginny didn't tell me that. Eli did.

We were in the restaurant, though it was closing around us. We sat at a table, surrounded by other, empty tables. The waitresses were sorting their tips, the dishwashers stacking trays. It was still raining; the windows were foggy and blue. You could hear the music, just barely, coming through the wall from the Red Room next door.

"Listen, I don't *make* her do anything," Eli said. He'd had his hair cropped; he ran his hand over a newly sheered crew cut. "Ginny does what Ginny wants—or have you been away so long you've forgotten what your little sister is all about?"

"To some extent, Ginny does what she has to do. What she gets paid to do," I said.

"If you care so much, then do me the kindness of taking

some cash off my hands. At least then Ginny can quit being nursemaid."

"Ginny's hardly a nursemaid."

"All I know is she watches over your mom like she's on duty, and she doesn't have time to breathe."

"Then you give her the money," I said.

Eli shook his head. "That won't work," he said. He sat back, speaking very slowly. "I'll write you a check and you hire someone for your mom. Don't cheese out on it, either. Hire a professional."

"I need time to think about this, Eli. It sounds wrong. I don't like taking money at all, for a start. And frankly, you aren't the most reputable character, and you're in a somewhat disreputable business."

"That's right. And if Ginny is willing to work here, where else might she work if she thought she needed to?"

"That's a startling thing to say about your girlfriend, to her brother," I said.

"People do what they have to when their back is against the wall, Sam. You've been fortunate in life if you haven't learned that yet."

I stood up. I'd had enough of him.

"I'll call you in a few days," I said.

"Take it now," he said, I thought a little urgently. "I've got a lot of friends in this town, Sam, and a lot of enemies. I've got some cash today; who knows where it goes tomorrow? Don't be dumb."

"Look, Ginny knows I don't have any money. She'll figure out it came from you."

"You know those tapes you heard? Tell her you represent the bands and she'll believe you've got the money."

I looked at him, and he answered my question before I could ask it.

"They're already cranking out albums," he said, "and are

managed by a guy who used to tend bar for me. That was a
long time ago. Today his annual income would pay for your
mother to spend her whole life in Club Med if that's what she
wanted."

"Fancy trick, Eli. How did you guess I wouldn't recognize
the bands?"

"Well, you didn't," Eli said.

"You dragged me three thousand miles on a hoax. Now you
want to give me money."

"If you came three thousand miles, I'd say you could use the
money."

"I don't like what's going on here," I said.

"We are talking about a small amount of good, clean cash."

"What if I say no?"

"I'm not putting a gun to your head. Do what you want."

And with those words I knew he was certain I would take
the money. I'd become like all the other people in his life,
predictable and in need.

"I'm not sure I want it," I said.

He smiled. "It's late," he said. "Let's not go back and forth
about this."

Then I felt something I never thought possible—I felt
somehow defeated, even as I unloaded Eli Igleton of more
money than I'd thought we were discussing. Much more, in the
form of a bank check, certified and made out to me because
he'd known all along.

TWELVE

The Renaissance notion of pilgrimage boats, packed solidly with madmen in search of Reason, was not entirely a myth. Throughout the fourteenth and fifteenth centuries, mentally ill people were driven from cities in Europe or placed on ships and sent out to sea. Then came hospitals, which were not so much hospitals as confining quarters for those believed to be insane, possessed, or otherwise unacceptable. They were dungeon cells, with all the characteristics you expect in a dungeon: extreme temperatures, flooding, dirt, rats.

This was described to me by Wilma, who had the night shift tonight. I'd gone to the hospital directly from my talk with Eli, feeling weary. Wilma had discovered me in the corridor, trying to find a coffee machine.

"Don't look so surprised, Sam. Even today most people conceive of the mentally ill as somewhat 'lesser than,' just by virtue of their disease," she explained.

"What is this, Freud?"

"God, no. Freud thought that women were retarded as civilized people. I never quote Freud."

We were sitting on two lounge chairs outside the nurses' station. It was the middle of the night, but Wilma was wide awake. In the past forty minutes I'd learned that a century and a half ago, cures for the mentally ill had included bloodletting, dunking in icewater, ritualized beatings, and painful restraining. When the insane were believed to be violent, they were chained to walls, to beds, to floors.

"If you go blaming your mother for what Ginny is up to, you won't help her or Ginny. Society teaches girls to want romance and children. And to please men with their bodies. If you don't believe me, go downstairs to the newsstand. I don't mean to pass judgment, but if you blame your mother for Ginny's problems, you are as primitive as the bloodletters and dungeon wardens."

I nodded.

"Do you know that your mother's biggest fear has always been that her children would be taken away from her? When your father died, she was sure she would lose Ginny. You might not think it's much, but she's done the best she could."

A headache was creeping toward my temples, and my coffee had gone cold. All I could think of was the Red Room and Ginny.

"Of course it's not Mother's fault," I said. "But something's got to change."

"Something is changing," Wilma said.

I stepped inside the hospital room and stood just at the door, my eyes adjusting to the darkness. There was a tiny light on the wall above the bed. It had a pink glow that made an arc against the blank wall. Through the window I could see the tall trunks of palm trees, deep black against the gray lawn. The breeze bent them westward, shaking the fronds. There was no more rain now. The sky had cleared. Far off, just beyond the freeway, the ocean broke moonlight over the beach.

"Sam," Mother whispered. I stepped toward her, steadying myself on the iron footboard of the bed.

"No," the whisper continued. "Over here."

I looked to my right and there was Celia, sitting in a chair. She held a book on her lap. She'd been reading it with a small flashlight, which she now shone in my face. I winced, putting up my hands.

"What are you doing here?" I asked. She clicked off the flashlight, and I found the wall for balance.

"Quiet," she said, a warning finger at her lips. "My daughter threw me out of the house tonight—*your* fault."

"Hardly," I said. "Anyway, I'm sure by now you're allowed back."

"Shhh!" Celia whispered.

In the armchair across the room was Van, deep in slumber. From Mother came soft, rumbling breaths.

"How is she supposed to rest when there are people here every hour of the day?" I said.

"Keep your voice down," Celia whispered. She punished me by flashing the light in my eyes again. "Don't be so ungrateful. You're forgetting that Van has been here every evening since your mother was admitted."

I looked at Van. His breath ruffled his long mustache, and I thought, not for the first time, that he had a wider and fatter face than any human I'd known. He was the type who sweated in his sleep—that much was clear from the condition of his shirt. Asleep, he looked much older. The moonlight slashed deep grooves in his cheeks and chin. His eyes disappeared beneath the hood of his brow.

"Excuse me," I said, whispering to Celia. "I didn't realize what a prize he was."

"Don't be so hard on Van, Sam. Oh my, your names rhyme. That means something—I used to know what. You don't know what it's like to be our age, to have grown children you never see. No, Van isn't perfect. Anyone can see that. But he cares for Lois."

"You could say the same thing about Mikey," I defended.

"No, no. Mikey seems acceptable because he has the camouflage of all those children, not to mention that silly house. Don't make the mistake of thinking that just because he's ordinary he's goodhearted. Lucy had one of those babies without his being even in the same city, let alone the delivery room. And when she says she wants something more from him, he throws money at her and tells her to hire help." Here Celia puckered her mouth and pretended to spit. "She already had *money.*"

"She told me she was broke when she met Mikey," I said.

"Temporarily," Celia corrected. "I was pretending to have cut her off."

"Oh, I get it. A joke," I said. "Ha ha."

"Whisper!" Celia demanded, but I knew I'd struck something in her. For a moment she paused, absorbed in thoughts that had nothing to do with me or Mother. Nothing at all to do with this hospital or this night. "Things were different then," she said finally.

I began to speak, but Celia readied her miniature flashlight. I gave her a look like *Don't you dare shine that thing in my face again,* and she shot me a glance that said, *What if I did?*

"Anyway," I said cautiously, watching her as I continued, "Van has a wife."

"Doreen?" Celia said. She whispered hard at me; it was as though we were having a screaming match in undertones. "She's been leaving and coming back for years. They live in two separate parts of a house, but hardly as man and wife. Sam? Sam? Why is it that you look so surprised?"

"I thought he was married to Doreen and he met Mother because he thought he was Napoleon."

"He *is* married to Doreen. I don't know anything about Napoleon. Why am I having to tell you this? Don't you ever talk to your mother? Love is complicated; things are always askew. You know, for a young man you have some very old-fashioned ideas. I certainly hope that Lucy knows what she's doing with you."

"What Lucy is doing with *me?*" I said. "Lucy isn't doing anything with me."

"Ha!" Celia said. She had gathered her bag, her coat, her umbrella. She stood, facing me.

"Don't go now," I said. "Don't drop a bomb like that and then float out of here."

"I cannot involve myself in my daughter's affairs," she said, sniffing. She dropped the flashlight into the pocket of her trench coat. "Just do me a favor, Sam—no matter how wonderful an idea it seems, don't get Lucy pregnant. Every time she falls in love she starts talking about more children, and frankly, there is world population to consider."

"I can only believe you will be punished someday," I said.

Celia laughed and went out. I sat down. I wasn't very good at this business of being a member of a family. I thought, *I hate, hate, hate being part of this mob of people.* I remembered what felt like millennia ago when Celia sat in the 737 cabin and told me that you couldn't escape from your family and that someday you always go back. She said that families are the most seductive and demanding of all scenarios. And that things go well only if you want it very badly and you are very lucky.

"You were right, Celia," I said out loud.

"She *is* right," came the voice of my mother. The surprise of her words knocked me forward. I wondered how long she'd been awake.

"It is just like you to pretend that you're asleep," I accused.

"You are in a bad mood," Mother said. She leaned on one elbow, taking her glasses from the table by the bed. "I don't blame you. If I had gone from a perfectly reasonable existence in Massachusetts to life in this household, I'd be in a bad mood too."

"I wasn't leading a perfectly reasonable existence," I said. "And I'm not doing any better here."

"Sam," she said, softly now. "What is it you expected to do? Haven't you realized yet that nothing is ever perfect? You keep thinking you can make it right again, but sweetheart, nothing was ever as right as you remember."

It was just that it was so late. It was just that I was tired. I leaned forward, resting my head against the table. I wondered what Mother meant. Maybe she was suggesting that things had been just as difficult even when Dad was around, that their marriage had been through its horrors and joys, that Ginny and I had been just as distressed and strange decades ago as now, that perhaps all families were more or less the same.

"I don't know what to do, Mom," I said.

She fitted her eyeglasses across her nose and stared at me. My mother certainly had two modes, this one sweet, intelligent, almost omniscient, the one where she knows me best and offers up an unending benevolence. She smiled beautifully and put her hand in my hair.

"You can do everything," she whispered.

When I left the hospital I realized suddenly that it was morning. Above me was a brightening sky, ripe with moon, a few remaining stars. A hint of sun cracked the horizon; everywhere there was stillness and expectation. I could see the freeway, the few cars that hurried along it, the trucks that moved solidly up the inside lane. There was no breeze or heat. It seemed the atmosphere had reached a zero ground, had emptied itself out and was ready to begin again. I took a cab back. The outdoors felt so vast and unending that when I got home and turned the key in the front door, it seemed as though I were entering the dollhouse of a giant.

I sat on the couch—my bed. Beside my foot was my duffel bag, stuffed solidly with clothes. I thought, *Who am I fooling? Why do I continue to pack as though I were leaving?* I glanced around the house and thought, *Get used to it. This is home, such as it is.*

I unhinged the couch and the mattress sprang out. Then the Henrys called, apologizing for waking me.

"I wish you had wakened me," I said. "That would have meant I'd been asleep."

"I'm afraid we got two pieces of very bad news for you, Sam," one of the Henrys said. I hadn't talked with them in almost three weeks, though they'd been gigging regularly, picking up work on their own. Bad news somehow seemed appropriate.

"Hi, Sam," I heard from another one. "We hooked up an extension here so we could all talk to you."

"Howdy, Sam," the third Henry said. "Brace yourself."

The first piece of news they'd read in the morning paper. At about two A.M. the members of The Fetish had been attacked in a parking lot as they were loading their equipment. A half-dozen guys, coming drunk from a club next door. They made the kids stack their instruments in a pile and one of the guys drove back and forth over it in a Bronco wagon. Then they beat them up, silently, thoroughly. "Stable" was their condition. "Gay-bashing" was the headline.

"I'll call them," I said. "I'll call their parents."

"I don't know if their parents will want that," one of the Henrys said. "I don't think they knew what their boys were doing."

"They weren't doing anything," I said. "They were playing music."

"Well, you give it a try," he said.

The second piece of news was that the Henrys had been

picked up by a scout and offered a contract, a large sum of money. The hitch was that I was written out of the picture. Which I expected and deserved.

"Well, congratulations then," I said. "*Of course* you shouldn't feel bad." I was trying to get them to stop apologizing. I explained that I really hadn't been so good for them.

"That's not true, Sam. We've been lucky to have you, and we might still be able to do it different. We're gonna make sure you get your rightful cut, and we haven't stopped trying to convince these fellas at the record company—"

"No," I said. "No, you go ahead and keep it. It's your money. I've got four new bands just by snapping my fingers out here. I have to go now, boys. I've got someone at the door, and you know how it is in L.A.—everything always on the move."

There had been a knock at the door. Three light taps and then a solid rap. Do burglars knock? Murderers? Would Eli knock? Would it be Lucy, having decided to leave Mikey? Or Mother, having decided to leave the hospital? Had Van's wife, Doreen, finally thrown him out?

At the door was Ginny. She was wearing a frayed sweater that hung off one shoulder, a T-shirt underneath, army fatigues hiked up with a belt. She held her uniform in a clump at her stomach, and all over her face was the sleepy, swollen look of a drunk. She walked past me, dropped onto the couch, and passed out in the very position in which she fell. I looked out and saw that she'd left her car door open. So that was it—she had fallen asleep in the car. I went outside and swung the Oldsmobile's door shut. Spoiled food on the back seat was beginning to have a bacterial edge to it, dozens of cigarettes had been crushed into the ashtray, and a half-bottle of champagne was lolling on its side.

I came back into the house, tripping on the doormat. I looked at Ginny, collapsed on the couch. I stood in front of her for a long time, and then kneeled on the carpet, close enough to smell the champagne.

"Hey, Gin," I said. She rolled to the left, an elbow bent over her face. A half-dozen silver bracelets slid down her thin wrist. Smeared lipstick made her chin pink. I put an arm under her and lifted her up against me. She was so light that carrying her was startling.

In her bedroom she woke a little. She sat up while I unbuttoned her cardigan, rolled a shoulder out of each sleeve. The T-shirt beneath was loose, stained with chocolate or coffee. A faded picture of Mickey Mouse smiled from her shallow chest. When I unlaced her restaurant shoes, I noticed raw blisters and no socks. Her jeans slid off easily. Her thighs were so thin they looked bowed. The skin around her hips was drum tight, stretched over the edges of her pelvis.

"Baby girl, you have to eat more," I whispered. I turned her onto her side, pulling a sheet to her shoulder. I lay down beside her on the bed. "Later we'll have a feast," I said, speaking to her back now.

I wondered if something other than alcohol was floating around in her bloodstream, and then I thought, not without a little bit of terror, that just a little while ago she'd been *driving*.

Ginny made a noise almost like she was going to cry but then didn't. I had drunk enough in the past to know what she might be feeling, that desperate need to escape your own sick body. After a few seconds she mumbled a thank-you. I kept my arm around her and floated in and out of consciousness. An hour passed. Another. The room was light with morning. Ginny woke, turned, winced.

"I had a dream just now," she said. Her words were thick and slurred. "I dreamed I was pregnant with Eli's baby. I think I liked being pregnant, except I was afraid Dad would be mad at me. In my dreams he is always alive."

"Go back to sleep," I whispered.

"I was . . . so . . . *big*."

I pictured Ginny with a pumped-up middle, handsomely pregnant, vaudeville fat.

"But look, there's nothing," she said. She waved a hand clumsily above her stomach. "Just piles of air where my dream baby was."

We fell asleep at just the time of day when Jasper, the dog, went on his run. When gangs of boys were outside, playing ninja warriors with broomsticks and waiting for the bus. Just as the dial of Ginny's alarm clock no longer radiated the luminous hours. We slept amid the sound of neighbors' radios buzzing with news reports, cars speeding and braking, doors shutting, music drifting from stereos anchored in the windows of apartment buildings, the hum of air conditioners, and children in mock wars.

I woke up, at first surprised by being in Ginny's bedroom, then just concerned that I might alarm her by being there. Her face was milky, her lips washed of color. She was probably still drunk. It was clear she would feel sick all day. I carefully unfolded my arm from around her, moving backward, crablike, to the edge of the bed. She was twisted beneath the sheet. Her hair rained over the pillowcase. Her naked foot hung out from under the covers.

"Some water," she said, just as I thought I'd escaped without waking her.

I crossed the living room. The front door was open—my fault. I must not have shut it last night. A hot breeze flew through the house; I could feel it even in the kitchen. The sun was out, high now in a noon sky. The air was scorched dry, with no hint of last night's rain.

I poured water for Ginny and then thought to take her orange juice instead. But of course there was no orange juice. I searched the refrigerator but found only a can of tomato juice, two wrinkled grapefruits, and a quart of milk.

Then, way on the bottom, back where the light flickered on a short circuit, I found four small oranges. They were not in great shape, these oranges. I took one to the counter and sliced it, assessing its juice potential. I sliced all four and got about half a glass from my efforts. I grabbed a paper towel, folding it in quarters to use as a napkin, I walked back through the living room.

Mikey stood in the open doorway, wearing golfing trousers and a cap. The expression on his face was a focused anger that worried me.

"Yeah?" I said, now standing still.

"I didn't know if I should knock," he said, gesturing at the open door. He had on a big, chunky watch and two rings on his right hand. Even in the pastel colors of his golfing outfit he looked foreboding, perhaps slightly criminal. His Popeye arms were pumped up to look large.

I walked to where he stood, took the doorknob in my hand, and turned it a few times. "Oh, you mean because the door is open?" I said, still playing around with the knob, making like I thought that it might be broken.

"Looks that way," he said. "We have something to talk about. You have some perversity over my mother-in-law? Now my wife? I think you ought to invite me in."

"Sure, Mikey," I said. "But first let's you and me fix this door." I put down the orange juice and told him to turn the doorknob slowly so that I could see if it caught. He stood there as I closed the door. The bottom lock clicked into place. I worked the latch as silently as I could, and then, when the moment seemed right, I told Mikey to turn the knob.

"It's stuck," he said impatiently.

"You're right. I'll have to call the locksmith. The entire door is jammed. Oh well. Thanks for coming over."

I raced for the back door and quickly worked the chain across it. I ran from window to window in the living room and Mother's bedroom, making sure they were locked, pulling the shades so Mikey couldn't see inside. He stood on the front doorstep, yelling, pounding his fists into the wood. I retrieved the glass of orange juice and took it to Ginny, who was now sitting up in bed, looking startled and confused.

"Here's some juice," I said to her.

"Who is trying to kill us?"

"Mikey. It's me he wants, not you. I don't know if I mentioned that he's Celia's son-in-law."

Mikey was yelling. He went around and around the house, banging on the windows and calling out obscenities. He got to where Ginny's room was and screamed that he'd kill me if I came near his wife. That he'd kill me anyway.

"Celia, the old lady?" Ginny asked. Her attention was on the windows.

"Older, not old," I corrected.

"I thought old people led peaceful lives," she said, just as the bug lamp burst all over the front landing. "You could have mentioned that you knew Mikey."

"Why should I tell you anything? You never tell *me* anything."

Another loud bang from outside.

"Jerk," Ginny said, and I didn't know if she meant me or Mikey.

I sat on the bed, feeling my heart pounding in my chest, my stomach queasy, my whole body alert. Between sips of orange juice, Ginny looked up, staring at the window, monitoring Mikey's course as he orbited our house, pitching fists and stones. I listened too, readying myself for the possibility that he might somehow get inside. My thoughts turned to household items that could double as weapons. To me this was all very unnatural, but Ginny's face held the wise look of someone not scared at all, just aware of potential harm. Almost as though she'd been through it all before.

The third time Mikey circled the house he banged on Ginny's window hard enough to break it. I told her I was calling the police.

"Don't," she said. "I mean it, Sam, please."

"He's out of control. This is dangerous," I said. "Where the fuck are the neighbors, anyway? Where's Hal and June? Where's Jasper the dog? This guy is crazy."

"You said 'fuck,' Sam," Ginny said, a little delighted. "I've never heard that from you." Then she looked at me seriously and said, "If you call the police, this will be much, much worse. They'll come and haul him away fast enough, but you see, he'll come back. And then it won't be a spontaneous thing—he'll be prepared; he might bring his friends. It's better to let him do his damage now. I can tell just by listening to him that he's not crazy. He's completely sane and knows exactly what he's doing."

"He's terrorizing us."

"Well, yes," Ginny said.

"He's going to kill us."

"Not even close."

But then came another loud crash.

Lucy called.

"Do you know what it's like to be married to a man with his own company? Every time you hate his guts, his secretary phones and accommodates his change in schedule, heart, interest, direction. You've got him down to feeling like a real scumbag and then *she* calls, saying it's no trouble at all to cancel the morning appointments, no trouble to pick up his dry cleaning, no trouble to have the car washed, no trouble. Every little thing he wants. Every *little, tiny*—"

I told her Mikey was tearing down our house.

"I know, I know, I know," she said.

Another window crashed. Mikey beat a shutter with a rock until there was a great snap of wood.

"Hear that?" I said, raising the phone to the window. There

was a boom. Another. I took the phone back into Ginny's bedroom. "Our house is collapsing, and Ginny won't let me call the police."

"I'm sorry, Sam. It's just that he's been accusing me of every imaginable thing and I thought, fine, I'll give him something to be upset about. So I told him I was with you last night."

"Lucy," I said, "I wish you hadn't done that."

Ginny raised her eyebrows and said, "Lucy?" She was dressed now: army fatigues and boots, a sleeveless black T-shirt. She laced a chain through her belt loops, wrapping it twice. "He just hit Dad's car," she said. "He dies."

"Your husband is beating my father's car to death. My sister, who was nearly in a coma last night, had a hangover and him to wake up to this morning."

Lucy made a sympathetic hum into the phone. "I'm going to have to leave him. I'm definitely, definitely going to have to leave him."

"That's real great, but why don't you come over here first and *get* him?"

"How can I, Sam? The window repair service is on its way. I got the boys off to school, but now Stacy has a temperature and I don't even know where my mother is."

"You mean he punched out your windows too?"

"Of course."

I heard shouting. I lifted the blind, looked out, and saw Mikey standing straight and looking a little bewildered. Ginny was running full gait at him. Every window in Dad's Oldsmobile was bashed in or splintered into webs of broken glass. The windshield, shattered like a puzzle, sagged inward, grazing the steering wheel.

Mikey and Ginny faced each other, screeching like monkeys. Mikey had yelled so hard his voice was hoarse. He coughed, forced his words, spat on Ginny. Van's car came barreling against the curb; there was a shriek of tires burning themselves into the pavement. By this time I was outside. Mikey saw me, jumped two feet into the air, and charged.

I ducked, racing around the end of the Oldsmobile. We rotated around the car, first to the left, then to the right. I watched his face distort with anger, his breath come hard, and the sweat roll down his neck. He vaulted the hood in a magnificent lateral leap and I stomach-dived over the roof, thwacking the radio antenna so that it sprang madly back and forth.

He swung his arms toward me. I headed for the grille. He feinted right, but I was on to his bluff and continued in the same direction. Now there was some distance between us. I took a breath and cut away, down to the left rear door. He rushed around the car, finally jumping onto the hood, and for a second I thought I was caught.

"Nothing happened!" I yelled. "I didn't touch her!"

He sprang for me and I curved around him, pulling my right foot onto the door handle and using it as a stirrup from which to leap to the opposite side. He climbed up the car and stood on the roof, knees bent, arms down, deciding on his next attack. I hovered near the back bumper, staring up at him.

"Lucy made it up!" I shouted. "She's on the phone right now. Ask her!"

"She called you!" he boomed. "I'm going to kill you!"

And then, just as Mikey shouted these words, I had this feeling, a feeling of gratitude really, that it was over. I was tired. One more time around the car seemed way too much work. It was good that Mikey was now going to leap onto me, kick me in the face, and then strangle me dry. Chances were that he'd think I was dead long before I was, and then I could rest some. I needed that. I needed to be left alone for a while; my world in Los Angeles had gotten way too complicated.

I readied myself for Mikey's jump, seeing it now as inevitable and even welcome. Maybe I could get a few clips in first. I am a big guy, true, and not in bad shape. But in high school it was chess team for me, not football. I've never had it in my nature to hit people. My impressionable years occurred during the sixties, and there exists within me a primal peacenik strain.

Mikey came at me, stretched in a dive, and fell across my chest in a lump of muscle and revenge. I was tossed back, rolling now on the hot pavement. I felt the heat across my cheek, my shoulders. I felt Mikey's forearm up under my chin, across my neck. He weighed a lot, more than I expected. The muscles he'd worked so hard on were making fast work of my jaw, my ear, my cheek. I did manage one swing: fist to stomach sculpture. It made him hesitate a quarter of a second before knocking me in the eye, reopening the cut Ginny had made days ago.

But then I saw a hand on the back of Mikey's head, huge fat fingers stretched over Mikey's scalp. It was as though God had come to pluck him up to the heavens, and for a moment we looked at each other, mortified, confused. We were punch-drunk and aching. Our mutual pain defined a type of bond. The hand was followed by another enormous hand around Mikey's throat, and he was carried back by his head.

I sat up, pulling my feet under me. When I began to stand, I wobbled some and sat back down. Van had Mikey against the car, his huge gut pinning him to the trunk. He hit him twice—accurate, determined blows. Then he swung him outward, sending him staggering across the pavement toward me. I shot to the side, leaned on my hands, and stood up, gulping air. Mikey swayed, his knees folding. He kneeled on the driveway and looked at me in a menacing way.

"You think this is over?" he said.

"I think it's over," Van said. He stood with his arms across his chest. He was pleased with himself, and he deserved to be.

Ginny raced at Mikey now, punching him in the shoulder, the back. Mikey turned away from her, swearing. I pulled her back, but she kept swinging.

"Bastard!" she yelled. I held on to her. "Let go of me, Sam!"

Van stepped toward Mikey. "You ready to leave?" he asked.

But he didn't need to say anything. Mikey was on his way down the driveway now, stumbling some. He got into his car, held his middle finger to me, and then sped off, sending dirt and gravel into the hot air.

I let go of Ginny, who went directly to the Oldsmobile. She put her hand on the hood and ran her palm gently over the shattered windshield. She looked so unhappy, surveying the damage. She brushed the door, steadied the radio antenna, ran a finger across the dished-in roof. The car looked as though a parade had marched over it.

"Does Mikey work at Eli's?" I asked.

"Sort of. I don't want to talk about it," she said. "Nice work, Van. You learn those moves in the Corps?"

Van nodded. There was a long pause, and then Ginny said, "Look what he did to Dad's car."

"It's so old," I said. I put a hand on her shoulder. "It's really a beater anyway."

"It's not a beater. I love this car. I inherited it from Dad," she said, which was a little sad because she hadn't inherited it from Dad at all. More or less, the Oldsmobile had simply fallen into her hands. I knew better than to correct her, of course. I had learned a little about how to maintain peace between us, and it had something to do with allowing for the occasional delusion in memory, the revamping of a history that was at once both shared and separate.

"What do you think, Sam?" Van said. He pointed at a long stretch of caved-in aluminum.

"Don't you guys touch it," Ginny said. She readjusted a mirror so that it no longer faced the ground. "I want a real car doctor."

Van nodded. He rubbed his hands against his trousers, eying the Oldsmobile as though he'd already completed a lot of work on it. Then he walked to his own car, fished in the back for a while, and pulled out a small suitcase.

"Your mother's coming home tomorrow," he said. He glanced at the front of the house, where glass lay in shards on the ground. The gutter hung from the roof at a forty-five-degree angle. "Maybe we could provide something a little better than this for her to come home to."

"This what?" Ginny said.

"This bringing of your, uh . . . unseemly affairs home with you."

"*You*, Van, are the unseemly affair," Ginny said.

"Don't start on that," Van said. "We're all supposed to make sure your mother takes her medicine. Half the time she goes into the goddamned hospital it's because she forgets the pills."

"She forgets them a whole lot more often if she's had a drink, which she is not supposed to have anyway, but I don't suppose we could count on you to keep her away from the booze," Ginny said.

"Ginny, please," I began. "He just saved me hours of unconsciousness."

"I don't mind," Van said, waving at me. He looked tired all of a sudden. The power he'd felt during the Mikey fiasco had worn him out. Even all his victory on that turf could not sustain him in a dispute with Ginny. His eyes were soft on her, full of defeat and fondness. "Let her speak. You don't hate me so much, do you, Virginia?"

"I hate you plenty," Ginny said. She studied a long scratch on the Oldsmobile's fender. Her face grew serious, thoughtful. "Sometimes you're okay."

The next few hours passed in a strange triumph over our defeat of the enemy, Mikey, who'd challenged our precarious homestead and whom we'd fended off like postmodern frontiersmen, sending him back, back to the recesses of eternal night, the dens of other supervillains, racists and inventors of new tortures, terrorists and international drug smugglers, Rushdie persecutors and those who put cleaning detergent in beagles' eyes. In silence we congratulated ourselves, regarded each other freshly, all of a sudden noticing little things—the colors of our clothes, the way we walked. Our conversation became a degree livelier, our gestures self-conscious, a touch more lavish, everything just slightly bigger.

I lapped up the excitement, feeling for the first time in a long while a sense of camaraderie. The cut over my eye had bled exuberantly all down my shirt, but I didn't change clothes. I dressed the wound, wrapped a bandage around my head, and celebrated the swelling. All the bruises and marks on my body were becoming comical to me. They seemed to map out the activities of my days; I almost enjoyed them. But there was also the fear that Mikey would return. Or that he would send over a similarly unbalanced appointee to hack down the sides and roof of our house, now that the windows were all gone.

The house was a punched-out version of its former uninspired self. Punished without cause, war victim, the house with its broken windows gave me a moment of heartache that couldn't have had anything to do with the house, really, but that erupted anyway, emerged and took hold. I drew long shards of glass from sills, seats of chairs, tabletops, carpet, cradling them in my thick-gloved hands and dropping them into the cardboard box Van and I had designated for glass. Van brushed the small slivers into a dustpan, vacuuming the rest. He hummed low under his breath, a habit that would usually set my nerves aflame but that under our temporary postwar enchantment was almost welcome.

Then I worked my way around the house, ducking between hedges, the sun glaring above. The phone rang with estimates for the car's repair. I heard Ginny insisting that competitors' price estimates had been lower, striking offers and counteroffers, and then leafing back through the Yellow Pages, searching for new garages to hustle for a lower price.

When I got to the third side of the house, there was Van,

standing above me on the inside, working a trowel across the frame of a window in the living room. He dug out the remaining glass, smoothed the wood, preparing it for new glass. He made slow, exact motions. There was a rhythm to his work, a stride that would make it possible for him to continue almost indefinitely, clearing window after window. I had not learned this manner of pacing and had instead scurried around the house as though there were a race. I was exhausted now, breathing hard. My hair was wet across my forehead; I felt some pain across the brow and I found myself thirsty all of a sudden.

I took a seat on a small patch of grass, resting my back against the house, knees bent, holding my gloves. Above me I heard Van's scraper stop, footsteps, the refrigerator door. Van came back to the window, leaned over, and handed me down a tall glass of icewater.

"I was thinking it might do your mother some good to get away from this place for a while," he said. "Trip north could give her a chance to get her feet under herself again. Breathe some real air instead of living in this pigsty."

I drank furiously, then took out an ice cube and ran it down my neck. "It's hot," I agreed.

"Severe smog warning in effect today and tomorrow," he said. I heard the clip of metal against glass, some tugging at wood. "The air quality is getting worse, and I know a place in Oregon so beautiful it would make you cry. You can fish all day. Guy I know bought a new car on the fish he caught and sold. No crowds on the beaches. Real trees."

Here Van stopped, studying the sickly-looking palm tree, dwarfed and yellowing with bad air, that struggled for existence in the yard next door.

"What's the matter, Van, growing tired of Southern California?"

"I'm thinking of your mother," he said.

I asked, "What about Doreen?"

"She don't care where I am. I'd have to keep it quiet that I was bringing Lois, that's all."

"Sounds sneaky," I said. I stood up, handing the water glass back through the window. Van didn't look at me. He let the glass stay where it was, just inches from his elbow as he worked steadily against the frame. He removed a long edge of glass, pulled back some putty, and studied it in his hands. I waited, but he didn't look up. He went on to the next segment of the frame just as though I weren't there. "Look, Van, what do you want? My permission?"

"I'll tell you something," he said, pointing the trowel at me. His voice became a low bellow, rising in volume as he continued. "I'm just tired of all the criticism from you and that sicko girl in there." He gestured behind him, where Ginny was speaking furiously into the telephone.

"I'm not saying anything," I said. I leaned close to the absent window, so close that I could smell turpentine on Van's hands, the solid wall of deodorized scent from inside the house. "You tell me you're not going to tell Doreen; I say that sounds sneaky. Big deal. I really don't care who you're married to. It's just that I refuse to pretend that the circumstances are entirely ordinary."

Ginny appeared suddenly beside Van, her mouth pinched. She said, "Who are you calling sick, fat man?"

Van looked at her, his expression sunken. He raised his great shoulders for a moment and then, dropping them, said, "No one. I didn't mean it."

Ginny and I glanced at him, then at each other, then at Van again. He looked all of a sudden outdone, deflated. I thought maybe we'd finally managed to convince him that he was as awful as he really was, which surprised and horrified me. Especially because I was beginning to like him.

"Well, you're right. I am sick," Ginny said. Her voice was

dressed for apology. She smiled some. "But I talked R.J.'s down three hundred bucks." She held out a page from a legal pad that she'd used to scratch phone numbers and prices on. She waved it proudly at Van and then went through an explanation of her bargaining tactics. She laid the paper on the sill, pointed at the figures, and explained how they broke down. I watched him survey the numbers. He was attentive to the details of dealers and repairmen, nodding through Ginny's account of conversations. It was exactly the sort of thing for which I have no patience, but Van faithfully studied the page of numbers as she explained them. Ginny touched his elbow, smiling fully. "So what do you think?" she asked.

"I think you're a genius," Van said.

THIRTEEN

■ ■ ■

I shook a carton of milk, tore the Open This Side side and also the Open From Other Side side. I drank in gulps, not even tasting it. Without windows, the house was like a tent, except every fly, every mosquito, every ounce of sun poured in. I sucked an ice cube, ran cold water up and down my arms, my face, neck, chest. I eliminated shirt, jeans, socks. In my boxers now, lying on the bathroom tile, the coolest place in the house, I phoned Pelzer.

"Are you all right, Arnold?"

"You know how much I hate you," he said. "But you call me anyhow. What do you want, Haskell? You want your cut for the night's performance?"

"I heard you got the worst of it."

"Yeah, me. I got the worst."

They'd given his right arm a compound fracture and sprained the other. His face was badly bruised, so much so that when I'd first called, the nurse said he was unable to talk.

"Are your parents around? Are they helping you?"

"My father isn't speaking to me. My stepmother thinks it's my own fault for playing at a gay club."

"That's ridiculous. You were just doing your job. We all need to eat."

"Yes, I'll mention that. Thanks loads. Why don't you write that down and send it to them?"

Van and I took shifts for the window work. When we weren't working we sat in what Van was calling his garden, now that he'd planted a new hedge and an olive tree in the back of the house. He sprawled in a lawn chair, his legs and arms glistening with suntan lotion. He had set the small television, the one usually in Mother's room, in the space where a window used to be. A blender rested on a plastic table next to him, so he could make diet milkshakes from powder that was part of some new nutrition program. A long black extension cord trailed into the house.

"Take a listen to this," he said. He nodded toward the TV and I glanced over. The sun was so bright that it was hard to see the screen. The newscaster was hazy in a blue background. I pulled my chair closer, leaned forward, and looked hard. They reported that Edgar Lawrence Igleton had been found dead in the hot tub at his Bel Air home. Igleton had been the long-time owner of the successful restaurant Eli's, and co-owner of a popular nightclub known by some as the Red Room. He was reported to have been electrocuted when a hair dryer fell into the hot tub while he was bathing. This was the fourth time in the past five years that electronic devices dropped into baths and hot tubs had been responsible for deaths in Southern California, the newscaster said.

I stammered, unable to complete a sentence. I said things like "How could . . . ," "Oh God . . . ," "Can't believe . . ."

Van shrugged; it was almost as though the news didn't surprise him.

"Does Ginny know?" I managed finally. I remembered how drunk she'd been, her dream about Eli. I'd thought she got a little carried away drinking, that's all. It had never occurred to me that anything more significant than that had happened last night.

"She will soon," Van said. "He's her goddamned boy-friend."

"It's hard to imagine Ginny having a boyfriend," I said.

"She doesn't," he declared. "Anymore."

The doorbell rang and Van huffed, rising from his chair. With great effort he pulled himself into a standing position. He raised the glass of chocolate shake that was supposed to make him lose weight, took a long swallow, and wiped the mixture from his mustache.

"A blow dryer," he said, shaking his head. The doorbell rang again.

"Van, I don't think you should answer it," I said. "It could be Mikey."

"Hope it is," he said. He walked to the side of the house, looked, and then came back to where I was, crouched behind the back wall.

"It's him, all right," he said. "Except now he's got a couple more with him."

"I can't take two fights in one day," I said. "Let's surrender this time."

I followed Van around the side of the house, taking careful, silent steps. We stuck close together. Van hesitated, whispering to me. "Here's our choice. We can psyche them out or we can trick them. Psyching them out means we come barreling at them looking like we love to fight and intend to crush their stupid brains with our knuckles."

"Let's trick them," I said. Van must have been having flash-backs to his Marine days. There was no way I was going to barrel after anybody. I touched the swollen spot on my fore-head. "You know I'm no good at this."

161

"Yeah, but you look all right with all the blood and guts on your shirt."

"I'm calling the police," I said, backing up.

"Don't be a girl about it."

"If I were my sister, I'd already be down there charging at them with a motorcycle chain and whooping."

Van said, "Look, here's the plan. I stay back here; you take a punch or two. When they're not looking I'll sneak up and club them over the head with a rock."

"What rock?"

"I don't know. I'll find a rock."

"Why can't you take the punches and I do the rock thing?"

"Because," Van said, as though that settled it.

I thought about what else we might do, like hover here silently until they left. But I had a feeling that was out of the question. The only way to fend off Mikey and his insanity was to meet it head on.

"This is not ideal," I said finally. I inched forward, winding my way around the house, sticking close to the wall. I felt my chest heavy with held breath.

But when I got to the front, I saw there was a white truck by the side of the road and two guys in work clothes pulling their toolboxes off the truck bed. Mikey was leaning against the truck, playing with a radio headphone and snapping gum. When he saw me he raised his hand, got in his car, and left. The two repairmen continued collecting their tools and bringing glass cased in cardboard from their truck.

"What are you doing?" I asked them.

"Windows," one of the repairmen said. He had an enormous black beard and a shaven head with dark stubble.

"I can see that, but . . ."

"We do windows for this guy all the time. It's a thing with him. A couple years back someone smashed up his nightclub so bad it took us four straight days to put it back right, and that was just the outside windows."

162

"The Red Room?"

"That's the place."

"Who tore up the Red Room?"

"Who knows? Look, relax, man, it's paid for." He looked past me to where Van, knees bent in karate fashion, made his way cagily toward the truck. "You want to call off the dog?" he asked me, nodding toward Van.

Ginny was flatbacked on her bed, spread out, her arms making a T. At first I thought she might be asleep, but when I peeked in I saw her eyes were open, staring at the ceiling.

"You can come in," she said, just as I was closing the inch of space of the open door. "Who's outside?"

"Window repairmen," I said. "Specialists in refenestration."

"I didn't know there was such a thing."

"We decided the situation demanded professionals," I said. I walked forward, hands in my pockets. I'd changed clothes and showered away all the tiny specks of paint and dirt, blood and window putty. I wore a pair of green-and-blue Bermuda shorts, a new shirt. For the first time in years my legs were no longer white. My arms, flushed with sun, stung a little. Ginny noticed my improved appearance. Eying my shirt, she said, "Nice duds." Then she said, "Are you in love with Mikey's wife?"

"No," I said, though truly I was beginning to have an odd feeling about Lucy, as though time away from her was a little impoverished. "Why do you ask?"

"Mikey has this jealousy problem."

"How do you know Mikey?"

Ginny sighed. She looked at me with apology. "He's at Eli's all the time—they have some sort of business arrangement, I don't know. I detest him; he feels the same about me. We don't get a lot of words in between the spitting and swearing."

"He has the most beautiful little girl," I said, for no reason, "named Stacy."

"Oh, God, you *are* in love," she said.

"I'm sorry about Eli," I said. "Ginny, I am so very, very sorry."

"What about Eli?"

"I thought you knew," I said.

"What happened to Eli?" she said. She jerked upright as if she'd been struck. "Sam, tell me now. Where is he?"

"It was announced on the news, Ginny. It must have just happened."

"Nothing happened to him," she said. "You're making it up. You don't like where I work, right? So what, is all I've got to say. Sam, really. Tell me you're pretending. Tell me nothing happened."

I stepped toward her, but she scooted back, out of reach.

"Say something," she said.

"Ginny, I . . ."

"Say he's all right!" she yelled.

"Ginny . . ."

"Say it!"

I shook my head.

"Say he's not dead!"

"I can't."

Ginny was silent. It was as though she didn't hear me. She pushed her hair out of her eyes. She made a half-pout, the one that fought tears, an expression that always killed me.

"I hated Eli for letting Mikey stay at the club all the time," she said. She had a wad of pillowcase clenched in her fist. She twisted the fabric, speaking slowly. "Also for being older than me and quirky and rude. For being impulsive and perverted and bad-tempered and arrogant and rich. For that goddamned club and for lying—the man was a liar. He was crass, really just . . . jaded and *foul*."

She stood up suddenly. Her eyes became fierce, determined. She was so angry and hurt that it was almost palpable.

She said, "I hated that he knew my every thought, every

goddamned thing I did. See that mirror over there? He gave me that. Christmas. I hate that mirror. When I look in it, I don't see me. I see him *looking* at me. He was always looking at me. I'm glad he's dead. I'm really, really glad he's dead."

She coughed. She took long gasps. There were so many tears she didn't bother wiping them away. They streamed over her cheeks, her chin, down her neck. She seemed suddenly so lost, as though Eli's death had cast her far away, to a place where not even gravity could find her.

Seeing her like this was breaking me.

"He knew this would happen. He knew and I hate him for knowing," she said.

"Knew what would happen?"

"Shh! Be quiet. Don't talk. Don't talk about it!" she yelled. "Go away now, Sam."

"I want to stay with you."

"Go away!" she said, her voice booming between us.

"No."

"You can't stay with me!" she cried.

"I'm going to stay with you."

"You can't. You don't know how."

"I'm doing it. I'm with you right now."

She turned, dropping to her knees beside the bed, crying more tears than I'd thought possible, her hands cupping her eyes.

I knelt next to her on the floor. I rubbed the back of her neck, pressed my fingers against her scalp. I glided a hand beneath her arms and lifted her gently onto the mattress.

"Leave me alone." She kept crying.

"I can't leave you, Ginny," I said. "I'd do anything for you, but I just can't leave."

Outside the repairmen called to each other. A pane of glass was brought to the window, steadied by gloved hands. I touched Ginny's shoulders. I rubbed her back. I brought her Kleenex and a cold washcloth. I brought her water. When she started shaking I pretended that nothing was wrong. That I was not worried, terrified for her. I pretended that everything would be all right and that we would keep it so.

"I'll help you," I whispered to her. "With everything."

"Just a new job," she said between tears. "Because I won't work for Mikey."

She told me how Eli had searched for a way into her life and she'd given him one, finally, when she confessed to him that she wanted to be a model. The first time she went to his house for a reason other than to sneak an hour in his pool was when Eli introduced her to his photography studio, all the equipment and supplies. He raised the folded metal legs of a tripod and stood it on the floor; he smiled at Ginny, who ignored him. He worked the tripod into position, pulling out more length from the metal bars and tightening the clamps, talking to Ginny all the while—and not getting anywhere.

"Hello, boys and girls," he called to her. "Do you have your listening caps on?"

Ginny sat on the carpet. Between her knees was a copy of *Mademoiselle*, which she scowled at, disapproving. She said nothing.

Eli unzipped a bag and took out film by the handful. He tore through the yellow-and-black cardboard and tossed the small, empty boxes at Ginny, gently but with exactly the same motion he would use to throw darts.

"The dining room has been transformed into a landing launch for Plutonic elves colonizing earth. Take a look, Ginny, there's one on your shoulder."

Ginny turned the pages of her magazine. He aimed film cartons at her and she rearranged her hair.

"How long you been taking pictures?" she asked. She knew he'd keep up with the boxes of film until she paid attention to him. He was like that. At the restaurant the night before he'd asked her if she wanted ice cream and then scooped it endlessly into a bowl, eleven scoops, twelve, until she acknowledged the absurd concoction he'd made, laughed a little. She was so used to the way he tried to amuse her that by now it had the odd effect of boring and comforting her at the same time.

"I started in prep school," Eli said. "If I took pictures for the sports teams, I didn't have to play on one. So I did the football team and the hockey team and, excuse me while I gag, the polo team. I went to one of *those* schools. Fell deeply and heartily in love with a girl on the cafeteria line, and when she was fired for her misconduct with me, I picked a fight with the headmaster and got expelled."

He came forward, squatted next to Ginny, and held a light meter to her face.

"What's that?" she asked when he unfolded a large round disk; it sprang forward, silver on one side, white on the other.

"Makes the light softer," Eli said, standing the filter in front of a set of large floor lamps.

"Maybe this is a dumb idea," Ginny said. She frowned into the magazine. "I don't even vaguely resemble these people. Not that I'd want to, either. This woman looks like she's made of marzipan."

"Well, you are not made of marzipan, Gin," Eli said. He loaded film into a camera, clicked the automatic winder, and checked the light meter again. "Whatever it is you're made of, it's a hundred percent and economy-sized and industrial strength."

"This shirt is ugly," Ginny complained. "It doesn't fit."

"I love the shirt," Eli said. He crouched down, positioning the camera. "Little smile," he instructed.

She looked into his lens with dread. She didn't smile.

"Perfect," he said. "Roll up your jeans an inch or two. Dump the shoes."

"My feet are too big," Ginny said, raising her high-tops for Eli's inspection.

The camera clicked away. "Nice with the sneaker," he said.

Later they stood together in the darkroom in his basement. It was big; it had purple lights that glowed as though from some other planet. There was a whole wall of sinks, and above them boxes of chemicals and paper, metal rulers, wax pencils, magnifying glasses. Across purple walls, hidden now in the darkness, were hundreds of pictures he'd taken over the years, of friends and girlfriends and dancers from the club, of strangers and people who'd become strangers over the years. Almost all were women, sometimes dressed, sometimes not.

"Let me guess. You photograph women for their majesty and grace," Ginny said.

"No, I photograph them because they let me."

"I hate you, Eli," Ginny said. "I hate you except you are not boring and you don't pretend."

"Here's a beauty," he said. He bent over a tub of pictures floating in chemicals. Ginny stood behind him. She watched over his shoulder as her face became clearer in the wet tub.

"They're not exactly *Cosmopolitan*," she said.

"You're way too interesting for that. Look at the one on the staircase. You're marvelous."

They brought dozens of pictures into being that day. Hours and hours of work in the darkroom. They were tired; they sat together with their feet dangling in the swimming pool.

"Let me take you to dinner," Eli offered. He saw the expression on her face change, the hesitation that always emerged when he suggested, in a way they both understood, that they spend time together. He looked at her, sighed with impatience, and then, in a voice that approximated hers, he said, "No chance, Eli. Go to hell, Eli."

Ginny slipped on her jacket. She held an envelope of pictures she'd selected to take to an agency.

"I don't like being mimicked," she said, her words slow and serious.

The sky outside the window had gone pink. Eli's hair reflected red light from the fading sun.

He said, "Sorry."

As she walked to her car, the evening emerging strong as a season, she heard his footsteps behind her.

"Hey," he said. "See you at the club tonight?"

She nodded. He managed to get a smile from her, which delighted him. He turned away, stepping across the gravel of the driveway as though he walked on high heels; he looked at her coyly like an old-time stripper on a stage. He shook to some music he was dreaming in his head. He unbuttoned his shirt and yanked it down, teasing with it as it slid across his waist. Hands in his hair, he did a twirl. He was on the second button of his fly when Ginny drove out of the driveway, watching him now in the rearview mirror as he continued his tease, down to underwear and socks.

We hadn't moved for hours. In her bedroom, amid the sounds of the repairmen fitting windows all over the house, with Van's TV game shows buzzing and applauding in the back yard, Ginny told me this story. She lay on the bed. I sat on the floor. A six-pack of beer, now empty, lay on the carpet.

"I loved him," Ginny said when she finished. "I thought he was the fucking tops."

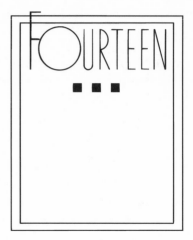

FOURTEEN

■ ■ ■

Lucy showed up, explaining how she'd been lost for forty minutes, roaming the neighborhood with a hand shadowing her eyes, squinting at doors and curbs and mailboxes, searching for a street number. At one point she stood outside a house similar to ours, though not ours, staring through a screen door, trying to get a fix on the figures inside.

"If Mikey finds out I'm here, we'll both be slaughtered," she said, gliding past me. She stood in remarkable contrast to her surroundings, like a piece of museum sculpture in a landscape of heaped cars and wreckage. She wore a skirt that stretched flat over her thighs, a winsome little blouse. The skirt was brown linen, the blouse a sheer cream silk. She was a woman with an imprecise and natural beauty, and wore jewelry that had been crafted, not set. Around her neck was a row of shells. A leather band harnessed her hair. "Good God, the heat," she said, fanning herself with her purse.

I brought her through the living room, where Mother's bags lay, still packed, left there after her return from the hospital.

Van had dropped off the bags and then taken her someplace by the ocean to ask if she would make the trip north with him. The question was one of great importance to him, a planned romance, a promise of future. It was almost like a wedding proposal, and I had wished him luck.

I sat Lucy in the kitchen and brought her lemonade with ice and just a little red wine. I'd positioned a fan in the window and a damp towel over the front of the fan. It blew air that was cooler, though not cool, into the small room.

"Your face," Lucy said, shaking her head. I sat next to her, leaning my elbows on the table. I wondered whether she always looked so good or whether she'd dressed for coming here. When she took a long swallow of her drink, I watched her fingers around the glass, the muscles in her throat. She closed her eyes and then opened them again. She said, "If you want to press charges against Mikey, I understand completely. If that's your decision, you have my support."

I laughed.

"Don't," she said, putting her fingers against my mouth. She seemed suddenly spooked. She said, "Nothing is funny here, everything is ruined. I feel, I've felt, that something terrible is happening. If I see or hear of one more person being hit or hurt or killed, one more thing being broken, one more part of this country being stormed or flooded, I will lose my mind."

"You think that Eli was killed?" I asked.

"Sam," Lucy said, in that same wise voice Ginny used. "A blow dryer in the hot tub? Come on."

"Happens all the time," I said. "They told us so on the news."

"Not to Eli."

"Why not? In addition to all the other glorious qualities this guy has, his sleaziness and his brilliant career, is he immune to electrical charge?"

"His hair was buzzed so close to his scalp you couldn't even see it. Who blow-dries that? Also, he made a very bad habit of

171

befriending the women he hired—I'm not talking about Ginny, I'm talking about a girl who disappears for ages and then shows up needing a little money. So he lets her dance a night or two, and the next day in comes the boyfriend or husband or whoever."

"You think a jealous husband killed Eli."

"I didn't say that, Sam, but I'm afraid that's what the cops will think."

"I'll tell you what. I think it was me who was nearly killed by a jealous husband."

"Yes, well, it would help if you didn't mention that to the police," Lucy said. "Anyway, I think it was another club owner. Eli went a little overboard infesting the competition."

"So you believe Mikey's rats-and-roaches story."

"I don't know what to believe. This blow dryer stuff is a little incredible. You should have seen his hair. I mean, it was *this* short," she said, pinching the air.

"I did see it, Lucy. It was a recent haircut."

"Oh, well, things change quickly, I guess. Don't give me that look, Sam. I'm telling you what I know."

I waited, watching her gather her story together. She'd surprised herself by being so unprepared. Her hesitations gave her away as much as what she said. She paused, glancing sideways. Then she said, "So I saw Eli, so what? Last night, after you left, I went back to the club. I wanted to see it—I don't know why. So I went in and had a drink. In fact, I had a Harvey Wallbanger, remember those? Anyway, it was all so changed, Sam; you might hate the place, but I'm telling you, it's the Ritz-Carlton compared to what it used to be. The Red Room at Eli's was a strip bar like any other, with girls who knew nothing but clubs and would never know anything but clubs. There's something different about it now. I don't know. I watched this one woman dance and she was so . . . so *good*. I thought she was a really talented young . . . person. Is that a crazy thing to say about a stripper?"

"You're a great liar, Lucy. But you are a liar."

I'd caught her and she knew it. She halted now, pushing her hair behind her ears. "Well," she said. She took a deep breath and held it.

"None of my business," I said.

"Okay, I wasn't in the club. It was his house, actually. But he told me about the club and it sounded pretty good."

I waited for her to finish but she kept on, misreading my silence as a demand for explanation.

"It was late," Lucy said. "I'm telling the truth now, Sam."

"Okay."

"Look, I hadn't seen him in years. I hardly wanted to see him in *daylight*. He is a very strange guy." She looked away now, fidgeting with her lemonade. She put the glass to her lips, then stared into it as though reading a fortune. "Once, a long time ago, he was a friend of mine."

"He made a business partner out of your husband. That was friendly."

Lucy looked surprised.

"It was on the news," I said.

"Well, that's half true. Really it was me that Eli made a partner. He gave me half the club."

"Any particular reason? I mean, was it your birthday or something?"

"Don't act slick, Sam, it's so unattractive."

There was a silence. Lucy looked at her watch, and for a moment I thought she was getting ready to leave. Instead she said, "I didn't want the club, and so Mikey and I agreed that once his business picked up we'd sell. But of course Mikey never *would* sell. Ginny knows better than me what's gone on since then. I really haven't wanted to keep track of the Red Room or anything associated with it."

"Is Eli really dead?"

"Yes," she said. "Eli is really dead. If anyone else in the universe died, there wouldn't be a question. But for some reason no one is quite sure with him. I phoned his parents to tell them. His mother answered—the guy's *mother*. She said, 'Oh.' Just that. It was remarkable, as though I'd told her the C train was running on time this morning. Or cotton sheets were on sale at Bloomies. 'Oh.' Then she said, 'I didn't know he was alive.' Can you imagine? To have a child wandering around and not know? The carelessness of it. It turned me cold and I felt like . . . *punishing* her or something. And so I said yes, your son is dead. And I held on to that statement; I didn't say I was sorry. Not another word. And then something terrible happened, Sam. You know what happened?"

Lucy's voice went quiet now. She leaned toward me, whispering. "She started to cry. And there was this flood of sorrow for all the years before. She said, 'If I'd known he was alive . . .' Sam, she *didn't know*. He'd just disappeared one day, and that was it."

"Don't tell me this, Lucy."

"Well, he always was a selfish bastard," she said, shaking her head. "Selectively generous, you know what I mean? He did plenty for other people, sure. But he did what he wanted, when he wanted, and in the manner he wanted. And he had no sense of responsibility."

"Sounds like you knew him well."

"Can we just stop this, please?" Lucy said. "Don't pretend you haven't guessed. Falling in love with Eli was the most wonderful thing I ever did, and it tore me in ribbons to give him up. But I did give him up, that's the point. I didn't let it end with Eli. Anyway, this was years ago. None of it matters anymore. Poor Ginny. I can only guess what she is feeling right now. I wasn't so much older than she is. What an asshole he is for always being with these kids. It's sick, you know that? These winter-spring relationships are a nice way of saying the guy's a prick."

She'd been twirling a lock of hair around one finger, winding it tighter and tighter up to her scalp. Now she let go; the curl wagged across her forehead. She took a long swallow of her drink. "How is Ginny taking it?" she asked.

"She isn't saying much. It's her habit under stress to take a sleeping pill."

I looked at Lucy. But she was having thoughts of her own.

"Poor baby," she whispered, and I wondered whether she meant Ginny or Eli. She put down her glass too hard, making a loud thud on the table. "Well, it looks like Mother is going to get her wish," she said. "I don't see how I can stay with Mikey now that he's gone to tearing apart neighborhoods and beating on people."

"You'll work it out," I said, without a lot of conviction.

"I don't know how to make anything better anymore."

"Then divorce him," I said.

"Divorce him, right. That would make sense, except that I have a family consisting of six people and he's only one of them. Sam, I'm *sorry*. I'm . . . ashamed. I look at this little place shot to hell and that handsome face of yours all banged up and I think to myself that this was done by the man I'm *married* to. He owns half a strip club and his partner is murdered —this is my *husband*? But I can't find a solution in breaking up another thing. I think it's just one of those situations that is tragic and impossible and really best to ignore."

She laughed, but her eyes went pink. She became quiet. Lucy was tough, tougher than I had thought before today. She sniffed and looked away.

"Use your bathroom?" she asked. I told her where and she raised herself gracefully, keeping her face stiff and controlled as she went off for a private cry. She left her bag on the table. Her wallet was open, showing pictures of her children, all with mussed hair and teeth at angles. I took the wallet, leafing from one plastic-bound photo to another. I tried to tell the twins apart but found it impossible. I searched for signs of Lucy in the children's faces. I could see how the twins resembled both parents, and Stacy certainly had Mikey's sturdy composition.

Bobby was different, smaller framed. He had red hair that would grow auburn through the years, just like his mother's. He had his mother's long eyes. Seeing the children this way made me think of them differently, more as a part of Lucy, like an arm, a leg. I folded the wallet back into her purse, walked down the hallway, and knocked softly on the bathroom door.

"Hey," I said, pushing gently on the wood. "I could be a bit more kind, yes?"

Lucy was leaning over the sink, rinsing her face in a pool of water. On the ledge above the toilet she'd put her contact lenses on a wad of toilet paper. Water had spilled down her skirt, making dark stains.

"Don't stand there," she said. "You'll think I'm ridiculous."

I rested my shoulder against the doorframe. She brought palmful after palmful of water to her eyes.

"Please go away," she said.

I put my hand on her back and left it there, unmoving.

"You have much bigger problems than me. I don't have any real problems." She struggled through tears. "I'm some dumb housewife."

"Lucy," I began.

"Seems like I used to have the excuse of being young, but that isn't going to work anymore. I mean, *look* at me." She raised her wet hands in front of her, chest high. "I'm so pissed at myself for spending so much time thinking how awful I was when there was nothing wrong with me at all. Now it's different. Now I really have become something horrible."

She splashed her hands back into the sink, pushing them deep under the water as though she were drowning kittens. Her mouth had turned puffy, it seemed, all at once. "Mother always knew what to do about everything. She picked all my clothes, my friends, every school course and vacation spot, every concert and restaurant, and now, now that I'm no one's little girl anymore, she yells at me because I can't do anything myself. The one thing I did was marry Mikey, and what a disaster *that* was."

She straightened and stared hard at the mirror. Her skin was dappled red. Water ran down her neck and arms. She took a towel, turned away, and held it over her face. She rubbed the towel over her neck and blouse, over the damp front of her skirt, across her knees, the backs of her hands. All this she did with a matter-of-factness, with hard, unyielding strokes, like a mother, impatient and a little punishing with a child who's gone out in the rain. When she got to her fingers she stared, frozen, at her wedding band and the diamond beside it. She took the rings off, studying them in her hands. Then she dropped them one by one onto the tank of the toilet, where they caught and reflected every speck of light.

"Give those to Ginny," she told me in a whisper. "Tell her you found them."

She turned away from me, fixing her collar.

"Come here," I said. There was a long silence between us. I looked at her back. She steadied her hands on the towel rack. I wanted to touch her, but it had nothing to do with pleasure. I could imagine the texture of her knees and thighs and hips and stomach, but even as she moved toward me, I thought that this feeling was arousal, yes, but of a different sort. More crisis than passion. I wanted us to see through one act together, one that had a beginning and an end. I wanted to draw a circle around us and declare that within that sphere we would have peace. I would ask Lucy only for what she offered, expect no more than all the pieces of herself she didn't know what to do with, all the small, forgettable fractions of time.

It's not much, I know, to want just the scraps of a woman's life. But I've learned that the tiny, unimportant bits of a person are sometimes the best treasure.

When Lucy was right near me I put my fingers on her damp mouth, over the line of her jaw, across her throat. We'd discovered the great absences in each other's lives. I concentrated on the feel of her against my fingers, on the softness of her neck, her forehead. I could give her these small concessions.

I knelt on the floor, taking the zipper of her skirt down with me. She put her hands on my shoulders; I kissed the inside of her thighs. And then went higher, beneath lace, elastic, a soft gray slippery fabric. I heard her above me, a single short hum, almost a song.

She rolled toward my mouth, everything at half-speed. I closed my eyes to feel the full pulse of her, to hear her above me. On her skin I smelled sunlight, the hazy weight of summer. I opened my eyes to Lucy, shining like the irridescent gloss of a seashell.

The first time I made love it was after several hours of swimming in a river at low tide. I thought then that all the smells of the river, the mud and algae, fish, water-soaked leaves, swollen branches, grass and sand, were the smells of a woman. I'd forgotten about that.

FIFTEEN

The police hadn't shut down the Red Room. It buzzed with the same lights, the same music. For three days it had managed to continue, seemingly unchanged by Eli's death. I arrived just after ten, while the crowd was still relatively quiet, but the door opened again and again, a few more faces wandering in each time. I sat at one end of the bar, trying to appear interested in the dancer, someone named Trinka, whose bright blond hair contrasted dramatically with a tan so deep she looked like she'd been rolled in mud. She had on a bizarre dress, long papery pieces of silver and blue fabric, hanging like fringe from just below her shoulders to just below her crotch. I watched her shake the dress around the dance floor, her nipples occasionally poking between the fringe. I hated this costume and wondered if Ginny had constructed it. She probably had, of course. I mean, that had been her job.

Mikey was seated at a table near one wall, talking with a group of men. They were ordinary-looking guys, in suits and white shirts. There were three of them, but they seemed to move in unison. They looked at me, considered me; all three rose from their seats as I went forward. Mikey began to introduce us, but the men walked off before he'd finished.

"Friends of yours?" I asked.

"They own Mama Best, at the other end of town. I'm trying to make amends with these people after all the problems Eli caused."

"Well, he's out of the way now," I said.

"We're all sorry about that, Sam," he said as we sat down. Mikey had on sunglasses, the kind they wore in the restaurant. He wore a silk jacket and a T-shirt with the name of his chocolate company, Sweeties, etched in what was supposed to look like lipstick across the front. His shoes were like bowling shoes, except they weren't bowling shoes, they were sneakers. When I got close enough, I saw that he had shaved his head to a blond stubble. The skin just below his hairline was so white it glowed against the rest of him. He lifted his lips in a grin, leaned back in his chair, and held out a hand.

"We can shake, can't we?" he said. "I'm sorrier than hell about what I did the other day. What an asshole I was, huh? But we took care of that, didn't we? The boys went over and replaced that glass?"

I nodded. I looked down at the table, where a catalogue of nudes in chocolate and other erotic candies lay open beneath an ashtray.

"Lucy gets these stupid ideas in her head, like pretending she's going out on me, and then I just don't know. I get a little carried away. Something about love makes you like that," Mikey said. He made a noise like a laugh, but it sounded more like a snort. "Have you seen this? It's the new catalogue. Take a look in there and see if there's anything you'd like. I've been meaning to send some of my chocolate over to you ever since Lucy and I had our little making-up talk. Things have been so crazy in here that I haven't had a chance."

He slipped the catalogue from beneath the ashtray, blew

some ash from a page, and handed it to me. I wondered what Lucy had said to convince him there was nothing between us. Mikey's recent work at the club had provided me with long, clean hours with Lucy, which I silently thanked him for. He pulled his chair closer, peering over my shoulder as I thumbed through the pictures of what he was now calling his "art."

"Take a look here," he said, showing a five-tiered wedding cake carved with naked women in various states of erotic pleasure. "It spins to a choice of wedding marches in English, Spanish, and Hebrew. Isn't that something?"

I turned the page. The music changed and another dancer came on, a narrow girl with red hair and breasts so large they commanded the rest of her.

"She's new," Mikey said, directing my attention to the stage. "Name's Carol. I hired her last night."

At just that moment the dancer was announced as Dolly. Mikey leaned forward and whispered, "Stage name—I recommended it."

"I had that feeling," I said.

"She's built to last, isn't she?" he said. I nodded, catching sight of Mikey's face as he all but drooled onto his jacket sleeve. I wondered where I'd heard "built to last" before and then realized it was an advertising slogan for some kind of pickup truck.

A woman came over, a leather purse slung over her shoulder. I recognized her as Madeline, though she looked different out of her stage costume. She wore faded jeans, cowboy boots, a leather vest. Her short hair was slicked back, and she wore loopy earrings. Her face was clean of makeup, except for her mouth, which was painted bright red and frowning now into Mikey's face.

"What are you doing?" he said. "Why do you have your clothes on?"

"Mikey, let me tell you something," she said. "I never thought I'd live to see the day when I shared a stage with a pubescent girl pretending to fuck a piece of fruit to 'Green-Eyed Lady.' "

I looked at the stage and saw that Dolly was doing exactly what Madeline had described.

"You're not *sharing* the stage. She's on now. You come later," Mikey said, as though explaining to a five-year-old.

"I don't think so," Madeline said.

"Madeline, honey, don't quit. Go get yourself a real drink. Take a rest. Don't tell me you quit. Look, this hasn't been a good week. We lost Eli. You're still suffering the effects. Besides, you already got paid for the week and you owe a spot at twelve-thirty. You're not going to run out on me without doing that spot, are you?"

"That's Eli's jacket," Madeline said. "And you look ridiculous in his haircut."

"Could you cover the spot?"

When she'd gone, Mikey sighed long and deep. He looked at me and then suddenly laughed and clinked his glass against my beer bottle.

"They get *soooo* snotty when they're in demand. The day that little girl walked into this club she was begging for a job, any job. Now she's particular about who's on stage. What a laugh. But listen, Sam, seriously, this is a clean club. We do very respectable numbers in here. I'd like to enlist your help, if you're interested. We really need Ginny back. She and I have had our troubles in the past, but I'm sure we can put those behind us."

"You're all for burying the hatchet these days, aren't you?" I said.

"Well, you know, I have a family to take care of, and this club is a mighty opportunity. We have to pull together. I need Ginny here doing the costumes, helping the girls out with their music, their routines. With Ginny back on board, maybe we can expand the place, you know? I'm sorry about how I've treated her in the past. Just a few days on my own here has taught me how truly essential she is to the operation. Do you know how much money we can all make together? Do you know just how great this is?"

"Really great," I said unenthusiastically. I looked into Mikey's catalogue, finding the pages increasingly ludicrous and nauseating.

"No, it's better than that! I mean, Ginny is a dynamo. You've seen my catalogue now, so you know I have a little something upstairs, and I'm sure you're great at whatever it is you do. Don't you manage acts or something?"

Madeline appeared at our table again. This time she pulled a wad of bills from her jeans pocket. She laid the money flat on the table.

"Okay," she said, thumbing through ones. "Are we even?"

"Madeline, please," Mikey said. "You're my favorite girl. What am I going to do without my favorite girl?"

Madeline said nothing. She didn't take a jab at him or spit on him or slap his groping hand away. Instead, she sighed almost mournfully, turning toward the door. She had a precise sort of walk, a balanced step without a lot of swing to it. Her boots, simple and dark, made her as tall as the men who watched her.

"I'm going to be honest with you, Sam," Mikey said, casting a last glance at her as she squeezed through a crowd at the door. "The business has its ups and downs. The money's great; there's lots of excitement, a nightly feast for your eyes. But I got to confess that there is not a lot of gratitude in these girls' hearts. They're tough, and they don't give a shit about you. You'd think they'd want you to like them. You'd think they might try to please you. But there's infrequent nookie perks, I'll warn you now. Maybe you'll be luckier with them. Eli was."

"You know what?" I said. I turned the catalogue toward Mikey and pointed to a pair of breasts in chocolate that approximated Lucy's. "Something about the shape of these looks awfully familiar."

"Don't fuck with me, man," Mikey said, begging just a little.

The funeral took place in a little mountain town east of San Juan Capistrano. The cemetery had a Spanish history, and most of the gravestones were carved with Spanish names. A woman named Catarina, one of the dancers at the Red Room, had made the arrangements. She stood with her husband at the service, both of them crying lavishly.

"He was such a nice man," Catarina said in a strong Mexican accent. "He hire me, not minding that I was illegal, and he let me work even after I had Sophia and Paulo."

Everyone nodded in agreement. These were people who hadn't known Eli at all, but they were friends of Catarina's and faithful to her grief.

"Don't be ridiculous, Catarina," Ginny said. Ginny was wearing the only dress I'd ever seen her in. Her skin was so white that standing in a cemetery, she could have been a spirit that had risen from the ground below. She slapped a mosquito from her thigh and said, "That wasn't being nice. You were good, and besides that, he didn't pay you when you didn't work."

"Is not true, Geeny," Catarina said. "He give me money sometimes when I was this big." She held her arm out to show how pregnant she'd been.

"No waitress ever made so much money," Catarina's husband said, sniffing into a blue kerchief.

"Waitress?" Ginny said.

"Shhh," whispered Catarina. "I never really tell him."

Afterward, Ginny and I went to a ribs place that apparently hadn't heard the West Coast had gone vegetarian and gravy hadn't even been a thought in fifteen years. The proprietress, a tiny square woman with tiny square eyeglasses, sat us in her best booth, which was decorated with red-and-white hearts, little cupids, and heart-shaped porcelain glued to a mirror on the wall. Plastic roses sprang from a teddy bear vase, and the glow from a block of candle made the velour seats extra crimson. Gravy came in molasses jars, and everything from potatoes to biscuits required it.

"It's delicious," I said when the proprietress asked. I mopped up gravy with a biscuit, having gnawed through a half-dozen ribs, mounds of potato, and a basket of something called hushpuppies, which were small logs of fried dough and corn.

"Very good," Ginny said, but she hadn't eaten much. The proprietress looked concerned. Ginny made a motion with her fork like she was going to eat and this pleased the woman, who brought us more butter.

"Ginny, you look so sad. You look like a kid's toy tossed out in a junk heap."

"Mmm," she said.

"I think that was a really nice funeral," I said. "I was quite moved, considering that it was entirely in Spanish and I couldn't understand a word."

"Eli would have liked it. He thought Spanish was a beautiful language," Ginny said.

"He spoke Spanish?"

"No, but he liked being confused."

"Ginny, have you ever heard of a place called Mama's Best?"

"Mama Best," she corrected. "It's a fat joint." When I looked confused, she said, "You know, fat women. Strippers have to weigh two hundred or better to work there."

"God," I said.

"You bring up a place and then you say 'Gaawd' when I tell you what it is."

"There were some guys from Mama Best in the club the other day," I told her.

"They wanted to buy the Red Room, but Eli wasn't game. Stay out of the club, Sam. Mikey's stupid and mean. Don't let his Howdy Doodiness fool you—he's a snake. He's probably at home right now shedding his skin."

"And Eli was a good, clean American boy."

"Yeah, he was pretty good. We buried him today, Sam, don't insult him."

"Sorry," I said. I looked at Ginny, but she was looking down at the table.

"What's your favorite memory of Eli?" I asked.

"Dunno," she said. She sighed; she fiddled with her fork, stabbing at the food she had no interest in, no hunger for. "I had a lot of nice times with him."

"Tell me one of them. Tell me about one happy time."

"Well, once when we were taking pictures, I guess. We'd blacked out the windows with dark sheets. Every door, every shaft of light. You don't want to hear this, do you?"

I nodded. I put down my fork and crossed my arms in front of me.

"We set the spotlights on stands, fixed a backdrop, moved everything. I had a stack of black-and-whites Eli'd done the day before, and they were all horrible, I thought. I looked like a goose."

"Did you complain?"

"Yeah, I complained. I said, 'Hey, genius, these really suck.' And he said, 'Here's the mirror. You do it. Sit in front of it, position yourself. Decide on your own light. Whatever. Tell me when you think you look okay and we'll take a Polaroid your way.' So I looked at myself in the mirror. Repositioned the lights, changed my hair. I told him how to do it and he took the picture. So I say that counts as my picture."

"Was it good?"

"I'd say I looked not bad."

"What did Eli think?"

"He was all wonder. He said, '*Ginny.* . . .'"

186

SIXTEEN

Eli's house was on Mulholland Drive in Hollywood Hills, with a view that stretched all the way to the sea. The hillside was covered with bougainvillea and Algerian ivy, with clusters of bamboo and a coral tree with blossoms like slices of persimmon. There were sculptures on the lawn, including a tall, elongated version of a woman with her hair standing straight up, her overlong arms sweeping across the grass and pointing toward the house. There was a steel rendition of a great Dane, lifelike except that it was about nine feet high and the drool from its mouth was made of blown glass and held there by tiny wires. The house jutted out over a valley of sparkling lights and trees, with so startling a vision of the ocean and city below that we sat without talking for a long while. Finally Celia broke our silence with the hundredth protest about going into the house.

"It's police business," she said.

"Not until they seal it off; then it's police business. I think we have some time before there's an investigation."

"But will there be an investigation?" she asked.

"Your daughter seems to think so."

"Leave it to Lucy to know every criminal activity in the city," Celia said. "Perhaps the investigation has already begun and they haven't had a chance yet to announce it."

"It's not an award. They don't *announce* anything."

Celia was dressed in a cotton skirt and blouse we'd just acquired from K-mart. Around her middle was an apron with "Cleanliness Is Godliness" written across the front. She had a hairnet, two curlers. I wore a mechanic's uniform, borrowed from Van, who apparently had been much thinner about two decades ago. The idea was that Celia was Eli's cleaning woman and that she'd lost her reading glasses in his house. I was her nephew, who had driven her after work to retrieve them.

"I just don't see why we have to go in," she said.

"This was your idea," I said.

Celia had suggested we take anything of Ginny's out of the house, just in case they opened up Eli's death for investigation. If Ginny got dragged into it, her whole life would be changed, Celia had said; there is nothing like an involvement with a murder victim to ruin a woman's future.

"We're removing Ginny's property," I reminded her. "In case they find any evidence. Don't tell me that you don't remember."

"Evidence of what? He had misfortune with an appliance."

"Fine, stay in the car," I said finally.

"If I sit here they'll get me first."

"*They?* They *who?*"

"The ones that got Eli."

"More likely, *they* will be the police. And if the police come, you know what to say, right?"

"I'm the housekeeper. I lost my glasses."

"And I'm the *nephew*," I added.

I told Celia that everything would be fine, and she sighed disbelievingly.

I had a key to the house, Ginny's key, which I'd slipped from her ring while she was on the phone. I went through the back gate and across a wooden deck where I saw the hot tub, lighted and uncovered, as though someone had just left it. The breeze picked up, rushing leaves across the deck. A few fell into the hot tub. I stepped forward and touched the water. It was cool, placid, nothing left in it of the electricity that had stormed through Eli's body.

The house was so well sited on the cliff that it felt as though there were no other houses at all, no neighbors, nothing to disturb. Eli's place had true serenity. It rested amid the sounds of insects and birds. Trees shaded the little garden, spotted with moonlight. A hammock, identical to the one at Mother's, was strung between two palms. I thought to myself that this was Ginny's hammock, installed no doubt for her. I wondered how many times she had trotted across this deck on her bare feet, a beer in her hand, calling out for Eli. I remembered what Eli had said about how she liked to use the pool, and I got a sick feeling as I imagined what might have occurred if she had been with him that night.

I went to the side door, peering through the glass beside it. Inside the house, a light glowed from the hallway. I could see the shadows of furniture in the vast two-tiered living room, a long leather couch against a wall and a cabinet full of electronic equipment. I turned the key in the lock and stepped carefully inside.

The cry of hundreds of animals boomed suddenly in my ears—leopards, mountain cats, boars, bleating calves, neighing horses, roars from bears and baboons, squawking parrots, and the trumpeting sound of dozens of elephants on a stampede. A spotlight flashed above my head; the sudden off-and-on of the light made it impossible to see. I reached forward, feeling for the alarm box. When I found it I hit every switch on the panel —which did absolutely no good whatsoever.

I tried to remain calm. I backed out of the door, pulled it shut, and hoped that would silence the alarm. Still the noise came booming from inside. The alarm was truly overwhelming, much fiercer than the one at Lucy's and worse, too, for so violently intruding on the silent, still night. I took Ginny's key from the door. I thought, *Fuck, fuck, fuck.* I thought, *How will this be explained to the police, when surely the cleaning woman would know the combination?* I thought, *What an idiot I am,* and then I looked on the key and there in Ginny's handwriting were the numbers 5291. I put the key back into the lock, rushed through the door, and stood in front of the alarm box, punching in the combination.

Suddenly the house was quiet again. The light dimmed and shut itself off. I found a series of electrical switches on the wall. One lit up the outside, another the living room, another the upstairs hallway. A small silver knob set the stereo going. When I hit the switch, a violin filled the air, delicate, hardly audible. I turned a dimmer switch, and the lights became moody or bright with the turn of the dial. I sent the violin up and down in volume.

Apparently Eli had collected contemporary art. Huge paintings, of a variety I like but have never understood, dominated the walls. Lights were positioned to show them off, and I saw that there was room after room of oils, watercolors, handmade paper, something done with wax. There were oriental carpets, beaten all to hell, and a noticeable absence of furniture, as though Eli had used the house solely for the paintings, which were crowded on the white walls between enormous floor-to-ceiling windows. Even the kitchen had art in it, a silkscreen made to look like a blackboard on which had been chalked, over and over again, "We must not make fun of conceptual art, We must not make fun of conceptual art, We must not . . ." A beautifully woven rug lay across the kitchen tile, designed to show the workings of human evolution, from tiny amoeba-like invertebrates through the beginnings of prehistoric man.

There was a lot of beer in the refrigerator, a box of Oreo cookies, and two gallons of milk. Inside the crisper someone had taped a photograph of iceberg lettuce. On the rack above was a picture of a sirloin steak, cut from a magazine ad. There were pictures of eggs in the egg rack, with a cardboard replica of a butter stick beside them. In each place you'd expect to find a particular type of food there was a picture of it instead. In the freezer a black-and-white photograph of lima beans was taped against one wall, also a picture of frozen waffles and a picture of Popsicles. But there was also a real gallon of ice cream and lots of 35mm negatives in plastic cases.

I checked the cabinets, but there were no photographs or magazine cutouts of food. No real food, either, I noticed. Instead there were hundreds of black-and-white pictures of Ginny. There was Ginny in spandex, kicking her leg up, back arched, feet clad in sneakers, hair falling to one side in a braid. There she was on the hammock, relaxing with a magazine. There was a picture of her in the shower, blurry behind a glass door. A full-face portrait, her hand beneath her chin. Her in the hot tub—a candid.

I waded through the stacks, able to determine more or less when they were taken by how long Ginny's hair was and how thin she was. The ones at the bottom were older. She had straight shoulder-length hair and about twenty-five more pounds to her, though she was thin even then. They were careful photos, with just a little worry in their subject. In the more recent ones, Ginny was much more relaxed, a little playful. One of the prints, which had been developed over and over again with different depths of contrast, was of her in blue jeans, hands in her pockets, looking down at a huge painting that was spread out before her bare feet. She had on her glasses, those thick black frames that dwarfed the rest of her face. As stupidly thin as she'd become, with every edge of rib poking out, there was still something compelling about her appearance, especially in photos. I could see now why she'd thought she might model, and also why she would never be a success at it. Her body did not express a will to please. There was no invitation in it. Her body only expressed itself, in a defiant and brave way.

I'd forgotten to bring a bag with me and had to search for a long time before coming upon a leather duffel in a closet. I dropped the pictures of Ginny into the bag, took the negatives out of the freezer, and carried the whole kit with me upstairs. The house was so pristine, so unlived in and cold, that it made me feel creepy. But through every window I could see the colors of Los Angeles. Skylights in the ceiling framed the patterns of stars. Where there wasn't a window there was a painting; everywhere my eye hit, something beautiful.

I poked around, rummaging through the linen closet, the bathrooms, the many sparsely furnished bedrooms, searching for signs of Ginny. I didn't find a scrap of her clothing or even an extra toothbrush, and it surprised me, made me reconsider what I'd thought their relationship might be. Way in the back, down a long hall, was a door I hadn't checked yet. I opened it, expecting to see the starkness of the other rooms, but instead I found what must have been Eli's bedroom, an enormous corner room packed full of everything the rest of the house lacked.

It was an incredible room, a long space that showed two walls of windows overlooking Hollywood's lights. Arching above was a high glass ceiling through which the sky revealed itself. When the lights were low, the walls filled with the night's dark blue, the stars clustered above. The view was so deep, so long, over the sprawling city that it became hard to distinguish the city lights from the stars. Here in Eli's bedroom Los Angeles became part of the galaxy, rising off the planet to the great distances of the sky, where stars charted themselves between the shine of other planets. The long, sweeping glow from cinemas and hotels, the small spotlit squares of tennis courts, the quivering chains of car lights, all the great rage of

the city was transformed by the distance into a false peaceful-
ness, rising from the edges of the horizon, challenging Ursa
Minor, Capella, Jupiter. The sight caught me off-guard, dis-
turbed me somehow. When I noticed a telescope in a corner, I
brought my eye to it and felt all manner of relief at Venus
glowing evenly through the lens, unaware of the disturbances
of the city, light-years below.

Even the more regular things in Eli's bedroom had an aspect
of the extraordinary. Beside the bed were a dozen or so alarm
clocks, all of them specialized in one way or another. One was
shaped like a motorcycle; another was a swingset that ticked
back and forth with the seconds. There was a lizard with a
pulsating throat. Next to a reading lamp was a stack of magazines, mostly photography magazines, with an occasional *Es-
quire* or *Newsweek* thrown in. There was a stack of metal boxes,
one of which I opened. Inside, wrapped in felt, were camera
lenses, automatic flashes, rolls and rolls of unused film, timers,
and instruments to check light.

A step led to an alcove in which Eli had set up an office.
Beneath a huge halogen lamp were promo photographs of
women in various states of undress. A grease pencil marked a
few. The rest appeared conspicuously unnoticed. When I
opened the closet behind the desk, a whole slew of photographs came flying at me. They poured over the file cabinets
and across the wood floor. Hundreds of pictures of women—
faces, half-nudes, full nudes. Sometimes just a part of a body, a
leg, a hand. This insanity of pictures, none of them promo
shots—who knew how many there were? The only thing for
sure was that I'd have to go through them, find the ones of
Ginny, and place them all in the closet again, a task that
seemed overwhelming.

"Hey there," I heard from the hallway. It was Mikey's voice.
He came striding in; Celia marched behind him.

"I couldn't deter him," she said. She glanced around Eli's

room, pausing to notice the domed ceiling, the walls of water-colors. She looked at a series of framed photographs hanging to her right. "These are very nice—Milton Greene's wonderful portraits of Marilyn Monroe."

"I see you're having a feast," Mikey said. He gazed down at me, kneeling in pictures of naked women, and grunted out a laugh. "Looking for Ginny?"

Celia gave me a sympathetic glance. Then she went back to her inspection of Eli's accumulation of contemporary art. "He did have an eye," she said, evaluating a print.

"I thought I'd try to keep Ginny from having to answer any hard questions," I told Mikey.

"Well, dig on through," he said. "If you see any of Lucy, pull them out for me. I'm here for the same reason."

"Lucy?" Celia asked, turning. There was an innocence to her voice, as though for the first time in a long while an aspect of the world had surprised her.

"You think he could know a woman and not take pictures of her naked? No chance, Ma," Mikey said, shaking his head. He squatted next to the photographs, shuffling through them. Picking up a stack, he lay the pictures one by one on top of each other. He took an extra second with those of women with red hair or gray eyes or any feature that vaguely resembled his wife.

"Put the contact sheets over there," he said. "They're gonna take longer."

"What are contact sheets?"

"The ones with lots of little pictures. Like this one."

"Hey, that's Ginny," I said, taking it from him.

"My daughter is in here?" Celia said. She spoke in a tone that I'd never heard before, stepping carefully toward the pool of pictures, her face clouded with dread. The cleaning-lady clothes were terrible on her, aging her instantly. She peered at the pictures as though into a casket. Dropping to one knee, she put her hand out slowly, and gently pulled at the corner of a photograph, separating it from beneath a tangle of others.

"That's great, Mom," Mikey said. He was looking at the picture of Lucy, bare-breasted, hair falling around her shoulders. "Good eyes."

"I recognized the forehead," Celia said. She brought the photograph close to her, staring disbelievingly at this very old picture of Lucy. "I want every speck of her out of this place," she said in a whisper.

We worked solidly, in silence. If you've ever been to an estate sale in which the owner of the house has very recently died, it is much the same. People drive great distances in cars with out-of-state plates. They enter quietly, talk in low tones, and creep around in careful, slow steps, as though silence might keep them from disturbing the dead, whose things they've come to carry off.

Years passed through our hands as we took photograph after photograph from the floor, from the cabinets, from a box we found beneath a laundry hamper, from the hamper itself, which had been used to house pictures. I saw Ginny at sixteen, bounding through the doorway at the restaurant, a knapsack over her shoulder, her restaurant shoes tied by the laces and hanging off the knapsack. She wore sweatpants from my alma mater, a bathing suit beneath. You could see how the muscles in her arms worked, imagine her breath coming swiftly, her fast stride. A recent photo, still smelling of developing fluid, showed her sleeping in boxer shorts and a tank top, her hands tucked beneath one cheek, her eyelashes making dark half-moons on her face. I handed a photograph to Mikey—one of Lucy just out of college, with so much hair you could hardly see her face, pink young lips, and a shirt that was a little revealing.

After that there was some discussion of turning the stereo on—Mikey's suggestion, which Celia vetoed.

"It doesn't have to be what I like. We'll listen to what *you* like. Classical stuff, Ma," he said.

"No," Celia said.

"He has an enormous record collection. You can choose."

"I don't want to hear anything," Celia said, "from his collection."

We unfastened trunk after trunk, finding them on the floors of closets, beneath tables, on top the wardrobe. Each was filled with pictures. Women, lots of women; landscapes, beaches, buildings. Cars. Streets. Playgrounds. Trash. Dinner parties. The pictures presented themselves tirelessly through the long hours. We searched, took away the ones we wanted, rearranged the ones we'd seen. We set the trunks aside when we were through. Already they took up a great deal of the floor.

It was late. I didn't notice the rustle of footsteps over fallen leaves, the door opening and closing, until I heard a few hesitant words, a call from downstairs.

We froze. I looked from Celia to Mikey. We moved slowly, like thieves, over the photographs, quickly and silently, placing as many as we could back into the trunks. I heard the call again. It was Ginny's voice. Then she appeared, wearing bicycle shorts and a windcheater, reflective tape in circles at her ankles. Dropping her knapsack at the doorway, she pushed her hair from her eyes. Sweat was visible across her forehead, above her lip. Her eyeglasses slipped on her nose. The Oldsmobile was still at the garage; apparently she'd bicycled here tonight.

"What's going on?" she said in a startled, unsteady voice. Nobody spoke. We listened instead to the endless sound of the wind outside, the heavy sway of palm fronds. "Who said you could come here?"

"Now don't get huffy," Mikey said. "We had a key."

"Who had a key?" Ginny looked from Celia to Mikey to me. She was spellbound at having found all of us there, the pool of photographs surrounding us. Her face was seized with a kind of dazed revelation, as though she'd just uncovered a bomb.

"Me," I confessed. "I took it from your key ring."

"To do what?" she challenged. "Raid the place? What do you want here? His pictures? Why?"

"Ginny, we thought we should take away any pictures of you that you might not want others to see," Celia explained.

Ginny walked to where I was sitting on a trunk beside the leather duffel bag, which was filled to the breaking point with pictures. She looked down at the bag, thumbed through a couple of the prints, and then stood facing me.

"Give me back my key," she said, and I handed it to her wordlessly. She looked at a stack of pictures next to where Mikey kneeled on the floor. They lay face down. She lifted up one of the prints. Then she went to a drawer in Eli's dresser and took from it an old stationery box bound by kite string, which had worn the edge of the cardboard. She brought it over to Mikey.

"Give these to Lucy," she said. "They belong to her."

The box contained snapshots of Lucy and Eli a long time ago. Nothing sexy, just pictures of them together.

"She doesn't need these," Mikey said, chucking the box on the floor. I could see his temper rising, the color in his face.

"They're *hers*," Ginny said. "She might want them. Or do you guys scrub everybody's history clean, whether they like it or not?"

"Ginny, let's just leave," I said, gathering the bag.

"Forget it, Sam. I came over here to spend the night. I wanted to be here just one more time. In his house, with his stuff all around, before someone got at it and changed everything. But I guess I'm too late for that."

"Don't be angry at your brother," Celia said.

Ginny wheeled around, her voice rising. "Who the fuck are you?" she demanded.

"Don't talk like that to her!" Mikey yelled.

"Don't tell me how to talk!" Ginny said, turning now to Mikey. Ginny spoke right into his face. "I'll say any goddamned thing I want, and I'll say this first, Mikey: how Lucy could go from Eli to some dirtball like you is more than I can understand."

"Ginny," I said. Mikey's face glowed red. His eyes were fierce, staring back into Ginny's.

"I'm Celia Lawson," Celia said, her voice calm. "Lucy's mother."

"Where's Lucy?" Ginny asked. She let go of Mikey and turned to me. "She doesn't know you're here, does she?"

"No," I said.

"I guess as a *favor* to her you didn't tell her. You know, she was there when the shutter was released," Ginny said, turning for the door.

"That's easy for you to say," Celia said, edging toward Ginny. "At least you've got your clothes on in these photos."

"So fucking what?" Ginny said. "Look, you guys can crawl around this room like dung beetles if you want, but I think you're all a bunch of cowards."

"We're trying to save you from potential embarrassment," Celia said.

"Don't!" Ginny answered from the doorway, yelling loudly now. "Don't try to save me from anything. Just go home. Go make hot chocolate and read *Travel and Leisure* or whatever it is people like you do. Oh, you make me sick."

She left the room. We three stood staring at each other. Celia cleared her throat and tucked a handful of photographs nervously into her handbag. Mikey dropped to one knee and continued through the prints, pushing the ones he didn't want aside. I couldn't move. All of a sudden I felt stuck just where I was.

"I think you'd better finish the job," Mikey told me. His

usual smiley manner was absent tonight. He looked at me seriously. "You'll be sorry if you don't."

I tried. I took twenty or so photographs and leafed through them. Beside me, picture by picture, stack by stack, Celia made her way through the collection. I sat back on my heels, wondering exactly what to do.

"Sam," Mikey said. "You leave any behind and there'll be questions later. There'll be questions anyway, 'cause Ginny's the one who was with him day after day, night after night."

"Questions," I said. My voice was croaky.

"Lucy thinks it was probably fixed, and I tend to agree with her," Mikey said. "The LAPD is slow because the cause of death isn't one of those that begs for inquiry. But they'll get around to it—I'm guessing now, but I'd say in a matter of days. You probably should never have come here but now that you've started, you have to finish."

"Of course he should have come here," Celia said, turning to Mikey. "Anyway, *you're* here."

"For me and Lucy it is a different situation," Mikey said. "True, Lucy and Eli's relationship was a decade ago, but I have a jealous streak that has once or twice been on police record. They'll look for a motive, and if they see a single picture of Lucy they'll have one."

"Well, maybe you *are* a murderer," Celia said. She stopped collecting photographs and shrugged her shoulders. "Maybe we should let these pictures remain."

"You pick them up," Mikey said. He leveled his gaze at Celia. "Or you go home. Or you think very hard where your daughter was the night Eli was killed, because frankly, I don't think any of us in this room know."

Celia went silent. Now two more surprises for her: that she did not know where her daughter had been, which to a mother such as Celia is a crime in itself, and that she had found, to her own embarrassment, a need for this man, whom she despised

but for whom, at least during the remainder of this one evening, she would do whatever was requested.

We looked at each other. I heard the charge of a generator
and a splash from outside.

"I think I'll go," I said.

"Take my car," Celia said. "I'll ride back with Mikey." She
removed a photograph from a stack.

I went downstairs, hauling the duffel bag with me, and
walked through a set of glass doors that led out to the yard.
Another entire section of the property had been illuminated
with pool lights. It was a nicely landscaped swimming pool, a
box surrounded by flagstones and fig trees. Ginny swam laps,
wearing the tank top and her bicycling shorts, her hair like a
mermaid's, floating out from her shoulders. I stood at the edge
of the pool, watching her make her way underwater from the
far end. She reach the side in a dozen swift strokes and rose,
heavy-breathed, to the surface.

"Ginny, I'm sorry," I said, squatting by the pool.

She looked at me, her eyes red with chlorine.

I told her, "You're right, what you said. Everything you
said."

I spoke hoarsely, stumbling some on the words. All of a
sudden speech seemed almost impossible. "I don't know what
was wrong with me that I thought there was anything to clean
up about your life. Four years ago you were a kid. Now you're
grown up—I don't know what to do around you anymore. I
can't pretend I'm not part of you, that you don't matter. I can't
help you or protect you. You're out there in the world and
anything . . . *anything* could happen to you. I know I'm in the
way; I know I've done everything wrong. It's just that I'm a little
scared . . . and I don't even know what about."

Ginny blinked. Her bangs were slick across her forehead.

"Anyway, you should know that right now I'm scared for
you, not that it makes any difference at all," I said.

I waited, but she said nothing. She stared at me, her arms

200

folded in front of her, hugging herself the way I could not hug her. An apology was impossible. I had done something that spoke more clearly, had more authority than any statement of regret.

"I'm going home now," I said.

I stood again. I left the sack of pictures on the flagstones, I turned away, catching a glimmer of the city lights, the bright horizon. The night was so pretty. I looked into the sky, and the moon went fuzzy before my eyes. I realized that I would have to leave this place, leave Los Angeles, even as it lay shining like a crystal below. I'd thought that by coming here I'd improve my business, reconnect with my family. The irony was that just the opposite had happened. My retreat from their lives years ago had been more complete than I'd known. I walked forward, feeling heavy, swollen. I had said goodbye to my sister.

I opened the gate. It slid noisily over fallen leaves. Mikey's car was in the driveway, parked next to and slightly behind Celia's, as if approaching Celia's car carefully, somewhat menacingly, the way the man himself approached his mother-in-law. I looked up and saw Eli's bedroom and the shadows of Mikey and Celia long against the walls. I thought about Celia, who, for her daughter, would return and return to a place she couldn't bear, would sift through photographs she should never have had to see, would work through the eleventh hour with a man she didn't trust. Who, in truth, she might really be a little afraid of.

Lucy's father was a doctor who saved thousands of babies, and Celia was a mother who had spent her life saving only one.

I reached into my jeans pocket for car keys and came up with Celia's Cadillac key ring and also something else, a wadded piece of paper that I unfolded in my palm.

It was the check from Eli. It was made out to me and signed at the bottom in the quick strokes of Eli's signature. I flipped it over and signed the back, writing that it should be made payable to Ginny. I was through making decisions for her. I thought, and almost said out loud, *Money is not to be traded behind Ginny's back. Decisions are not to be made for her.* I walked back through the gate. The pool was an oval medallion, dominating the large garden.

"Sam!" Ginny hoisted herself out of the pool and ran forward, water rushing from her clothes. She stood in front of me, her arms cradled around her, hair clinging to her scalp, her neck. Huge eyes. The lights from the pool blossomed around her. Her hands, her shoulders shook. I stopped, watching her breath burst from clenched lips, her words arching forward. I held out the check for her. She didn't see it, her eyes were so fixed on my face. "Sam, if you're planning to go somewhere," she said, her chin trembling, "please take me."

SEVENTEEN

■ ■ ■

The gym where Lucy works out is on the ground floor of a luxury hotel, encased in glass, crowded, and from the outside entirely silent. If you sit on one of the benches framing the small, square courtyard outside the gym—though they don't call it a gym, of course; it's a club—you hear nothing of the music, the sound of lead weight meeting lead weight, the whir of chains running through stationary bicycles, of rowing machines spinning currents of air. The courtyard is secluded, quiet, with shade from a tall fir. A rock garden provides, in miniature, a perfect landscape.

Across from where I was sitting, inside the quiet glass, Lucy worked a machine that simulated a staircase. She walked up and up stairs that folded beneath her and rose again. She wore a black leotard that tugged at her hips with each step. Her legs were shaped in aquamarine tights; the muscles in her calves tensed and relaxed. In her hands she held three-pound weights; her shoulder muscles quivered as she raised and lowered them. I watched her ponytail bob with her movements, the sweat gather across her back, wetting her leotard. Her face was serious. She looked like a traveler burdened with luggage and late for a plane, moving as quickly as possible to the departure gate. Gripping the weights, she pushed down her heel, all concentration and purpose. The stairs collapsed and rose again, always meeting precisely the same spot on her sneaker.

I finished my sandwich just as she switched from the staircase machine to the treadmill. I watched her short-strided jog, noticing her thighs, the muscles tense, swollen. She fiddled with the radio headset that, along with a sweatband and elastic, held back the intrusive strands of her auburn hair.

I ate an apple; she did twenty-five push-ups, perfect as a soldier.

The weather was hot and dry; traffic on the way had been certain torture. But here in the courtyard, amid the cool rocks and shade, there was luxury and opulence and a sense of peace I'd not yet encountered in this city.

Lucy stretched, chin to knee, chin to floor, chin to knee, and straight. Chin to shoulder, chin to chest, chin to shoulder, and straight again. Then she saw me.

She did not look startled, as I would have expected. She did not look angry or alarmed. She walked to the front of the gym, rearranging her earphones so they hung around her neck and keeping her head level, her eyes on mine. She did not smile at me so much as acknowledge my presence, accepting it instantly and without opinion. She stood next to the wall of glass, staring right at me. I walked forward. We were inches of thick glass apart; we couldn't hear each other or touch.

She stood inside her world of movement and effort and people. And I stood in my unpopulated, still, and silent garden.

She told me I could remain, but only if I behaved. The children have one thing and only one that they all like to do together. Every afternoon at exactly this time they go swimming, the four of them plus Lucy. They are not to be taken by anyone else. They are not to be taken by a nanny and watched by the teenage lifeguard on the ladder above, a guy with a tan so bronze he looks not white, not black, the color not of any race but of a lifestyle.

They are taken in Lucy's old Buick, a car she owned before she and Mikey were married, that she bought with money she saved tending bar in New York. The Buick has a hundred and thirty thousand miles on it and is the only one of the cars that is big enough, really big enough, for all the kids. They arrive in a car that only Lucy drives, and they are looked after by her.

"This is their time," she said. "So don't expect a lot of attention from me."

"Understood," I said, flopping stomach first into a lounge chair.

Lucy stood in the shallow end of the pool, letting Stacy swim to her again and again, her chubby arms, encased by air pillows, slapping the surface of the water.

"Kick your legs!" Lucy called. The pool water lapped at her hips, where there was a line—more or less a line—between the emerald film of her dry swimsuit and the deeper pine color darkened by water.

"Watch this!" one of the twins yelled. "Mommy, watch!"

It was Paul. His name was stitched across his swimming trunks; that was the only way I could tell.

"Perfect!" Lucy called.

"Watch, Mommy!" Bobby said. He tried the same dive but ended up on his belly with his neck arched, his eyes shut, his nose wrinkled as though he'd just landed in something foul-smelling.

"Watch, Mom!" the other twin yelled. He cannonballed off the diving board, splashed big, and came up grinning.

"Terrific!" Lucy said.

"I'm kicking!" Stacy said. "You aren't watching."

"Of course I am. But you have to kick *up,* Stacy, not just into the water."

"Oh," Stacy said. She latched onto her mother, wrapped her arms around Lucy's neck, and hung there, catching her breath. "You didn't say *that.*"

There was a playground next to the pool. It had two swing-sets, one for little kids, with wooden seats with safety bars, the other with rubber slabs held by chains. There were two slides, a spinning wheel, a jungle gym shaped like a dome. There were ponies on thick springs, basketball nets set in a miniature court. Stacy played in the sandbox. She made a city out of buckets, rocks, her shoes. She carved roads and stop signs into the sand, built hills and lakes.

"Can I play?" I asked.

"You may *not,*" she said in what I thought was a very good imitation of her grandmother.

The twins were engaged in a serious game of one-on-one basketball. Lucy was the referee; she had a whistle, which she used occasionally, not to call fouls as much as to stop them from socking each other or biting each other's ears off, which seemed to be as much a part of their game as scoring points.

"Only my daddy plays with me in my sandbox," Stacy said.

"Very wise," I told her, and she looked up to the sky and said, "Yes."

"You can play with *me,*" Bobby said.

"What are you doing?"

"I'm, um, I'm . . ." Bobby looked around as though searching for an answer on the ground. "I'm not doing anything," he said brightly.

"How about a push on the swing, or I catch you off the slide, or how about seesaw?"

"Yes!" He went charging for a swing.

On the way home there was ice cream—actually frozen yogurt—and then Lucy delivered all four children to a babysitter, who gave them dinner on the back patio. We said goodbye to them; Lucy hugged each one and told them she'd be home soon.

"There is one secret to children," she said as we got into the car. "Exhaust them before they exhaust you."

"You're a great mother," I told her. The afternoon sun glowed on her cheeks. I noticed for the first time that she had freckles on her eyelids.

"Great mothers don't make dinner dates with single, cute, younger men."

"Sure they do!" I said.

"Just so the place is dark," Lucy said. She reclined her car seat so that she was almost lying down, her hand on my thigh. "Right here. Left at the bottom of the street."

We went to a small diner in Beverly Hills, not the most discreet place until you go into the very back of the back room and realize how easy it is to hide in one of the booths, amid lights suitable for nocturnes.

"How did you know about this place?" I asked. We slid into a booth, high-backed, private on three sides.

"This is where stars come to be seen not being seen. Lately it's gone out of vogue, but I think for tonight it will suit our purposes."

"Are you always so concerned about being seen?" I teased. I squeezed her naked knee beneath the table, tugged some on her skirt.

"Not unless I'm having an affair," Lucy said.

"I don't think I like that word."

"Maybe vegetarian lasagna?" Lucy said, assessing the menu.

"I suppose *affair* is better than *vegetarian lasagna*. How about friends? Or does that sound too much like Ernie and the Cookie Man?"

"Cookie *Monster*. I hear you and Mom and Mikey spent last night ransacking Eli's place."

"More or less," I said.

"But you'd still like to be *friends?*" she said. She held the menu in front of her so that I couldn't see her face.

"You're mad at me?" I asked.

She said, "I'd like to die of embarrassment . . ."

"Over pictures? Pictures are no big deal."

"I would like to die of embarrassment, but dying would be way too good for me right now."

"Lucy," I said. I got out of my side of the booth and slid in next to her. "Don't worry about it. It doesn't matter."

"It matters to Mother. To you too, I bet. Admit it."

"No."

"Well, it matters to me. It seems I've spent half my life making mistakes, the other half correcting them. Anyway, seeing those photos must have thrown you."

"Not really. You want to know what has thrown me? Not knowing where you were when Eli died. Obviously, you know what happened, who did it."

"I didn't do it," Lucy said.

"I never thought it was you. But you must have some idea."

"No, Sam, I don't. No idea at all," she said. She looked closely at the menu. "I really want the cheesecake, but the scale will not be forgiving."

"How about the guys from Mama Best?"

"Don't know."

"How about someone from the Cat Club or Eve's Parlor?"

"Well, well, you've been getting around."

"I don't know where Ginny was or where you were the night he died," I said.

"Not true. You know I was there."

"How do I know that?"

"Because I *told* you," said Lucy, rolling her eyes. "Some detective you are."

"Please. I don't have to be given a blow-by-blow account, but just the basic stuff about what happened that night."

"Can't tell you," Lucy said.

"Why?"

"Sorry. Be a pal and order the cheesecake so I can have a bite of it."

EIGHTEEN

...

Mother stood over the ironing board, which was being used for once for what it was designed for. A white blouse sleeve hung limply over the edge. An iron steamed above. Mother listened to the radio, humming along.

This is how I remember her best—not a very glamorous recollection, but one that I can recall easily at any day or time, able to remind myself instantly of every detail of her: her sturdy legs, her slim hips, her back, which was long enough to be disproportionate to her height. I saw her as she was, without the influence of other people. Her eyes focused on the seam of a sleeve, the positioning of a collar, but something in her face suggested that her concentration lay elsewhere—on the trip that was before her, on a detail of the vacation catalogues she and Van had leafed through together. Maybe she was thinking about me and Ginny. Or maybe about something that had nothing at all to do with me or Ginny or Van or anyone. Just her.

She looked so pretty, with her hair done, a little lipstick. I'd been watching her, through this blouse and the one before, ironing and folding, tucking each item of clothing carefully into her suitcase beside a stack of walking shorts and half-slips and sandals. She always took a small bag of makeup with her, not the expensive kind but the stuff that is sold in the aisles of Walgreen's and Dart Drug. Seeing that little bag of powders and creams could break my heart instantly, as it did while she packed for her trip.

They were going north on the coastal highway, a route that maybe everybody in L.A. has taken at one time or another. Mother and Van had spent a lot of time in a bookstore. They'd bought a picture book of the western coastline from Los Angeles to Seattle, a field guide to birds, an elaborately illustrated album of wildflowers, a color guide to seashells. They had fishing gear and camping gear. Ginny had recovered the Oldsmobile from R. J. Olds and waxed it glossy while I changed the oil and a few spark plugs.

"It's beautiful," Mother declared as I pushed the suitcases into the trunk. She had a wicker picnic basket loaded with food she'd prepared with Ginny—sandwiches, fruit salad, a lemon pie—which she wanted in the back seat. I tucked the basket next to an ice chest and the books. Ginny and I had scrubbed and vacuumed the upholstery, shampooed the carpets, emptied and polished the ashtrays. An impressive job; from the inside, the car almost seemed brand new.

"Mom, wait a second," Ginny said, knocking the screen door aside and jumping three steps to land in the driveway. She held out a shoebox packed with ten or so cassette tapes, all labeled in her writing. "Okay, these two are theme songs from Academy Award–winning movies. You know, *On Golden Pond, Chariots of Fire,* the ones you like. This is Louis Armstrong on one side and Dinah Washington on the other. This one is a mix of stuff, Rosemary Clooney, Fred Astaire. I got Marlene Dietrich and Tony Bennett . . ."

She held up a set of three tapes marked with a pink dot in

the center, two marked with blue. "Pink means classical. Blue is opera, and I know you hate it but I only taped the *highlights.*"

"Thank you," Mother said, putting a hand on Ginny's cheek.

"They're not the best recordings, but they'll do," Ginny said. She peered into the back seat as she spoke, inspecting the books, the basket, the rain gear in a corner. She scanned the trunk, rummaged behind the suitcases, and brought out a large flashlight, some flares, and a canister of foam for temporarily filling a flat tire. "You know how to use a flare, right, Mom?"

"You showed me yesterday," Mother said.

"And the 800 number for Triple A is right here," she said, pointing at the lid of the trunk, on which she'd written the phone number in indelible marker.

"Yes, honey."

"And you have all your pills?"

Mother nodded. "And prescriptions for more in case I lose them," she said.

"Okay," Ginny said, slowly backing away from the car as though it might explode. "Don't drink and drive. It's the law."

"We'll keep the flask low," Mother said.

Van's Subaru appeared from around the corner. He pulled it in against the curb and took a small suitcase and a load of camping gear from the seat beside him.

As I waved, he came forward, smiling. He looked very happy. He was slimmer than I'd come to think of him. The diet milkshakes must have had some effect.

"You sure you want to take the Olds?" he asked. He flipped his fishing hat forward and rubbed the back of his scalp.

"I don't mean to be insulting, Van," Mother said. "But that little car of yours has always scared me just a bit."

"Scares me, too. The repair bills. Here," Van said, handing a cluster of tulips to her. "They're not as pretty as the wildflowers we're gonna see."

Mother squeezed his arm. She admired the flowers.

"Here we go," she said, almost like a song.

"Mama," Ginny said, hugging her.

When they left, Ginny waited by the window for a long time, staring out at the empty road in front of the house. They say there is a bond between mothers and daughters that is unlike anything men can understand, and maybe that is right.

I heated a plate of fries, doused it with ketchup, and went in to sit with Ginny.

"Mother is not coming back," she announced. She had her elbows on the back of the couch. She leaned forward and took a french fry from my plate.

"How do you know?"

"I know," she said. "I mean, she'll visit. We'll see her. It just won't be the same."

"Mmm," I said, not knowing at the time that she was precisely correct.

"You want to know why Mom went away?" she said. She held a fry between two fingers, chewing at the end as if it were a cigar. "I mean, one reason? Because she knew that otherwise we would stay with her. It's really that simple. She left because we wouldn't. I don't think she could have done anything more to show us how much she loved us."

"She's only been gone an hour," I reminded her.

"Oh no. She's definitely left," she said. "We're going to get a call next week or the week after or whenever, and Mom's going to say she is happy where she is, the truth of which won't even matter."

At the time I didn't understand, though I grew to know very well what Ginny meant. In some ways, I suppose, Mother had already left us, left us with her legacy and her ghost. Ginny and I had lived for so long with Mother's voice in our heads, in houses that were hers, had known so well all of her dreams, that we had occasionally mistaken those dreams for our own.

And then they had become our own. We were part of her. Or maybe now it was she who was part of us. She would become for us every antique postcard, every forties movie, every old band song. In her absence we would fill our minds with her, ruminate on and love her differently and completely, always wanting her back.

"Ginny, we'll see her a week from Monday," I said.

"You're not listening," said my sister.

Mother had said one thing to Ginny, and one thing only. When she'd hugged her that last time, she had leaned away for a moment and looked seriously at her daughter.

She said, "Sorrow is exhausting. It is the one thing in the world, Ginny, that has the ability to sap all that beautiful energy of yours."

"I'm sad you're going," Ginny had said.

"You mustn't be. Listen, now; I've never had any advice to give except this. I know from experience: sorrow is like fire. It spreads, consumes, lays waste to everything in its path."

Ginny went into her room and stayed by herself for a long time. I wrote a letter to Pelzer, enclosing a small check. The night outside was noisy with birds. Ginny took a shower. She trudged around the house in jeans she'd painted fuschia and orange, with elaborate etchings in pen. Holes fist-sized, holes small as a coin. Her T-shirt hung thigh length.

She papered the living room carpet with classified ads. In her left hand was a red pen for circling jobs that interested her. I watched her from the couch as she circled two ads: one to work at a catering service, the other to manage an ice cream store.

"What do you really, *really* want to do, Ginny?" I asked. I sat down on the rug with her. "Regardless of talent or experience, regardless of competition?"

She thought for a while.

"You can say anything, no matter how dumb it sounds, but it has to be the absolute truth," I said. "Modeling?"

"I admit that I used to have an interest there," she said. "But now I see that it's impossible and humiliating. I could be an antimodel, maybe. I'd like a picture of me ripping up something by Laura Ashley. Or setting fire to all things Lycra."

"An actress?"

"Yuck. All those people *looking* at me."

"A detective?"

"I've grown wary of police."

"A social worker?"

"I practically *am* a social worker," Ginny said. "Maybe, *maybe* I could be a photographer."

"Of course you could be a photographer. Why not?"

"I don't know. Seems like everyone I know is having their picture taken. Not taking a picture."

"Eli took pictures," I said.

"Yeah, but he was Eli. And I'm, you know . . ."

"All you need is the equipment," I said. "And we know where to find it."

We drove to Eli's just as the stars appeared overhead, reflecting in the mirrored sides of office buildings; just as the temperature fell to a tolerable degree and all the streetlights flicked on, awakening the need to go somewhere, anywhere. On the side-walks, people walked more slowly, a little closer. Friends clowned in the open-topped back seats of Volkswagen Rabbits and Fiats and Jeeps. We drove into Hollywood Hills, the ocean swirling below us in olive green and cobalt, the wind pushing the driest breeze across the city.

"You wouldn't call this stealing?" Ginny asked.

"Not at all," I said. "There's thousands of dollars' worth of equipment that is going to go to some bank that doesn't want it. They'll sell it for ten cents on the dollar to a business that couldn't care less, which will in turn sell it to a secondhand store that overcharges for the merchandise. In fact, you are stopping them from swindling some poor sucker who walks in the door with his MasterCard in hand. Believe me, Ginny, you're doing everyone a favor."

At the top of the hill we took a right, another right, and then drove down Mulholland to the hidden driveway that led to Eli's house.

"Thank you for going with me," Ginny said.

But at the bottom of the driveway we discovered a long stretch of tape between two trees, barring our entrance. The tape was yellow and black; POLICE BUSINESS was stamped across it.

"Oh God!" Ginny said, her hand over her mouth.

"Don't worry."

"We can't go in there."

"Sure we can."

"Please, Sam," she said. She was spooked, her face white. "Get back in the car. You'll get in trouble."

"No trouble," I said, ducking under the tape.

The door was sealed shut and bolted with a police lock. I circled the house, eying the windows. Ginny stomped behind me, protesting all the while.

"Sam, come on," she said. "I don't like being here with this police crap all over the place. It's spooky. I don't want the stuff anymore."

I jumped up, reaching a rafter that hung just below one of the upper-floor decks.

"You're gonna hurt yourself," Ginny said.

I pulled up, trying to find a place for my feet.

"Wait," she said. "Look, if you're bound and determined, I'll show you a way in."

216

I gave up my grip and fell onto grass. Rubbing my hands where they were sore from holding the wood, I followed Ginny down a hill. We stepped behind a hedge and sidled up to the house to avoid the sharp branches. There was a clearer area where the branches had been worn away, and here Ginny crouched down, her sneakers bordering a window well.

"There," she said, pointing at a tiny window. She pushed her leg into the well, kicked the latch, and gently nudged the window open with her foot.

"I can't fit," I said. "I think I'm better off climbing up."

Ginny leaned back, lowering herself toward the window.

"I'll go," she said.

"No, Ginny . . ."

But she was already halfway through the opening. She continued down, disappearing through the mouth of the window and into the dark basement of Eli's house.

I heard her land on the floor. A light went on in the basement, and then she disappeared. I made my way back through the hedge. She opened a side window to let me in.

"It's upstairs," she whispered.

"I know. Ginny, look, I'm having second thoughts. There's this slide show in my head at the moment, and it's featuring us with handcuffs. Police have this terrible habit of rounding up suspects, taking fingerprints. All that stuff you see on *L.A. Law*. I think it's a bad idea for us to go any further. Let's go home."

"I never even wanted to come in the first place," she said. "But now that we're in, we're in."

"I think, Ginny, that we ought to just buy whatever you need."

"With what? I don't have a job anymore."

I opened my wallet, took out Eli's check, and handed it to her. It had been creased and folded too many times and was worn at the edges from having been carried about for too long in damp pockets and hands.

"I've been wanting to give you this. I know it's made out to me, but that's only because Eli knew you wouldn't take it. Given the circumstances, I think you'd better cash it in sooner rather than later."

Ginny stared at the check, her brow furrowed, her mouth slightly open. "No," she said, pushing it my way.

"Ginny, take it. What's it matter anymore?"

"He always gave women money. It was his way of being adored. I don't want to think of myself as another woman who wandered into his life, got shortchanged by him in one way or another, and was compensated with cash."

"So don't think of yourself that way. Think you're Princess Diana if you want, but keep the money."

"Nope," she said. She ripped the check.

"Ginny!" I tried grabbing it from her, but it went in pieces to the floor.

"It's not right. It's not how it was."

She said this while I was scrambling on the floor, retrieving bits of what had been a small fortune.

"Ginny, you weren't even supposed to know about the money! I was going to say it was mine, to get a nurse for Mom so that you didn't have to always be taking care of her. It was an arrangement that had nothing to do with you. Really."

"That was the plan, was it?"

"Well, yes."

"Good plan," Ginny said. "I'm going upstairs."

We came home with a back seat full of film boxes, tripods, filters, camera bodies, lenses, foam, developing pans, chemicals, spotlights. While we were clearing out the stuff, bringing down crate after crate, Ginny talked. She talked nonstop. She laughed. She seemed oddly joyful. And I got the feeling that in Eli's house, surrounded by his things—his clothes and bathtowels and coffee mugs, his mail and bicycle gear, his chairs, records, plants, his paintings and his white, white carpets—it had been her habit to be joyful.

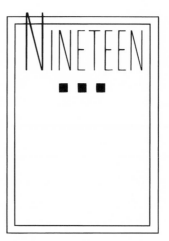

NINETEEN

Lucy and I had draped a blanket over the hammock so that it dropped down on either side, forming an A-framed tent of sorts. We settled under the hammock, between walls of blanket. Inside there was room to sit or lie on the grass. A night breeze came from each of the long ends of the hammock, but the blanket kept us warm, made us cozy. A flashlight formed a circle of light against a corner of dark wool. It was enough so that we could see each other's faces, our skin, shining, dark, full of shadows. Lucy's eyes were black, her freckles undetectable. Her hair, in ringlets, framed her face.

"And then I'll unhook your bra and move it slowly up, not off entirely, but just enough so I can see the roundness of your breasts," I said, continuing a long conversation that focused on the same. "I'll kiss you where your ribs disappear beneath that arc. I'll touch your nipples with my fingers. Then my tongue."

We'd been telling each other, word for word, movement for tiny movement, how we would make love. In our rigged tent, we sat, legs folded, hands quiet and waiting. We had not kissed or touched.

"It's about time we offed my bra," Lucy said, recalling the last thirty minutes of conversation. "We've been through a lot with that bra still on."

"Are you even wearing a bra?"

"No, but that's okay. Go on, I'm enjoying this part."

I leaned forward. It was enough now. I couldn't keep on without touching her.

"I'll kiss your ankles," I said, and did.

"I'll bury my face in your lap," Lucy said, her eyes steady on mine, her hands reaching forward.

I felt how small her mouth was, her soft lips, the curve of her tongue. She closed her eyes, sinking onto me, and I smiled. I touched her face, lingering at the pulse beneath her chin, at the base of her throat.

Later, still in our tent, I put an arm beneath the small of Lucy's back and raised her toward me. With my finger I separated all the parts that are her. I kissed her thighs, her hipbone. I traced the brilliant decoration on her stomach, the marks of all her children.

"After Mikey and I were married I still thought about Eli," she whispered. "I couldn't drag myself away from him entirely. I couldn't rid myself of the feeling that I'd left behind some part of me when I left him."

I kissed her belly button, moving my fingers across a line of whiter skin below her tan.

"I wanted it back. It had been years, and I still wanted something that I was sure I'd lost or that he'd taken from me. So I went to his house. And you know what? I hadn't lost anything except him, and I wanted *him* back."

I kissed higher and higher, moving up Lucy's ribs as though they were a ladder, tasting her skin.

220

"But at the time I realized that I had made a mistake; it was that simple. I had left him when I shouldn't have. I was just twenty-five when Eli and I split up. Who knows what I was thinking then? I didn't want a man like Eli because I thought he wasn't good enough to be my husband. He was good enough to be my lover, but I didn't want him to be the father of my kids. And so, like an idiot, I left him for Mikey. Years later I went creeping back. One night. One time. And we made Bobby."

I kissed the back of her neck, the line of her collarbone. I thought of Bobby; I could see now how much he looked like both Lucy and Eli. I pictured his lopsided smile, a trait he shared with his father.

"I'm going to tell you something terrible," Lucy said. Her voice broke and I thought she would cry. I pressed my cheek to her cheek, but there were only a few stray tears, which stopped as quickly as they'd begun. She said, "Bobby is my favorite child."

I wrapped my arms around her and held her tightly.

"He's a wonderful boy," I said.

"His father . . ." Lucy hesitated. "Mikey won't pay any attention to him. Even when I was pregnant, I think Mikey knew it wasn't his child. We never talked about it. It was the great unsaid thing between us. Mikey wasn't there when Bobby was born. His sister was getting married, so he went to her wedding in Cleveland. Mother never forgave him for that, but the fact was I didn't want him at the birth. They say babies all look alike, but I'm telling you, nothing could have been more obvious than Bobby's paternity."

"Do you talk about it now?" I asked.

"God no. But Mikey never changed his diaper or gave him milk or pushed the stroller. Mikey is the type of man who will retrieve his daughter's stuffed bear in a thunderstorm at night on a highway if he has to. But he won't say good morning to Bobby, and that poor child is dying inside."

"He's happy, Lucy. He comes running up smiling."

"He tries to please."

I kissed Lucy on the mouth. Her lips smacked of salt. I kissed her eyes, her forehead.

"I can never leave Mikey, because he didn't leave me when I insisted on keeping that pregnancy. He held my hair for me when I puked in the mornings because of a child that wasn't his. He waited the patient months we couldn't make love because I was either too pregnant or too sore. And when Bobby was a little baby, crying in the night, Mikey brought him to me. He didn't hold him himself, but he brought him to me."

"Did Eli know?"

"He gave me half the club so that we would never have money problems, so that his son would never go without. He promoted Mikey's business, and he kept his distance from me because he was afraid of Mikey's jealousy. Not that Mikey would hurt him, but that he'd hurt the baby."

"Mikey wouldn't do that."

"Of course not. But Eli didn't want to take the chance. He saw Bobby one time—a random meeting in a supermarket in Ventura, of all places. The twins were walking then. I had Bobby in the shopping cart. Eli came up, didn't even look at me. He looked right at Bobby, leaned over, kissed him on the cheek, and walked out. I didn't see him again until last week."

"And what happened last week?"

Lucy sat up, rubbing her eyes on her shoulder.

"Last week a blow dryer fell into a hot tub," she said.

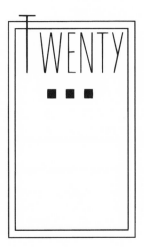

Ginny was in the living room, watching television. It was three o'clock on the hottest day of the year. You couldn't get away from reports of low air quality, fires, warnings of dehydration. Outside, kids put dry ice on the road so it steamed like a firecracker. Down the block someone had burst a fire hydrant.

"Ginny, we'll dry up like lizards unless we go to the beach."

She had pulled all the shades and was bellyflopped in front of the television. She lay motionless on the carpet, her T-shirt made blue by the television's glow.

"Thunderstorms predicted," she said. "Meanwhile, there's mealworms."

We watched Channel 73, formally called "Of Natural Interest" but known throughout Southern California as the stinko channel because of an early attempt by the network to provide viewers with scratch-and-sniff cards to accompany various programs on science. The talk-show host Ginny was watching,

Rudolph Sill, was himself a subject of fascination. He was weirdly dressed in an off-red shirt and a leather tie that matched his white hair. Listening to his guest's answers, he sucked a finger. His skin was yellow, which was not the fault of our television. He was only marginally less bizarre than Dr. Trevor, whom he interviewed about killings across the nation.

"In 1982 at the Prande Museum at Royce College, an anthropologist impaled one of his graduate students with a Balinese spear, used centuries earlier among warring tribes. It was a bizarre act, not clearly a murder at first, but sexually based."

"The student was a woman?" Sill asked.

"A young woman."

"Of course she was a young woman," Ginny said, rolling her eyes. She used the top of a mayonnaise jar as an ashtray, tipping the long ash of her cigarette. She yelled at the TV: "Why don't you say, *young, hot woman with pulsating thighs and breasts?* God, do they have to make it sound so appealing? Every demento-head in the city is sitting in his living room right now getting hot over the idea of primitive domination games. God, I hate this show. I hate you," she said to the screen.

There was a commercial break for—no joke—a trucker urinal. Then one for a chemical compound that takes lipstick off shirt collars. A free gift with your subscription to *National Geographic.* Molson is the beer of choice.

"If I order chicken wings, will you eat them?" I asked. The night before she'd stayed up all night, mixing chemicals into trays, hanging photographs to dry. There were half-eaten apples here and there but no sign she'd had anything substantial.

"Oh, Sam, how can you eat those poor little hens' arms?"

"How about a pizza? You never eat, Ginny."

"I eat."

"Marshmallows out of the bag is not eating. Cornnuts is not eating. I would say you eat like a bird, but of course birds eat much better than you do."

She stared at the television screen. "You watch," she said.

"The next murder in L.A. will be a busgirl done in with a samurai sword."

In the kitchen I moved bottles of developing fluid, wax pencils, paper, rulers, and assorted other supplies from the table, then got a towel and wiped clean the scarred wood. I assembled some food for dinner: a bag of spaghetti, some mushrooms, tomatoes, a chunk of cheese the size of a softball.

"We're having pasta," I called. I filled a pot with water and set it to boil. I melted butter in a pan. "According to the instructions, this should take twelve minutes," I said.

Over the sink Ginny had strung wire and clips. The photographs hanging there were dry now. They were self-portraits, black-and-white. In the pictures her face was shadowed in different ways. Her eyes were round, sunken, so large and dark it was hard to find the center of them. The face in these pictures held my attention, startled me just a little. I took the pictures from the line, making a space for them on the kitchen table, away from spattering oil and steam from the stove. Ginny came in, turned the gas flame up, and read the cooking instructions on the back of the spaghetti bag.

"All of Santa's elves couldn't make this in twelve minutes," she said. She sliced cheese, using the phone book as a chopping block.

"Your photographs are excellent," I told her. I leafed through the stack, pulling out the ones I liked particularly.

"Automatic timer," she said. "You have forty-five seconds to pose after positioning the camera. It would be better, of course, if I had a model."

"These are so sad," I said. "And strange. They don't look anything like you."

Ginny walked to where I was standing. She gave the photos a hard stare.

"Inside myself," she said, "that's what I look like."

■   ■   ■

At eleven-thirty Celia phoned me, waking me out of a deep and satisfying slumber.

"Life is short, Sam Haskell," she said. "Try to stay awake for some of it."

I heard some background noise and then the muffle of Celia's palm over the receiver.

"I know this is way beyond the call of duty, but could you drive me to the airport?" Celia asked me. There was more noise, the sound of Lucy's voice. "I'm leaving tonight. It's the end of my life here in California. I'm willing you my car."

I sat up. Steadying the phone between my shoulder and chin, I shook out a pair of pants and pushed a leg through.

"Sam, are you listening?" she whispered. "The police were here. They think it might have been Mikey. They took him away, is that too perfect? Nine years I've been wishing for him to go, but I never thought it would be in a police cruiser."

"Mikey couldn't have killed Eli," I said, searching for a shirt. "That's ridiculous."

"We can't talk about it now. The important point is that Lucy is still not going to leave him. Am I right that this is *the* final straw? I've done everything I can. I'm going back to New York."

It was Lucy, not Celia, who was waiting outside the door, her arms folded across her chest. She wore a leather jacket over a pair of spandex tights and high-top Nikes. Her socks were regular men's athletic socks, with purple bands above a tube of white. They drooped to her ankles. She'd pinned her hair so that it made ringlets on the nape of her neck. It shone red and gold against the porch light.

"Don't do this," she warned as I came to the door. "They're just asking Mikey some questions. He's not under arrest or anything. Celia wanted an excuse to leave and now she has one."

She dropped her arms so they slapped against her sides. She was angry in that way I'd seen before. Afraid, too, I suspected. I took her hands in mine, drew her near me, and kissed her between words.

"Celia has the habit of dramatic entrances and exits. I refuse to let her fly the red-eye on the foggiest night of this century. Don't kiss me now, Sam, I'm talking. I'm not trying to be unreasonable, it's just that it's not my personal wish to see my mother frighten herself into a heart attack at forty thousand feet."

"You're afraid to fly, aren't you?" I said, smiling at her, kissing her eyelids, her nose. "Just like your mom."

"Me? I'm terrified. That's why I never do it. Celia *says* she's afraid, but I notice she gets on the goddamned plane," Lucy said, pushing me away. "Stop. Someone will see."

"Ooooh," I said, pretending fear.

Inside, Celia was making her way down the long stairway, dragging a suitcase with her.

"Oh, great," Lucy said. She hopped up the stairs and took the case from her mother. "Ruin your back first and then get on the sky inferno."

"I wish you wouldn't call it that," Celia said, shaking her head.

Lucy hooked a thumb over her shoulder. "You can't see diddly out there," she said. "Electrical storms are imminent— call weather info and you'll see I'm right. Mother, think about it logically: planes are heavy; the air weighs nothing. One little tiny problem and—"

"They fly every day," Celia said. "I've read that you are safer in a plane than you are in a car."

"That's mile by mile, not hour by hour."

"What is she talking about?" Celia asked me. She draped a sweater over her shoulders. "Can someone please explain what my daughter is talking about?"

"She doesn't want you to go," I said. "Don't punch me, Lucy."

The phone rang twice and then I heard someone else's voice, a female voice, speaking into it. We waited as a girl a little younger than Ginny came into the hall, bringing a cordless telephone with her.

"It's Mikey," the girl said, handing the phone to Lucy.

"Nella, this is Sam," Lucy whispered, gesturing my direction. "Sam, this is . . . oh, forget it."

She took the phone, turning away from us. "Hello? Yes, darling, I'm here," she said, seating herself on the staircase.

"I babysit the kids," Nella said and shrugged her shoulders.

"What nerve, taking you in for questions," I heard Lucy say into the phone. "Listen, Celia insists on going back to New York. No, it has nothing to do with you. Of course no one else is here. Just me and Celia and Nella. The kids are in bed. Well, they *were*."

We all looked up at a child's face peering through the railing below the banister. It was Bobby, clad in light blue pajama bottoms. He sat at the top of the stairs. I noticed that someone, probably him, had drawn on his feet with red marker.

"I'm sorry, Mikey, I can't hear you. I think the phone is broken." Lucy ran her fingernails over the receiver, blowing on it at the same time. "Did you hear that? Hello? Mikey, I think our line needs work . . ."

She hung up delicately, then dialed a recorded message and left the phone lying on the stairs. She looked up at her son. "What's the matter, sweetheart? Did we wake you?"

"Is Grandma leaving?" Bobby asked.

"Yes," Celia said. She took the handle of her suitcase and nodded at me to open the door.

"Mother, you can't leave," Lucy said, struggling to take the suitcase. "I need you here."

"Los Angeles is not my home," Celia said. "It doesn't even feel like home."

"It never does to anybody," Lucy said. "Not even to the people who live here. That's part of the city's appeal."

"I don't find that appealing."

"Mother, *please*, you can't ask me to make a decision all at once like this. I will do something, I promise, but not all of a sudden," Lucy said. I watched Celia's face and thought perhaps Lucy was gaining ground with her.

"One day you want one thing, the next the other. You've always been the same." Celia sighed.

"He's my husband," Lucy said. "And he's in trouble."

"He has always been in trouble," Celia said. "How much trouble does he have to be in before you are willing to call it a day?"

"Just not right now," Lucy pleaded. "Oh, Mom, please don't go."

"We've talked about it," Celia said seriously.

"I'll get Bobby some milk," Nella said, backing toward the kitchen.

"If you leave, then what will I do?" Lucy said. Her forehead broke out in lines, her mouth seemed to shiver on her face.

"I don't know, Lucy. What have you been doing for the past nine years? Do *that*," Celia said. She wrenched the suitcase away as Lucy wiped her eyes.

Bobby ran down the steps and stood in front of me, his face alert. "Do you want to see my turtle?" he asked.

"Not now," Lucy answered for me.

"I'm three feet," Bobby said. He leaned forward and I picked him up, which pleased him. He smiled at me and then unbuttoned the breast pocket of my jeans jacket. "But that's small for my age."

"I bet you're nine or ten," I said.

"Nope."

"Ten or eleven?"

"Nope."

"You're not as old as I am?" I said, feigning shock. "You're not thirteen million four hundred and twenty-five thousand, are you?"

Bobby squealed. He leaned forward, whispered "four" in my ear, and then turned toward his mother, his face alight. But Lucy had sat down on the floor next to the phone, which repeated the time over and over again. Her hands were pressed to her face. She rocked back and forth. Celia had left for the car.

"Mommy is crying," Bobby said. "Can I come to the airport?"

"Sure," I told him, fitting my jacket over his tiny shoulders.

"Put something on his feet," Lucy said between tears.

Lucy held Bobby in her lap and played a game with him in which she pretended to be blind and he had to describe everything he could see from the car.

"A truck with cars on its back," he told his mother. "A palace of cinnamon."

"That's the Palace *Cinema*," Celia said from the seat behind. "*Cin-e-ma*."

"Please, Mom," Lucy said. She had put on sunglasses for the game and held Bobby's hand as though she needed his protection, which in some ways I thought she did.

"Grandma, were you always old?" Bobby asked.

"Yes, always," Lucy said. She laughed at her own joke.

"No, Robert," Celia said. "Your mother made me that way."

Bobby kissed Lucy on the point of her chin. "By magic you will be able to see," he announced and made twirling motions in the air with his hands. He tried to sound out a drum roll, which he accomplished only with help from the rest of us. Then he waved his invisible magic wand, and when he announced his blind mother's recovery of sight, she flung off her glasses, doing a stellar job of acting astonished at sight, vision, colors.

"And now you're all better!" Bobby said proudly. "Whaddya see, Mommy?"

There was a pause. I switched lanes onto the access road to the airport. A Pan Am jet rumbled downward, landing with precision on the runway.

"I see Sam," Lucy said, smiling at me.

I spent the night on Lucy's couch, a yellow, overstuffed six-seater. When I awoke, one of the twins was staring at me, his face concerned.

"I think the phone is for you."

I took the phone from him, sitting up.

Mikey's voice: "I'm in jail for murdering a guy and you sleep with my wife. Now you tell me, is that a smart thing to do?"

The other twin had joined his brother and they watched me from the opposite side of the room. They sat at either end of a window seat, perfectly identical, like two china boys. I spoke quietly. "I didn't sleep with her," I whispered.

"I don't care if all you do is drink tea and talk about medieval fucking history, this is my one phone call for the morning and I'm telling you to get out of my house."

Stacy arrived now, wearing pajama bottoms that were way too big for her, so that she tripped over the trailing cloth at her ankles. She held a doll upside down, its hair brushing the carpet. She stumbled toward me, and I bent over to roll her pants legs.

"Mommy's sleeping," she said, putting a finger to her lips.

Mikey was yelling through the phone now. With the kids around, I didn't dare take the receiver from my ear.

Bobby ran in, saw me, jumped five feet, and landed on the couch. He hunkered down under the covers and hid, hugging my leg.

"If you are in *my* house with *my* family when I get out of here this afternoon," Mikey warned, "if you are anywhere near my wife or my kids, I'll kill you."

"Oh, Mikey, why do you *do* this?" It was Lucy's voice now,

coming from another extension. She sounded sleepy and sad. I could tell that she'd been crying.

"Honey, is that you?" Mikey said. "I'll be home this afternoon. I was just telling Sam the good news."

"You're not going anywhere," Lucy said. She sighed. "They tape these phone calls. Now that they've got it on record that you threatened someone's life . . ."

One of the twins yelled, "Postman!" and all four kids screamed and ran to the window as a postman in beige walking shorts and a camel-colored shirt and cap made his way down the flagstones.

"Oh God," Lucy said. "Sam, would you tell the kids not to terrorize the mailman? I'm hanging up now, Mikey. Please try to behave so that someday, somehow, you get out of jail. Sam, is Stacy putting her arm through the mail slot?"

"Yes," I said.

"Get her away from the door," Lucy said.

"Don't you touch her!" Mikey said.

A half-hour later Lucy came downstairs in gym shorts, tights, and a bright orange hooded sweatshirt. She held an exercise mat under one arm and two five-pound dumbbells.

"Pay no attention to me," she said. "I look like a witch."

"What do we start with? Sprints? Sit-ups?"

"We start with groveling and apologies for my hideous behavior and that of my mother and my husband. We start also by saying that Nella will be here in fifteen minutes; I drive carpool today, and you are out of your mind."

"Well, that's it. Celia's gone," I told Ginny. She was in her room, feeding blue fabric to the tiny point of her sewing machine needle. The last track of Donizetti's *Lucia di Lammermoor* had run its course, and the record spun silently round and round.

"Gone where?" Ginny said. Her hair was knotted above her

head. Her glasses swept low across her nose. The sewing machine had a tiny light bulb just inside the motor that controlled
the needle. It was shorting out slowly, blinking now with the
movement of the machine. Ginny eased the pedal with her toe.

"New York," I said. I fell backward onto Ginny's bed. There
was a notebook on the pillow, filled with inked words, crossed
out and rewritten.

"Give me that," she said, reaching for the book. She ripped
out a clump of pages she'd been working on, creased the center, and sat on it.

"What are you making?"

"Shirt."

"What did you write?"

"A letter to Eli. I realized today that in all the time I knew
him, I never wrote him a letter. I know there's nothing I can do
about that now, but I thought I wanted to write one to him
anyway. A letter I would have written if he were alive and
could read it. Don't laugh."

I told her she was wonderful.

"Don't make fun," she warned.

"Is there some sort of code I'm supposed to use to compli-
ment you? Regular words seem to have the opposite effect."

I watched her work, sliding cotton through the machine
inch by inch. She wore a tiny silver chain around her neck. She
concentrated, studying the fabric closely. I'd almost begun to
enjoy the way she ignored me, the way she was able to blank
out her surroundings and focus on whatever task she decided
was crucial.

"The police took Mikey in for questioning last night," I
said.

"Waste of time," Ginny said. She let the machine come to a
slow halt, the needle raised, as she fished in the drawer for a
new spool of thread.

"Have they been here?"

"Yup."

"What did you tell them?"

"Nothing," she said. She switched spools and pressed gently on the foot pedal. "There was nothing to say."

"Did writing a letter to Eli help at all?" I asked.

Ginny pushed a mound of cloth away from her, smoothing the part being sewed. Then she stopped, took her glasses off, and laid them down.

"No, Sam," she said. "You want to know what would help? It would help if you would just sit there and be quiet and let me finish this collar."

"Okay," I said. I moved off the bed and went quietly out of the room.

"Sam," I heard, just as I closed the door. I looked back inside. Ginny had turned in her chair and now faced me. "I didn't mean leave. I meant stay—just not so many questions."

I was sitting cross-legged on the floor, hunched over the phone, speaking to Lucy. It was midnight. The windows were pitched high; cool air swept through the house. Mikey had been released after questioning—no arrest had been made. Lucy, poor kid, had been stuck with the enormous task of explaining to him that I'd slept on the couch. She told him that I had been too tired to drive home after taking Celia to the airport. This, in fact, had been more or less the case, but Mikey needed some convincing.

"Then what happened?" I asked Lucy.

"Then there was the usual fighting and yelling," she said. "He's at the club now."

"Who yelled? Who fought?"

"I did most of the return yelling. Mikey was more on the offensive. But remember, it's me who went out on him."

"You admitted it?"

"Of course I didn't admit it. I told him that if he hadn't been imprisoned, you wouldn't have slept on the couch. Therefore it was his fault. And of course I failed to mention any of the important details about you and me. God, I'm getting sick of lying. It's such *work*."

"What do you want to do instead?"

"Leave him."

"Do you mean that? Tell me, Lucy. It matters."

"No, I guess not," she said after a long while. "Do you hate me? Look, I know you're going to get disgusted with me at some point. Now wouldn't be too soon."

"How about instead I come over tomorrow night while Mikey's at the club, kidnap you, and have my way with you?"

"That would be wonderful, Sam, but I think the best I can do at the moment is give you a maybe."

I looked for Ginny and found her stretched like a cat in the long hammock, her face tilted away from me. She was staring off into her favorite spot above the horizon, an area just to the left of the Little Dipper, where I had searched many unsuccessful times for an interesting star that was the reason for her attention.

"Finish the shirt?" I asked.

"Yeah."

"Couldn't sleep?"

"There's an eclipse tonight," Ginny said.

"Balzac wrote *Cousin Bette* in six weeks. You can be sure he wasn't sleeping much. I understand that Handel wrote the *Messiah* all night long. And of course you know about Van Gogh. Insomniacs do great things, Ginny."

"What time is it? The moon is scheduled to disappear at one-thirty."

We waited, me on the grass and Ginny slung out in her hammock. And then it happened, like a moment of sorcery; the moon shrank back into a dark cloud. I had seen an eclipse before, but I was amazed anyway; I felt enchanted by stars, by sky, by galaxies and gravity. I was ready now to believe anything about earth and light. I could believe that the sun was guided by a chariot, that lightning was thrown like a spear. I didn't dare make a sound. I stayed silent, alert, still. The moon became a thin piece of lunar white against a long black sky.

"I don't think I can stay here anymore," Ginny said.

"Here where?"

"This house. This city. I want to leave, but then I think that's exactly what Mom did after Dad died. And look how much good it did her."

"She sounds as though she's pleased with her life. More or less."

We'd received a letter, two postcards, and a box of saltwater taffy from a beach town in northern California. She signed her last message, "Love and happiness, Mom."

"You could start something new here," I said. "You could move house, get a new job. Go to school if you want."

"It doesn't matter what else I do or where I work or live. As long as I'm in L.A. I'll be Ginny who works at Eli's. I mean, that's how I feel."

"Move back east, then? Or to the Midwest, where no one knows you. You'll just be Ginny with cameras around her neck. Ginny with the light meter."

"Yeah," she said. "You're nice to say that."

I'd been rocking the hammock for her, swinging it gently backward and forward. I stopped now, steadying it.

"When the police came, what did you say, Ginny?"

"I wasn't with him," she said. "I told them that."

"Lucy was with him, wasn't she?"

"Yes, probably. Eli's motorcycle was parked at the restaurant, so they figure he must have gone off with somebody. They figure whoever it was killed him or knows who did."

"You didn't tell them—"

"No," Ginny said. She looked uncomfortable.

"Who else saw her with him?"

"Nobody," Ginny said. She looked at me. "I'm sure no one else saw."

TWENTY ONE

▪ ▪ ▪

The night Eli died, Ginny and Eli had been together as usual after the club had closed, the workday ending with dawn. Ginny sat on a bar stool, studying the account books, trying to find an error Eli was sure existed somewhere within his hundreds of scrawled numbers. Her uniform, replaced by a pair of jeans cropped at the knee and an overlong T-shirt, lay in a heap on the stool next to her. Thursday nights she waitressed. Fridays was a split shift. Saturday it was the club exclusively. She knew every square foot, every procedure of the place—which refrigerators needed scrubbing, which chairs needed a bolt tightened, which spotlights could use new filters. The club was empty except for a porter named Hector, who was polishing the floors. The buzz of his electric broom sounded vaguely in the distance and then stopped altogether. He dragged the machinery into a closet and called out goodnight as he left.

"Hector needs a new one of those," Ginny said, glancing

238

up. "Also a raise. He's been here nine months and not a dime increase."

"Fine," Eli said. He stood between the serving bar and the dance floor, in the spot the barmen worked. A tea towel hung over his shoulder; he'd swapped his contact lenses for glasses. He studied the long rows of gin, vodka, rum, whiskey, ouzo, tequila. "Did you know that champagne was invented by the Benedictine monk Dom Pierre Perignon, who was the head honcho at Saint Peter's Abbey in Hautvillers in eastern France?" he said, coming to where Ginny concentrated on her numbers.

"Found it," she announced, using an eraser against the page.

Eli watched her record the correction in the ledger book. He waited for her to finish and then said, "He was blind, so he had a heightened sense of taste and smell. This is 1690. At the time wine bottles were stopped with a piece of wood wrapped in hemp and dipped in olive oil. The dom realized that the bubbles in wine would never stay unless the bottles were more tightly sealed. He got the idea for corks from two Spanish monks who stopped in for the night at his abbey."

"Uh-huh," Ginny said, punching the buttons on the calculator again. "Let me just add this one more time."

"It was an alchemist in the Middle Ages who discovered the distillation process. He was trying to figure out a way to transform ordinary metal into gold. I bet you didn't know that."

"Nope," Ginny said.

Eli reached into a refrigerated cabinet beneath the bar and drew out champagne, a big dark bottle. He opened it with a tremendous bang, the cork flying skyward. Ginny looked up, surprised; she dropped her pencil. Eli poured the champagne into two tulip glasses. He was drunk already, but with tiredness, not alcohol. He handed a glass to Ginny, holding his own gently, with appreciation.

"I want to toast the best friend I ever had," he said, clinking his glass against hers.

She looked at him, leaning like a wave toward her, the man

with whom she'd fought and worked, negotiated and settled, whom she had cared for and neglected, made secrets with and kept secrets from. She held his eyes for a long while. It was somehow determined just then, on that random night of their working and being together, that she would be part of him forever. Their union, however unable to be named, had a quality to it. Ginny lifted her glass to her lips in a slow but sure gesture.

"Someday, when some other man has you, I'll have to kill myself," Eli said.

"Maybe there won't be some other man."

He brought himself close to her and then stopped, hesitating, careful now. He moved back, his fingers grazing her elbow, wrist, palm. He let her go and then stared at her. She waited, suddenly worried that she had said something wrong. She had heard stories of this, long friendships that derailed like a train, vanishing in wreckage before disbelieving eyes.

"Ginny," Eli said. "You're too good for me. And too young. In a few years you might not even say hello to me on the street."

"I wouldn't say hello to you now," Ginny said, smiling at him.

I was lying on the couch, listening. Ginny finished the story and went to the kitchen for something to drink. The armchair where she'd been sitting had patchwork on the seat cushion. An ashtray, balanced on the torn left sleeve of the armpiece, held a half-dozen cigarettes, all with the faded mark of her lipstick.

She came back from the kitchen with a glass of water and a couple of hayfever tablets.

"Eli walked me to the car, and there was Lucy in the parking lot," she said. "She'd fallen asleep waiting for him. You should have seen his face. I thought he'd pop."

"What did she do?"

"I don't know. She was asleep. I got in my car and took a dose of these." She swallowed the pills, making a face. "Driving home, I was completely wasted. How would I know that champagne and Allereze would mix like that?"

"So you don't know where they went?"

She shook her head. "I didn't ask Eli what he was going to do. He'd been pretty private lately, and when I saw Lucy in the parking lot I thought maybe that was why. Now I'm not so sure."

"What do you mean, he'd been private?" I asked.

"Just that he'd been keeping to himself more, and I think he'd been hassled by some of the principals from other clubs. Eli was one of the few independents I know of; most other clubs are owned by groups. There'd been a lot of pressure on him to sell the club to them."

"You mean to the Mafia?"

"What's the Mafia? It's not guys in slick hair and brown suits anymore, Sam."

"But you think these guys might have been out to get him?"

"Not 'out to get him.' God, you really have a cowboy-and-injun mentality. I'm just saying that Eli had pissed off a very big couple of guys. That's all. He refused to sell the club or form any partnerships, other than with that idiot Mikey. To top it all, you want to know what he did in the beginning of the summer as a joke? *As a joke* he released a hundred lab rats in the kitchen of a club a mile down the road."

"I heard about that," I said.

"Who'd you hear from? Mikey? I knew it," Ginny said.

"Where did Eli get lab rats?"

Ginny shrugged. She said, "The only thing I know is that every time people pressured him to accept some kind of deal, he always refused and then pulled one of these pranks. One time he paid all the dancers in a club not to show up. Another time he disguised himself as a health inspector. Stupid, yes, but that's the kind of stuff he did. And nobody liked him any better for it. One night, when I first started doing the costumes for the Red Room, five guys walked in, all in suits, all in white shirts with the buttons bursting below their necks. They each had one beer, paid for it; for all I know they tipped the barman. Then they stood everyone in the center of the club and systematically broke every window, every glass, bottle, lamp, picture frame, you name it. Didn't touch a soul. Didn't say anything. Just tore the place to ribbons and then left, calmly as you please. Eli never told me why. And you know what else? It never made the papers. Not a mention."

"What about the night he was killed—anything strange happen that night?"

"Just that when we came out of the club, there was Lucy. They have a pretty complicated history; maybe they'd started something up again. Who knows? Last thing I remember was him bending over Lucy's car, looking at her through the open window. You know, I used to think he was such a jerk, but that morning I would have done anything to be the woman in the car, the one he was waking kind of carefully."

"Ginny . . ."

"I'm fine; I'm getting over it all," she said, a little too quickly to be believable. She got up. "I'd better go to bed. New job tomorrow. I can't say I'm excited about working at a fish house, but the tips are supposed to be good."

Now I was the one who couldn't sleep. I sat in my couch bed, making out images in the dark living room. A clutter of knickknacks, tall baskets stuffed with dried flowers, stacks of yarn, papers in piles. The bookshelves were filled with everything but books: flower vases, a cookie tin, garden tools, an umbrella, a radio, wire hangers, a sweatshirt, a clock.

I tried not to think about Eli and Lucy. There was no point in guessing at what their relationship had become. Lucy had told me that things were long over between them, and I had to believe that. But what I couldn't believe was that she didn't know anything more than she claimed about Eli's death.

Beneath Ginny's door I could see a shallow stream of light, flickering from the television. The news carried a lot of information about Eli's life, the club, his various dealings. Ginny had been watching all the reports, looked for any mention of murder in the papers. There really wasn't any evidence. There were lots of fingerprints all over the house, too many different sets to make a case. The blow dryer, of course, was scrubbed clean from being in the hot tub. What the police had was his body, with a very bad bruise across one shin. And the fact that he'd practically shaved his head and therefore would never use a dryer. If he'd been anyone else, there would be no investigation. But Eli had been a figure, known by lots of people for all sorts of different reasons, and so the death, which would not otherwise have earned more than a mention, had become a possible murder that fed the media. Which Ginny now suffered from.

I got up, pulled on my jeans, and tapped at the bedroom door. I waited, but there wasn't any answer. I knocked again, then pushed open the door. There, standing before a long mirror, was Ginny. She had on earphones connected to the television, which explained why she didn't hear me. On the screen, a news report showed pictures of Eli's house, which looked even more impressive on film. Ginny had a handkerchief in one hand, a ball of cotton in the other. She'd been trying to take off makeup and stop herself from crying at the same time.

I went to where she stood, took the earphones, the cotton from her. I switched off the television and placed myself behind her, turning her shoulders so that we were both looking at her reflection in the mirror. She was a tall stalk of a girl. Her legs sprang from her hips in two thin bows. Her pelvis was quite visible. Her stomach was scooped out, and her tailbone easy to see, even beneath her shorts.

I ran a finger beneath her wet eyes. "Part of why you feel bad is because you are so tired," I said.

"I never sleep," she said. "It's like a curse I have. As punishment for being so generally awful, I am sentenced to a life of acute awareness."

"If we went away for a while," I said, "it might help you feel better."

"Sam, you keep thinking I *want* to feel better. But I don't. I don't want to get over it or through it or whatever you are supposed to do with sadness."

"Eli wouldn't want you to be this sad," I said.

"He doesn't get a choice."

In the mirror she was so frail-looking. Her voice contrasted with her reflection, and for a moment I thought that she felt the same way I did, that she knew she could not continue the momentum of her grief. She would eventually have to give it up, or it would hollow out whatever was left of her. But for now she was capable of owning that sadness, of maintaining it intact alongside all the rest of her life's disappointments. Right now she could do anything. I half expected her to wheel around and fix me with a look that commanded my exit.

She surprised me by being quiet. By letting me hug her. She looked down to the floor, avoiding the mirror. Her hair drooped forward, and I brought back a handful and let it slide across my palm. I put a finger on her back, found a vertebra, and then counted upward from vertebra to vertebra, defining her sharp architecture. I stopped when I got around to her collarbone, which was a decisive ledge above a sunken shadow of skin. I turned her around and held her close to me.

"I'm very ugly," Ginny said. "I am afraid of how ugly I am."

Her ribs were so tightly sprung against her skin that for a moment I was frightened too. Not of her ugliness, because she was not ugly at all. She was a rangy beauty with spirit and grace. But I was afraid of what might happen to her now that she had lifted away all the blurry distinctions of flesh and fat. What more could she eliminate in herself, if all of the physical molding had been reduced to a minimum? I touched her chin and she looked at me. I thought I saw something in her face, a look of credence and solace. And I wondered what I could ever have done to win from her even a moment of such surety.

"You are beautiful," I told her. She began to speak, but I hushed her. I moved away and really looked at her, at her skeletal frame, her tower of legs and arms, her firm and serious shoulders. "You are beautiful, and someday a man you love will tell you so, over and over again."

I spent the next day rounding up work for what remained of my Boston business and keeping Celia up to date on the latest events, which she'd been monitoring from New York. It was one of those lazy days that seemed to stretch forever, and I was relieved when Ginny came back from her new waitressing job, which somehow meant that the day had concluded.

"I smell like a fishing boat," she said. She held her arms away from her sides, looking down at herself as though she'd been contaminated.

"Shark? Or swordfish. Definitely a saltwater variety."

"If I still reek after this bath, you have my permission to roll me in cornmeal or set me on ice in a window."

Ginny soaked in the tub and I watched a movie involving a lost ship struggling in a storm. The television screen was filled with wild ocean, torn sails, and a panicked crew. At the first commercial break Lucy called.

"I think the captain is to blame," she said. "I think he steered them wrong."

"They might have hit an iceberg—no, that's *The Titanic*. What's the one where they hit a spacecraft?"

"They took Mikey away," Lucy said.

I turned off the television. "When?"

"After supper. The kids were awake."

"Lucy, honey," I said.

She said, "They watched the whole thing, uniforms, handcuffs, and all."

In the morning we left the kids with Nella, who came with another girl, Alice. Alice was Nella's lab partner, whatever that is, in biology class. They arrived at the doorstep with big textbooks, folders of notes, detailed, time-consuming drawings that showed the inner workings of various organisms. Alice was a tiny girl, but her extensive orthodontia caused her grin to be something of a spectacle and made her seem taller than her five feet. Nella, in a leotard and jogging suit bottoms, was a perfect replica of Lucy. From behind the two women looked very much alike, except that Nella was narrower and her hair was done in a long braid that divided her, shoulder to buttocks, into two perfect sides.

"If they get out of hand, confine them to the basement," Lucy said, nodding at the twins. They were leaning their shoulders into each other and pushing football fashion, making football grunts. In Paul's arm was Stacy's doll, which was serving for the moment as a ball. "Really, Nella, you aren't going to get any work done otherwise."

"This one is so *cute*," Alice said, grinning at Stacy, who sat in her lap, a biology textbook across her chubby knees. "Someday when I have a child, I want her to be just like Stacy."

"My daddy makes chocolate out of this," Stacy said, pointing to an illustration in the anatomy chapter.

"Oh, I don't think so," Alice said, laughing. "What an imagination she has!"

Lucy sighed, gathering a Dunlop bag, a cooler. "Back by seven," she said.

Already the sun was strong, warming the driveway so you could feel the heat through your sneakers. I took the front wheels off the bicycles and fitted the bikes into the back of the Cadillac. Lucy made room for the rest of our gear.

"I need a lot of exercise," she said. "A simple gym workout won't counter this stress. I need miles behind me, exhausted muscles, possibly overexposure to the sun. I need to sweat out every drop of water in me and replace it with Evian."

"Oh, I see, this is more of a transfusion than a bike ride."

"Exactly," she said.

We cycled many miles north, along a path by the ocean. Most of these miles I spent several lengths behind Lucy, who could keep a pace. We stopped in a place where tourists strolled along the boardwalk, licking ice cream, buying T-shirts. I was exhausted. I told Lucy we should get some lunch, but she said no, she couldn't eat. Instead we sat on the cool part of a stone wall, passing a jug of water between us. Our bikes leaned against each other, dusty from the long ride.

"Do you mean we have to do that *again?*" I asked.

Lucy nodded.

"Would our circulatory systems forgive us if we took a taxi home?"

She smiled, gulped water, squeezed my hand. A roller skater passed us, her legs swooping from side to side, her back bare except for the tiny string of a bikini top.

"Don't stare like that," Lucy said. "I already know what you're thinking."

"What am I thinking?" I said. I pulled my shirt off, using it like a towel to wipe the sweat from my neck.

"That I'm six years older than you. And that she doesn't have any stretch marks."

"Oh that," I said. I smiled. "I'm always thinking *that.*"

"Don't tease. I hate it when you tease."

"Who's teasing?" I said. I leaned my leg against hers.

"I mean it."

I touched her chin and turned it so she was facing me. "You want to know what I was really thinking? I was really thinking that I'd like to settle in Los Angeles, if anyone manages really to do that."

"Sam . . ." she said.

"The music scene is very good here, and I think with the blues festival coming up it's a good opportunity to start establishing a reputation," I said. "Boston is only a tiny city, and I can barely stand New York. It makes sense for me to be here now. You know, it's funny, but I feel for the first time in my life that I can really do something with myself. Not a moment too soon, I suppose."

"You're going to do great," Lucy said. But she said it as though I were a terminal patient and just didn't know it yet.

There was a silence, and I kissed her.

"I told Mikey that when this whole thing is over, I'll go to a marriage counselor with him," she said, pulling away.

We watched the sun move toward the ocean. Soon it would be evening and Lucy would be home feeding the children. She would wait for the lawyer to call. Or Mikey. She would wait until they told her she could fetch her husband from the police station. And she and Mikey would drive home together, her telling him how worried she was for him and not telling him where she'd spent the afternoon. Under these conditions she would attend counseling?

"I'm not sure I understand why you would see a counselor," I said finally. "The point of counseling is to be honest."

"I want to be honest," Lucy said. "I think I used to be."

I braced myself for what would come next. I looked at her arms, thin beneath the short sleeves of a tennis shirt. I looked at her thighs, smooth and square; at her face, which was suddenly new to me, as though there had never been the hundreds of kisses or the details of her beneath my fingers.

"Sam," she said, "when it is all over, will you believe, will you *remember*, that I was very, very fond of you?"

"Fond of me, Lucy?" I said. "You're *fond* of me. How nice. How nice that I inspire in you a feeling of fondness."

"Please, Sam . . ."

She kissed my neck, my jaw, my throat, my chin. She was suddenly all over me, holding me tighter than she ever had.

"I know you don't believe me, Sam, but I didn't use to have affairs."

"I don't believe you," I said. I laughed—I have no idea why—and kissed her hair. "When exactly do we begin this ending?"

"Soon. Not yet." She looked at me for a long time. "Oh, God, now what am I doing? Forget I said anything."

I nodded, keeping my arms around her. There would be a time when she would tell me it was over, I was sure. But I had a feeling that that time was far off, and this afternoon there was only the sun pricking my back and Lucy's long body next to me. There were miles of bike path back to the car, and the two of us were exhausted. The sun was going down, and all I knew just then was that it was time for us to go home.

"He doesn't have an alibi," Lucy said. "The kids were asleep. The babysitter was asleep. He wasn't seen by anyone until he showed up at your house. And some of your neighbors are willing to testify that he was in a rage."

"Lucy," I said, "what can I do? Tell me anything at all I can do."

"The lawyer says that if the prosecution finds out I was at Eli's house, they'll drop all other suspects and try to get a conviction on Mikey. It'll look like Mikey went to Eli's, found me with him, killed Eli, and then went to the house of my other lover to kill him."

"It's circumstantial," I said. "It won't stick."

"It won't stick if all they prove is that Mikey was at Eli's house. But if they find out I was there—well, things could be different," she said. "They'll call it a crime of passion, not pre-meditated but certainly second-degree."

"If you were at the scene of the crime, then why can't *you* tell the police that it wasn't Mikey?" I asked.

"I just can't," Lucy said, after some hesitation.

"Why not?"

"First of all, because I don't know that it *wasn't* Mikey," she said. "I was at 'the scene,' if you must call it that, but I didn't see what happened. Quite frankly, Mikey doesn't know with a hun-dred-percent certainty that it wasn't *me*. He takes my word for it."

"And you take his?"

"He didn't do it," Lucy said. "This was a professional job. Whoever did it had no idea I was there—that's why it went wrong. I hid my car just in case Mikey came around. The murderer didn't bother to look for it, but the police found tire tracks matching my car, which you might have noticed is no longer in the driveway, because they've impounded it. When they asked Mikey who was driving the car, he said he was. He told them that his car needed work—which he proved just by showing it to them—and so he'd taken my car. How is that for a good husband?"

"Lucy—"

"Lucky for us your neighbors can't tell white from pale blue. Lucky, too, that I let Mikey get me that stupid car, which I detest. I could have been driving the Buick. What would we have done then? What if I hadn't been so afraid that Mikey would find me and left the car in the driveway? See how close Mikey and I are to getting caught, when we never even did anything? See how close I was to *dead*?"

"Lucy, please—"

"No, Sam. Don't try to make it better. Just let's not talk about it anymore."

■ ■ ■

When I got home Ginny was watching the coverage of the investigation on the stinko channel, which had been doing a fairly thorough job because it gave Rudolph Sill the opportunity to interview strippers and up his ratings. Ginny made hate noises at Sill. Her face went white whenever Eli's name was mentioned.

I cut tomatoes, peeled carrots, sliced radishes, tore lettuce, added a Dijon dressing from a bottle. I'd received a long letter from Pelzer, which I read while grilling two cheese-and-onion sandwiches. I brought it all into the living room.

"Supper," I said, taking a seat next to Ginny. She didn't move. I bit into my sandwich, pushing an onion back between the bread. "Letter from Arnold. His parents felt so guilty for not visiting him in the hospital that they bought him a whole new set of drums. He sends his regards."

"Mmm," she mumbled. I handed her the letter; she dropped it in her lap but kept her eyes on the television. In the corner of the screen, above the newscaster's head, was a small photo of Eli. He was smiling. His hair was the color of wet sand, and he wore a tie.

Ginny said, "They're flaking out on this investigation."

"If you have ideas, tell the police."

"I can't tell them, Sam. Don't even talk about it. This is much worse than you think. I was talking to this guy named Bernard—his partner and him own Pal & Co. You heard of it? A gay place? So anyway, Bernard says to me that he thinks it was a hire from out of town and that someone here paid for Eli's murder. Mikey is the fall guy. I have to agree, Sam, that it does look that way."

"Mikey hasn't made a statement yet. He'll come up with some way of defending himself."

"If he tells the cops who he thinks might have done it, he'll be killed," Ginny said. "Even if he tells them and he's wrong, he'll still probably be killed. Whoever murdered Eli has decided that Mikey is the best one to pin it on. They could have picked

251

anyone—they might have chosen me at one time, but somehow I got lucky and they're happy to let Mikey be the one. Basically, he's a sitting duck."

"Then we have to testify. We can't let the guy go to jail."

"No," Ginny said. She looked exhausted. Every muscle in her face was tensed. "We do nothing. Listen to me—if you come forward, you will bring it all down on top of Mikey. If he's smart, he's hoping he gets not guilty due to insufficient evidence. But if he says anything to point the finger elsewhere —if they even *think* he's breathed a word—he's a dead man. Maybe not immediately, but soon enough. Sam, he's got four kids. A wife. There will be no end of horrors for him if any of us talk."

"He's not smart enough to figure this out."

"People get pretty smart when their lives are at stake," Ginny said.

Here is what Lucy told me.

Eli had wakened her by touching her cheek with his finger. When her eyes opened, he smiled, stood back, looked at her.

"Tell me to leave if you want," Lucy had said to him. It was a night like any other; the same taillights slid along the freeway, the same colors lit the boulevards. Ginny's Oldsmobile made the same sound it always did, idling at a traffic light outside the club. Eli waited until the light changed and Ginny drove off before getting into the car with Lucy.

"I never watch a space rocket take off, not even on television," he said. They sat close together in the car, hands over hands and knees and thighs. "I think about every sound and rumble, what every hiss means, convinced that the thing is going to explode. And then I think that my pessimism will cause it to explode, and I think about those astronauts and how I'm killing them with my imagination. I don't think about

Bobby, because if I do, I'm sure somehow I'll jinx him. I don't think about you because—"

"Because I'm already jinxed," Lucy said.

They left the freeway, turning up a steep hill, leaving the city below. The cars, the giant buildings, receded, becoming smaller and smaller. Lucy pushed the car into a low gear, climbing the steep grade. Farther on she looked over her shoulder, seeing trucks coming up from the orange groves, the harbor lights now tiny like bulbs on a Christmas tree, miles and miles of low, flat rooftops. Beverly Hills was a toy below them. They were above all that now. Eli put his hand to Lucy's cheek, and she kissed his palm.

"I have the feeling you get at just the wrong moment, when you realize that what you're dreaming is a dream," he was saying. "And you don't want to wake."

They drove to his house without even a question.

Lucy sat on the bed. Eli stood at the opposite end of the room, puffing a last bit of cigarette before stamping it out on the bottom of his shoe. He wore a pair of Levi's fraying at the cuffs, green sneakers, no socks. His jacket, once very elegant, was old now. Lucy recognized it from long ago, before he'd torn the lining, worn out the sleeves.

"It's good to see you," he said after a long silence.

Lucy slid her shirt over her shoulders, kicked off her sandals. "I guess you know I've been spending time with Sam." She looked down at her body, brushing a piece of lint from her stomach. "Mikey's got some outside interests."

"Don't bet on it," Eli said, stepping very slowly toward her. He shrugged his jacket from his shoulders, knelt before her, and touched her knees with his hands. He moved closer, letting her wrap her legs around him, letting her arms browse dreamily over his own, her fingers work his shirt buttons, sweep over his chest, around his neck, through his hair.

"Bobby looks more and more like you," she said. She held her hand against his stomach. The moon, shining through the skylight just over their head, was heavy and yellow. Lucy imagined them naked beneath the sky. "He's like a time bomb waiting to go off."

"Tell me about him," Eli said. "Every inch and detail."

"He's got your cat grin," she said. "He's got your wide feet."

"What's his voice like?"

"A little boy's voice."

"He has freckles like you," Eli said.

"You have freckles."

"But he has your eyes."

"How do you know?" Lucy asked. "You only saw him once."

"I remember."

Lucy exhausted every bit of information she could about Bobby, describing the things he'd say, what he liked to do. She did imitations of him, talked about his friends, the TV shows he liked. He'd been the sort of baby who refused to be weaned, she told Eli. Piglet was his favorite stuffed toy. He chipped a tooth on a sled the winter before, during a trip to Lake Tahoe. They fell asleep talking, and when Lucy woke she saw Eli standing at the window.

"What's the matter?" she asked.

"Nothing. The pool lights are off."

She was sleepy; her eyes were closed. She said, "Come back to bed."

"I just want to see if someone is down there," Eli said.

She heard him go outside; he called Ginny's name. There was the sound of someone swimming in the pool, of the whirlpool being turned on. After a while she got up. She considered joining Eli in the pool, but she was still very tired, too tired, and so instead she went back to bed. She fell asleep dreaming of Eli gliding through the water, of Bobby playing in the swimming pool, of all her children making their brave dives.

"Anyway, that's what happened," Lucy told me. She was angry, and I knew it. She pushed her sunglasses onto her forehead and squinted at me impatiently. We were in the rose garden, a small bit of landscaping to the side of her big house. She had delivered the entire story while pruning a bush of mauve-and-crimson flowers. She hadn't looked at me once. The only break in her conversation occurred when she bent over to drop more stems on the pile at her feet.

"So when you found him, he was already dead."

"Yes. But that was hours later," she said. "Look, Sam, I've told you now. He went outside looking for someone. He didn't come back. I think he thought it was your sister."

We looked at each other. Then Lucy turned back to the rose bush.

"Thank you, I just had to know," I said. I was relieved. Lucy couldn't have invented the story. There was no way she could know about the pool lights or how Ginny used to sneak into his pool at night.

She glanced at me sharply, then asked, "Why trust me? You know perfectly well how duplicitous I am."

"Oh, Lucy."

"Before you came over here today, you were thinking that I might have killed Eli. Admit it."

When I didn't reply, she said, "I have a lot of watering to do."

"I'm sorry, Lucy. I guess my imagination got the better of me."

"I'm very busy . . ."

"I'll sweep the drive," I said.

"It's okay. I'll do it later."

"You must need something done. Cut the firewood? Dig the 'taters? Slop the hogs? I don't blame you for being mad at me, but let me make it up."

"Really, Sam, I'm not in the mood," she warned. She bent toward the bush, inspecting the petals of a flower. Her shorts were of the jogging variety. Her hands, in gardening gloves, were enormous, seeming to belong to a body other than the one in sheer nylon shorts. I followed her to the driveway, where she deposited a mound of thorny stems in a garbage can.

"I don't see why it matters so much to you anyway. You hardly knew him," she said, tugging on a long cord of green hose. "What you are forgetting, Sam, is how fond I was of Eli. If I'd thought there was anyone else out there that night, I would have called the police. But the only person I saw swimming in the pool was Eli."

"And you didn't see him get out?"

"No, I didn't. I admired his stroke, and then returned to the pillow. I was exhausted, Sam, and I'm getting exhausted now."

A silence fell between us. I watched Lucy maneuver the hose over a bed of small flowers. Then I remembered what Eli had said about how dark the pool was without lights.

"Poor Eli. He probably didn't know what hit him, it was so dark," I said.

"I guess not," Lucy said.

"Was the blow dryer still in the socket when they found him?"

Lucy dropped the hose. She looked at me a little strangely, then shrugged her shoulders.

"Of course," she said.

She turned away from me. I did not talk and she did not talk. And when I left, it was as though somehow I'd gone from being on the inside of her life to belonging way at the sidelines.

Which was fine, I decided, driving home.

TWENTY TWO

■ ■ ■

I had thought that I knew Lucy very well. After we made love, when I was lying beside her, I felt that we were very close. I couldn't imagine that there were things she would not tell me. When she spoke so openly about her faults—"I have a disease that prevents me from saving money"; "I am wretchedly jealous of younger and more beautiful women, which means I essentially have no friends"; "I hate sports—this aerobics stuff is just a prophylactic for obesity"—I thought this showed honesty. Just a week before, she had opened the front door wearing a nightdress that must have been her mother's, a facial mask over her nose and cheeks, and I had thought that it was a sign that our love had grown deep enough to allow such casualness.

But Lucy was very good at making a person feel that he was important to her without that's being the least bit the case. She was studied in a certain type of elusiveness, which was difficult to spot because she seemed always to care. She had asked me around as often as she could. She had listened when I talked. She'd never complained about the time I took from her, never

minded where we went or where we didn't go. We had stuck
pretty close, and it was painful to realize that there had always
been such a gulf between us. They say that love is blind, but it
must be deaf too, because I could not hear all the lapses in what
she said to me, hadn't paid attention to the careful way she
managed me, the same way she managed any of the other
complexities in her life.

But now she said that she had seen Eli swimming in the
pool when the pool lights were out, which I knew, from Eli,
was impossible.

When I saw Mikey he seemed smaller somehow. His skin had a
gray hue, and his hair was dirty, falling over his forehead in
greasy wisps. We were in Eli's office, which Mikey had adopted
as his own. The room had two chairs, an overhead light, a
table. There was a desk in one corner, and a filing cabinet. The
tile was the color of sea foam. The walls were old and many
times painted. Mikey sat in a chair, smoking.

I said, "I know what is happening. I can't think of what to
do."

"That's two of us," Mikey said.

"How is Lucy taking it?" I asked, as though I didn't know.

"She's pretty tense these days," he said, looking away.

"She's probably very worried for you," I said.

"Worried," he repeated, as though he weren't sure what that
word meant.

We were awkward and quiet with each other. Mikey
seemed distracted, as though he wanted to get back to whatever work there was to be done. Coming here had been a whim
on my part. Perhaps not the best idea.

After a long time, he said, "Tell Lucy not to do a thing.
Don't act like you don't see her. You want to talk about being
worried. I spend nights imagining what will happen if she says
a word to anyone."

"She won't—"

"She's obviously said something to you. Listen now. Don't talk. I know and you know. That's one too many. Now get up out of that chair, and when you leave, talk like we were discussing how she's getting along. On the way out the door say, 'I had the car looked at and it's running fine now.' Say, 'You owe me a hundred for the repairs.' Got it, Sam?"

"Yes," I said.

And then I said something I hadn't expected to say. The words came faster than I could stop them. They were more deliberately and surely spoken than I would have intended if I had thought about speaking before I did.

"You think Lucy did it, don't you?"

"Car repairs," Mikey repeated. "And nothing else."

Ginny was fired from her restaurant job for failing to report a waiter who'd stolen six salmon fillets. She thought this was unfair, and when her defense got her nowhere she cursed at the management so much and for so long she was pushed out of the restaurant and had her knapsack thrown after her.

It sounded bad, but this was positive improvement, I was sure. For a moment, you see, she had not been thinking about Eli.

"It's a sign you're not supposed to be working in the service industry," I suggested when she returned home, fuming. "I have several checks coming from Boston, so mellow out on the money front."

"Pisses me off," Ginny said. She had a refrigerator packing box that she'd found down the road. Tomorrow was trash day, and she rummaged through the house, collecting garbage. She pitched magazine after magazine into the tall box, dragged it five feet, and pitched more. She tossed out unopened sweepstakes offers, empty bottles, paper towel rolls, dried-out potting soil, cereal boxes, Styrofoam take-out tubs, film tubes, pictures she didn't like, last week's *TV Guide*. "My job was waitress, not cop."

"That's right," I said. I was taking up the carpet. Ginny and I had decided to remove every bit of green shag in the place, and I was on my knees, tools in hand, overalls stretched over my shoulders. "But I honestly think your waitressing days are numbered."

"If they want security they can pay for security. Nobody at three bucks an hour has to turn in criminals."

"It's not easy to start something new, and I know the competition for photographers is very tough. But Ginny, I have a feeling that if you got out there and really made a case for yourself—"

"The assistant manager didn't like me. Typical—the manager hires you and then some assistant schmuck kicks you out on your ass."

"A newspaper might take you on, for example. Or you could go to some sort of art school."

"The assistant had a face like a truck. The guy was a dog."

"Did you know there's a hardwood floor beneath this?" I asked.

"No kidding?" she said. She let go of the box and in an instant was beside me, hovering over the spot where I was kneeling. Beneath carpet foam, in the square foot I'd pulled up, was pine.

"Oh my God, Sam," she said. "You've made a discovery. You're like Columbus." She tapped the wooden floor with her knuckles. "Do you think we'll recognize the place without Dunkin Donuts bags and Carpet Fresh all over? Do you think you can hold that pose just a moment while I get the camera?"

I took up the floor in the bathroom using a hammer and chisel. I bought paint and rollers, spirit and brushes. I tightened the toilet seat so it didn't move on the bowl, changed the washers in the sink. I bought a new shower curtain, put up a towel rack. I planted geraniums and tulips in a window box bought from a gardening center, feeding them with a mixture that prolonged flowering. I replaced broken door handles, fixed a cabinet drawer that was in need of repair. I hauled anything extra, broken, unidentifiable, or useless to the dump. I was attending to matters at home.

I phoned Mother.

"Ask Ginny to visit," I told her. "Have her come up for a few weeks, anything."

"Hello, Mother, how are you, Mother, so good to hear your voice, Mother. Sam, you're always in such a rush."

"I'm not rushing."

"You're practically panting. Do you miss me? I miss you."

"Yes, sure, Mom."

"Does Ginny miss me?"

"Terribly. I think you should have her come up right away."

"It's just a little cabin, but there is a room, tiny though it is . . ."

"Whatever," I said. "But insist."

The kitchen cabinets were sticky with roach killer and old spills. I cleaned them and I bought new tile, grout, caulking. I measured out the bathroom, unwound the molding strips. I did not stop except to eat. The house had become for me both a form of diversion and a focus. It reminded me to think about my family, and it kept me from thinking too much. I concentrated on one task at a time, measuring out my energy in work on floors, ceilings, light fixtures, plaster.

Celia called. "You don't think Lucy was *there*, do you?"

"I don't know, Celia. I'm laying tile."

"You don't think Mikey *did* it?"

"No," I said. "My adhesive will congeal if I don't get back to work."

"It couldn't have been him, I suppose, but *why*, Sam?"

"I don't know. But the timer has gone off and the tiles have been scored."

"I don't trust his lawyer," Celia said. "I had a long discussion with the fellow today and he didn't impress me. He seemed like just the type of shifty character Mikey was likely to hire."

"He'll do the best he can," I told her. "Can I remind you, Celia, that this adhesive was not a skim coat?"

"They're not looking for other suspects anymore. The lawyer won't talk about it, even to me!"

"Celia, I have to go."

"Why?"

"Because I have grout all over my hands."

"Sam, don't you hang up that phone!" she said. "Lucy won't return my calls; Mikey won't answer the phone. Why won't anyone talk to me!" She was yelling now. She was tired, and I could hear that tiredness even through the phone lines. "This lawyer isn't up to snuff. The police don't seem to be doing anything. I think they're all ready to let Mikey go to jail!"

"Celia, please—"

"Don't treat me like I'm some silly old lady. I'm not silly. This is my family. They are going to lock up my son-in-law, and I'm just not going to let them do it. I'm not going to let this shabby investigation come to a close. I'm calling the travel agent right now—"

I said, "Give it a few more days, please."

"—and then the lawyer. I'll file a countersuit that will break records."

"Celia," I said. "You've got to stay out of this."

"Why? Why must I? Does anyone other than me care if this man goes to jail?"

And then I said something I perhaps shouldn't have. I said it because I couldn't think of anything to stop her from doing exactly what she planned. I said, "Celia, Lucy may have been involved."

"Lucy did it?"

"I didn't say that. I said she might have been involved."

There was silence at the other end of the phone. A long silence and then a whisper.

"Why would my daughter be involved?" she asked in a calm tone that gave away nothing. She could have been asking anything—where to get a good lobster, the best place to shop for patio furniture, the temperature of the ocean, which newspaper I preferred.

"Bobby is Eli's kid. There's a lot of history between Lucy and him. I don't know what went on, but she was there that night."

"Bobby!"

"That's true. If you don't believe me, ask her. Ask her outright and come back and tell me if I'm wrong. Celia, I don't know what happened that night, but Lucy was there. And no matter how innocent she may be, no one's going to believe her. It'll look either like she did it or like she and Mikey did it together. We all have to stay quiet, I think."

Celia was repeating something, over and over again. I listened carefully, and then I could hear.

She said, "Dear God." She said, "Then we won't discuss this any further."

Ginny had her feet on the dashboard, a straw in her teeth. She'd cut holes in it like a flute and was blowing so that the straw made a noise.

"Was it this exit or the next?" I asked.

"Next one," she said. "Otherwise we'll end up in Malibu."

In the back seat were several boxes, my duffel bag, which I'd given to Ginny, and a sack of her own. Ginny was going to spend two weeks with Mother, who claimed to greatly enjoy fishing and the cabin by a lake that Van had picked for them.

"Are you going to marry Lucy?"

"Lucy already is married," I said. "A lot more married than you might think."

"Are you two quits?"

"Not quits, exactly."

"What are you going to do while I'm gone?"

"Well, you know the drain system in the house does need repairing."

"Oh God, will you stop with the fix-it crap? You *could* go with me to visit Mom," Ginny said. "God knows when you'll see her again."

"I'll visit soon," I told her.

"That's what you always used to say. You know, someday it won't be so easy to get all of us together. When I get back I'm going to find a real job, get an apartment of my own with only my stuff in it and friends who come over sometimes for dinner . . ."

"Oh, so you will be eating then?"

"Sam, I eat now. I just don't eat what you want me to eat. You're just like Eli, worrying about every morsel I put in my mouth."

She took a Mounds bar from her knapsack and tore through the wrapper. "Toll booth," she announced, nodding at the sign.

I reached below the radio to where a sack of change nestled.

"Did you ever think that maybe Eli and you ought to have been, you know, *together?*" I said.

"We were together."

"You know what I mean." I tossed her our sack of change. "Find a quarter in there."

"Well, it wasn't exactly love at first sight," Ginny said. "And sometimes if you don't take up the chance to be romantic with a person, the chance leaves you."

"True enough," I said.

"Besides, I knew that I'd have to work with him later, and what if he did something really terrible to me and I'd have to see his face every day at work? I couldn't stand that. It wasn't a pride thing, but you hear horror stories, Sam. I read this play once where the guy tells his girlfriend he's going to rub her in butter and then make passionate love to her. He comes in with this tray of butter sticks and she lets him put it all over her. But then when she's all naked and her whole body is dripping with butter, he just leaves her like that. Walks right out the door. The next day she finds out he's steady with a cheerleader."

"What did she do?" I asked, slowing for the toll.

"Shot him with a gun," Ginny said. "Here's five dimes."

We collected her ticket at a window that had, I noticed, bullet-proof glass. I'd begun to notice things like that. The trains were being announced loudly and incomprehensibly over a speaker system. We exited through the door marked PLATFORM 3. Amid the great noise of the station, the train engines and people, calls from conductors and so many hurrying feet, Ginny turned to me. She kissed my cheek, a hard kiss, so I felt it afterward. She said, "Be careful, Sam."

And then she disappeared, ducking into one of the many silver train cars.

It all happened so quickly, I hadn't realized she was saying goodbye. I had encouraged her to leave, but now she was so suddenly gone. It seemed terrible to me. I had to find her again, say goodbye in some other way. I thought of how she had said, "Be careful." Be careful of what? It occurred to me that there were many ways to be careful; which one did she mean? I wanted to ask her; I wanted to hug her once more. But she was already inside the train with all the other passengers, who were busy shifting luggage onto seats and racks, dragging it along the narrow aisles. I could not find her among so many people. I could not make a sound loud enough for her to hear me. I walked along, looking through the windows. I leaned forward against the glass, using my hands to shade out light, and really searched. I went from car to car and back again. I checked the doorways, called her name. But an official-looking guy in a blue uniform was asking all visitors to leave the train, and I still hadn't spotted Ginny.

I wanted to find her so badly. I wanted to ask her this one question. On a day like this, when she was so clearly happy, optimistic, looking forward to her trip, I didn't want to bring up Eli's murder—but maybe she knew something that I ought to. In my mind, I replayed the way she'd said, "Be careful."

Now the station official was walking toward me, his shiny shoes articulating every step. I was holding open the doors as they were trying to close. He was calling out something, this man in the shoes. I was prying open the doors, pushing my body through, tripping over a conductor on the inside of the train, who was using one hand to push me back out, the other to work his walkie-talkie.

I ducked past him, jogged up an aisle, dodged a child, slapped the pushbutton on the door. The train was moving now, gaining speed. I entered another car, scanning the seats. I thought I'd found her in 45F, but that was a much older woman, one whose hair had looked the same. The conductor was after me. I was running through another car. I heard her call me just as a second conductor approached from the front.

"Ginny!" I was leaning over her now, one hand on the arm of her seat, the other on her shoulder, catching my breath.

"Jeez, Sam, what's the matter?"

"What am I supposed to be careful of?" I asked.

"God, I don't know. Getting clubbed by this guy behind you, I guess."

It was the man in shiny shoes.

"I've brought the medicine!" I yelled. "She forgot her pills!"

"It's true," Ginny said to the conductor. "Just the same, you can hit him if you want."

I rode with her as far as Santa Barbara. It took two hours,

during which we talked, played a game of miniature checkers in which all the pieces were held to the board by magnets. We drank Cokes, laughed at things I can't even remember. You can't erase the damage you have caused or hold back love once it's loose. But on a train going north you can let the landscape bleed together in greens and blues outside the window. You can forget for a moment. You can watch someone smile and think she's beautiful. You can be with her and miss her at the same time, and you can leave her on the train and take the memory with you. Keep it like a gift. Protect it from all the intrusions of coming days, the immediate crises that go on forever and rob you of that train ride, during which you didn't have to ask yourself if you were happy.

Lucy's Buick was parked outside the house. I found her out back, lying in Ginny's hammock. She was asleep or faking it. Her eyes were closed, her lips parted.

"You're a great friend," she said when I was close enough to smell the suntan lotion on her skin, the lemon scent of her hair. "You tell my mother something that I thought was private between us. Then you go running off."

"Here I am," I said. For all the heat of the afternoon, Lucy was spotless. Her creamy skin looked cool in a summer dress. She had a healthy flush to her face, but no sunburn. Seeing her now, her eyes still closed, her lips parted, looking almost asleep, I could see how much she resembled her mother. I could envision her at sixty, at seventy, striding through her life just like Celia did. They were survivors, these two. They were impenetrable and perhaps untrustworthy. But if you stuck by them, there was the promise they would save you from whatever it was they were always saving themselves from. And if you left them, you left them forever.

"I had to tell her, Lucy. She was practically chartering a flight."

"You didn't have to tell her *that*. You could have made something up."

"I'm not so good at making things up," I said.

She handed me a piece of paper on which was written "Shhh . . ." The paper was the sort that children use to learn to write.

"Came through my front door this morning," Lucy said. "Would you be scared?"

"A bit," I said, examining the note. "Where are the kids?"

"At home. Nella's watching them."

"You left the kids with Nella?"

"Yes. Mikey is at the club."

I sat on the hammock and took Lucy's hands in mine. "You aren't going to let Mikey go to jail," I said. "Are you?"

"It's not up to me, Sam," she said. She looked at me, eyes big, with their big doe lashes.

"You've messed up a lot in your life—I'm not being judgmental, I've done the same. But you are going to do this one right, aren't you?"

"What are you suggesting?" Lucy said.

"Tell them it was you, if it was. Tell the truth."

"*Me?* It wasn't me," she said. She sat up, pulled her sunglasses down onto her face, gathered her purse, slipped her feet back into her sandals. "You think you're so smart, but Eli was killed by one of these stupid mini-mobsters you don't have to pay five figures to for murder."

"Oh yes, I heard the rumor about a guy brought in from out of state. Did you know, Lucy, that ninety-five percent of murders are done by a person very close to the deceased? A husband, a wife, or a lover."

"You're the Columbo, not me," Lucy said, standing now.

"And when you pull the plug on the pool lights at Eli's house, you can't tell who's in the water. So I don't know how

you could have looked out the window and seen Eli swimming."

"Thank you for that bit of information, Sam," she said.
"Who told you that?"

"Eli did. Ginny used to swim there, and she liked it dark."

"I'm sure she did, but I can tell you that it is perfectly
possible to see who is in the pool even without the lights. Eli
just didn't want you thinking he was a peeping Tom."

"Lucy, I'm saying that for your own good, you should come
clean. You imagine you're going to be able to forgive yourself
for this, but what if this time you can't? How much can you
carry around with you before it's just too much?"

"You don't know what you're talking about," she said.

I took her by the elbow and sat her back down on the
hammock, harder than I meant to. She wrenched away from
me, but I kept hold of her.

"Let me go," she said flatly.

"You are too good a mom to leave your kids in the house
with a teenager when notes like this are coming through the
door. I wish you'd stop lying to me. Lucy, I'm in your corner."

"Get off me," she said. She was squirming out of my grasp,
and it wasn't right to hold on to her. So I let her go and put my
hands in my lap. She stood up quickly.

"You've graduated into a real asshole," she said. She dug
through her purse, finding her car keys. "I only came over today to say goodbye."

"Let me ask you this, Lucy," I said. She'd gotten as far as the
side of the house, walking toward her car as fast as she could
without breaking into a run. "In five years, how will you feel? In
ten? If you say nothing, what will you do in fifteen years? Will
you think about it still, or will you discard all of us who know a
little about your past and just keep meeting new people, who
will believe what you want them to believe?"

She didn't pause or stop or turn around. She went to her

car, got into the front seat. I jogged down the front lawn and caught her just as she was pulling away.

"So that's it?" I said, speaking through her open window. "You're just gonna scoot off?"

"I admit the note was a scam, but everything else is true. I have no idea who killed Eli. It wasn't me—I was simply in the wrong place at the wrong time. Occasionally, just occasionally, I find myself in the extraordinary position of not being at fault. I didn't do it and I don't give a good goddamn if you believe me or not."

"I don't want to be buried in your past," I said. "And I think you're going to regret this."

"Let me tell *you* something. This has nothing to do with what I'm going to regret; it has to do with *your* schoolboy guilt," Lucy said. "You feel bad, like you have some debt to Mikey for sleeping with his wife. If I tell them I was there when Eli was killed, if I tell them I had something to do with it, then *you* have your conscience relieved for having convinced me to do the 'right thing.' It's not the right thing, but you're too stupid to understand that. You probably don't even understand the irony of what you're asking, either. You want to use *me* to pay back Mikey so you feel better. You're a coward, Sam, and that's what you started as."

"If I know Mikey didn't murder Eli, isn't it my duty to say something about it?"

"Your duty! My word, listen to you," Lucy said.

She drove off then, speeding down Sun Dial Street. I planned to look away, to turn my back and walk into the house, just in case she caught a glimpse in her rearview mirror. I didn't want Lucy's last memory of me to be the startled, sad, ruined expression that I knew was on my face. I didn't want her to credit herself with having had the last word, for having hurt me. And so I turned. I saw the front window of Ginny's room, with the corner of the curtain just hanging through; the line of glow-in-the-dark ducks outside the front landing; the wrought iron rail that was so ugly. I tried to think about these things and only these things, my physical space in the universe as Lucy took off down the road. But the crash gave such a tremendous bang. There was a smell of something burning, the long blare of the truck driver's horn, and all the distance between me and Lucy's car.

I am running now. When I remember Lucy's crash, I remember how long it took to run that hundred or so yards to the corner of Sun Dial Street. It was as though that last dozen yards would never end; I felt Lucy receding even as I closed the distance. In my dreams, my nightmares about that afternoon, I never close that distance, or see her face, or take her from the car, no matter how near I come, how fast I move.

I am finding my way through torn doors and chrome twisted out of shape and glass that comes away in my hands. Lucy's name is everywhere around me, echoing in my head. But I am silent. There is no one to hear me. How precious Lucy is to her mother, I am thinking. I am thinking that there are two lives that must be saved, Lucy's and Celia's. You cannot give a daughter life without risking her. You cannot love someone without giving that person the power to break you in two.

In my dreams I never kick the door open, never get my arm around her shoulders, never mumble over and over again how wrong I was, how sorry. I never take her to the grass, where for a moment I think she is dying. I think, *She is dying, and I have killed her.*

EPILOGUE

I keep some photographs of Lucy in the cellar. They are old photos that Eli once took, head shots of Lucy when she was in her mid-twenties. Old as they are, I keep them because I have no others. Our affair was so discreetly conducted that I have nothing else whatsoever to remember her by. The photographs are in the cellar, in an old steel milkbox from the days when milk was delivered by truck. I also have a news clipping that reports the continuation of the investigation into Eli's murder after Mikey was acquitted.

Mikey was so far from being convicted that the case never even made it to court. It was an unsolved murder, if it was indeed a murder. Sometimes I think Eli just tripped and fell into the hot tub and Lucy panicked and fled. Other times I think it was truly a mob-related thing. But whatever happened to him that night, it was quickly forgotten. The last time I looked at the clippings, the entire event, with the exception of Lucy's accident, seemed unimportant. Not even Eli's death mattered to me anymore. The only thing that mattered was that the pretty

272

woman in the glossy black-and-white prints, a woman who spent hours every week correcting any flaws in her body, had taken six months to walk without crutches after an accident I had caused.

She never blamed me. The crash knocked her so badly that she remembered nothing about it, not the conversation we had or what she hit or even why she was in Sun Dial Street. She remembered that we had an argument in her garden a few days before and that I suspected her. When she recalled this, she seemed to find it funny. She laughed, and in that laugh I heard all her innocence. I visited the hospital every day until she was out of danger, and I telephoned her once a year later. When she answered, I hung up.

I have a wife now—Claire. She is a gift, and like a gift she came out of nowhere. In the mornings, after long hours asleep with her, I make breakfast. By the time she comes from upstairs I've put out cereal, bowls, fruit juice, a pot of coffee. I am waiting for her. She knows how to read music, sculpt ice, make a perfect fire so it burns clean, which apples are good for pies or sauce or eating. At work I miss her just a little, and when we are together we reach for each other in unison.

Claire hasn't seen the photographs and clippings, doesn't even know that they exist or that I've kept them. She divorced a guy named Benjamin long before I met her, and when we discuss the past I focus entirely on her relationship with him, what it was. I pretend that I have had no serious relationships or that they were certainly nothing compared to my marriage to her—which is true, the second part, that is.

Claire is a musician. She plays flute with an orchestra, but she says, she *insists*, she likes the pop music acts I represent. I admire Claire; I find everything she's done with her life impeccable. Ben was a drinker, and Claire would not have children with a man who drank.

"But you still love him, then, right?" I ask. "It was an intellectual decision to leave him, not a decision from the heart."

"Oh, Sam," she says to me. Even in the dark, in bed with the blankets around us, I can see her roomy smile.

When I moved in with Claire, I tried not to think of Ben, who had been with her before in this same house, within these same walls. I tried not to think of her "past," as she called it, of the men who happened along between the divorce from Ben and the time she met me. I feel a strange kinship with Ben, who was more or less a permanent fixture, like myself, while all the other men were just passers-through. Not that there were so many—I'm not saying that. I'm not accusing Claire of anything at all.

It's just that I know how much the past can weigh on you.

Occasionally I wonder what more has happened in Claire's life than what she tells me, what thoughts she has even now that she does not mention. Once in a while a piece of junk mail from some ancient mailing list will arrive in the post addressed to Benjamin McLean, and it makes me feel there must be unfinished business between them. Or that somehow, because he was here before me, he belongs here and I do not.

I rarely ask about Ben or anyone else. But because I have secrets from Claire, I suspect she has secrets from me.

"Want to know a secret?" she asked one night, and I thought, *No, no, no.* She said, "I've always wanted a really good-looking husband like you. I know you are supposed to love someone's soul or spirit or feel you share values or have the same background or something. But honest, Sam, I love it that you're tall."

I wish I had met Claire long ago, before I met Lucy or Celia, Eli or Mikey. Now that I'm with her I have no interest in any other woman, any other person on this earth, except Ginny and Mom. Lucy would not have seemed so special if I'd been with Claire. She wouldn't even have caught my attention, really. She'd be just like other women we know and are friends with, the kind of woman Claire would describe upon meeting by saying, "Isn't she lovely!" and I would nod, not knowing what "lovely" means but knowing she must be if Claire thinks so.

This is what she said of Ginny when she came from Illinois for the wedding. Ginny's a free-lance photographer now and lives in Chicago. I guess she's pretty good, because I've seen her work in magazines.

"Do you ever think about him anymore?" I asked Ginny at the reception. Claire was changing out of her dress, and the family was in the living room. "About Eli, I mean."

"Not really," she said. "Once in a while, I suppose."

"Like when you go swimming?"

"*Swimming?*" Ginny said, and looked at me oddly. "No. Only if I meet someone named Edgar or pass a sign that says EXOTIC DANCING. Then for a millisecond, I admit, he crosses my mind."

She smiled. Claire was right. Ginny did look lovely. She'd gained weight, and there was a softness to her expression that was new.

"Really, Sam, it's better that I don't think of him." She stepped back, took a sip of her drink. "Let's go sit with the others," she said.

"Wait, Ginny," I said, following her.

"It's your wedding, Sam," she said. "Let's make it a happy day."

"Just one question," I said. Ginny raised an eyebrow. "If the pool lights at Eli's house were off, could you see from inside the house who was swimming in the pool?"

"Oh, Sam."

"I know. I'm ashamed I'm asking you."

"Does Claire know how strange you are? Well, what did she expect, marrying into this family."

"Seriously, Ginny."

"If we are going to play 'who killed Eli?' I don't want to talk about it."

"Please. Just this one question."

She looked at me and sighed. After a moment she said, "I suppose you could see who it was if the moon was bright. Otherwise, there would be some guessing involved. On a moonless night, forget it." Ginny glanced across the hall into the other room, where Mother was talking excitedly to Van. Van wore a bow tie that was lost beneath his chins. He looked very happy. He and Mother together looked very happy. "They are so weird," Ginny said.

Ginny had only one comment about Claire. She said, "If I could choose to be another person, I think I'd be her."

I know what she means.

Now that I'm married, I can see that if I were to go to jail on Claire's behalf it would be no different from her going to jail. To confess that it was me, not her, or her, not me, would be pointless. Pedantic. No matter how it went, we would both suffer in the way that families suffer. Our capacity for individual grief left years ago. And when we have a baby in September —a girl, we are told—I imagine that our union will deepen even further, to a place I don't yet know.

I have never told Claire about the conversation that took place before Lucy's accident—only that it happened outside my house and that it was terrible. Unforgettable. She is understanding. She thinks she knows the whole story now, or maybe she realizes that there are great omissions but she doesn't mind. It is like her to allow me that room, not to ask questions or put pressure. The fact that only I know what was said that day— that it is my own secret—is a positive burden. All of this makes me a little crazy, and I know I need to tell Claire everything— not for her, but for me. I need to write it down and give it to her, word for word, just as it happened. Just like this.

ABOUT   THE   AUTHOR

Marti Leimbach was born in Washington, D.C., and grew up in Maryland. She was graduated from Harvard University in 1987, and then spent a year as a Regents Fellow in the Writers Program at the University of California, Irvine, during which time she completed her first novel, *Dying Young*. Since its American publication in 1990, *Dying Young* has gone on to be published in twelve other countries and was the basis for a major motion picture released in 1991. Marti Leimbach is married and currently lives in London.